THE
Lost
ROYALS
SAGA

SEASON OF THE WOLF

RACHEL JONAS

CONTENTS

THE LOST ROYALS SAGA

COPYRIGHTS

Published May 27, 2018

WRITTEN AS RACHEL JONAS

<u>THE LOST ROYALS SAGA</u>
The Genesis of Evangeline
Dark Side of the Moon
Heart of the Dragon
Season of the Wolf
Fate of the Fallen

<u>DRAGON FIRE ACADEMY</u>
First Term
Second Term
Third Term

<u>THE VAMPIRE'S MARK</u>
Dark Reign
Hell Storm
Cold Heir
Crimson Mist

**WRITTEN AS RACHEL JONAS
& NIKKI THORNE**

KINGS OF CYPRESS POINTE
The Golden Boys
Never his Girl
Forever Golden
Pretty Boy D
Mr. Silver
Sexy Beast

SAVAGE KINGS OF BRADWYN U
Break the Girl
Cold as Ice

DESCRIPTION

*The dragon within Evangeline mourns, but her wolf
has one thing in mind … revenge.*

When the Sovereign caught wind of there being a forbidden hybrid living in Seaton Falls, he came to collect her. What he didn't know was that Liam, her warrior, was more than willing to sacrifice himself for the only girl he's ever loved.

But saving her meant losing a part of himself, his true form—his dragon. This transformation has compromised his mission to protect his soulmate and future queen, and time is no longer on their side.

It hasn't been long since Evangeline accepted her abilities, but she must quickly learn to rely on her own strength if she's ever going to fix this. Her survival, and Liam's restoration, depend on it.

The foundation of Seaton Falls has been shaken and a new day is on the horizon. An influx of outside shifters preparing to wage war, and the arrival of a few highly-anticipated guests, are only the beginning.

Maybe the odds have finally shifted in the clan's favor.

Or … maybe they've just been set up for an even harder fall.

Thank you for your purchase! I would love to get your feedback once you've finished the book!

Please leave a review and let others know what you thought of

"Season of the Wolf"

Come hang out in the newly created "Shifter Lounge" on Facebook! https://www.facebook.com/groups/141633853243521/

We chat, recommend YA paranormal romances, and engage in other random acts of nerdiness. Once we're fully up and running, there will be tons of giveaways, exclusive ARC offers from me, and guest appearances by some of your favorite YA authors!

For all inquiries, please contact me using my primary email address:
author.racheljonas@gmail.com

CHAPTER I

Evie

Silhouetted trees resembled statues beneath the night sky.

I cleared the rail of my balcony, driving both feet deep into the snow when I landed. Naked and chuffing warm breath into the chilled night air, cold scattered across my skin in stinging pricks. With a quick scan to make sure I was alone, I ran.

Hard. Fast.

Faster than any normal human could even fathom until I cleared the newly-built wall surrounding our property—a feature I still hadn't gotten used to.

There was no time to slow down, shift in peace. I had to make do on the run.

No turning back, Evie.

You can do this.

You have *to do this.*

It wasn't lost on me that the odds of penetrating the

Sovereign's camp again were slim to none. There was no telling what I'd face when I got there, but I was going anyway. Whether this endeavor would be a failure or success, I'd try.

I couldn't afford to overthink things. My focus and intentions had to be singular.

This was for Liam.

Bone shifted over bone in a series of painfully sharp jolts, cracking beneath my skin as my feet trampled snow. I muffled a scream, replacing it with a low growl that resonated from my chest. It was all I could do to weather the pain.

With what felt like an explosion in my spine, I was on all fours, staring at fur covered limbs as I sprinted through the woods in full wolf form. The air's scent filled my nostrils and it was different from before—what was once one smell, now broken down into many.

Glancing back, I kept the pace. It wasn't lost on me that, last time I took off like this, I ended up with an arrow through the leg and Liam was taken; another reason I felt compelled to right the wrongs. Had it not been for me, had it not been for him protecting me, none of this would've happened.

I shook off that last thought, doing all I could to dispel any useless emotions. Guilt was definitely useless.

My eyes focused miles ahead, to the clearing where I stashed a bag with two changes of clothes during my dry-run. Once I made it that far, I'd be on to phase two—boarding a bus headed north.

North to track down the Sovereign's army.

To track down the witch that hexed Liam.

I knew the success of this mission was farfetched, and probably the dumbest thing I'd ever done, but she was the only one who could fix this.

The only one who could fix *him*.

At first, when I spotted light from above, I thought I imagined it, thought the moon had cast an odd hue with these keen eyes of mine. Trudging ahead, the strange orange glow flickered in my peripheral, strobing between thick trees now.

Not the moon.

Dallas.

I picked up speed, packing snow to the ground with my paws, leaving deep tracks that brought to mind one of many reasons it would have been ideal to shift into my dragon.

But ... she'd been silent for weeks.

There was no trace of her strong presence, the surge of energy pulsing from the center of my chest, through my limbs. She'd practically disappeared, retreated to some distant place within to mourn.

I suppose to her, the loss of Liam's dragon *did* feel like death. It was the link connecting her to him, and now, it was gone. Acknowledging her despair made me lose my breath every time. The tightening in my chest was a dead giveaway.

Intricate details of Dallas' flaming wings were easily seen now as he closed the distance between us. My clean exit hadn't been as clean as I imagined.

"Turn back," he called out into the night, gesturing toward home with the wave of his hand.

Those words went in one ear and out the other.

"Evangeline!"

I ignored him and stayed focused on the black bag that came into view. I'd tucked a watch inside one of its pockets, a means of keeping track of when the bus would arrive. If I had to guess, I was cutting it close.

Thanks to Dallas, I had to alter the plan. Instead of stopping to change, I now gripped a canvas strap between my teeth, deciding I'd try to lose him first.

The thick underbrush of the woods suddenly thinned and the town's lights glittered on the horizon like distant stars. There was no way I could run the streets looking like an overgrown Husky.

Especially not with a backpack dangling from my teeth. People would assume I'd eaten someone's kid and, needless to say, *that* wouldn't go over well.

There weren't many options, and when Dallas swooped in front of me, I knew he was equally aware of my plight.

"What do you think you're doing?"

That question flitted through my thoughts and each of my motives came rushing in. Short answer: I was doing this because, if I didn't, I'd die inside. The options were to be proactive and do all I could to find this witch, to bring her back so she could fix things, or continue to sit by watching, waiting for him to wake up.

And if he didn't …

Don't think like that.

I tried to shove the thought aside, but it'd been harder to get rid of lately—the longer it took Liam to show signs of life.

I wanted to scream at Dallas, to yell for him to get out of my way. However, as my wolf, I wasn't afforded the convenience of verbal communication. When he slowed in front of me, I darted to the left, narrowly dodging his reach … and a tree.

"Are you trying to get yourself killed?" he asked, his voice fading behind me for only a moment until he caught up, nearly matching my speed. "Because if you're doing what I *think* you're doing … alone," he added, "you may as well just run out into traffic, kid. Death by semi-truck would be a walk in the park compared to what Sebastian will do if he gets his hands on you."

Truer words had never been spoken. I was certainly at the top of the Sovereign's list of people he wished to end with slow, painful torture. However, what Dallas, and maybe others, failed to realize was that being in limbo with Liam's life hanging in the balance for weeks was just as bad. Maybe even worse.

The flare of light beside me dimmed and I glanced in that direction, toward Dallas when he darted away. For a split second, I thought I might have convinced him to let me continue on, but that moment was fleeting.

The sound of wood splintering seemed to come from every direction. It wasn't until I was rolling through the snow with the sky tumbling around me that I realized the noise had been straight ahead—a tree Dallas leveled in my path. Likely, with one blow from his shoulder. Without enough time to react, I tripped and barreled toward the thicket of bushes that finally stopped me.

My head spun and I now stared at my paws in the air. Snow crunched to my left, followed by a rugged face covered in blondish scruff popping into my line of sight.

"You all right?" he had the nerve to ask, that drawl of his making the question seem all the more cynical. It didn't help that, judging from the tension in his jaw, it took everything in him not to laugh.

Smug bastard.

If I could have told him to '*suck it,*' I would have.

Instead, I righted myself and sat, shaking off the temporary daze ... and all the snow I accumulated on my fur as I rolled.

Dallas circled me now with no flames shrouding his tall, broad frame, only the lava moving in his veins for warmth.

"Sorry I had to do that, kid, but ... Elise would kill me if I came home without you." He smirked again. "Plus, Hilda and I kinda like having you around, too, so you can imagine how rough it would've gotten at the house if I hadn't stopped you."

Dallas wasn't the most expressive person in the world, which made it even more surprising to hear him admit such a thing.

His large hands came to rest on his waist and he let out a breath, eyeing me as I sat there, still panting from the run.

And maybe a little from the rough fall, too.

Our gazes locked and there was a softness behind his I hadn't expected. Perhaps that look meant he *wasn't* totally oblivious as to why I'd taken such a risk tonight. Seeing him with Elise over the past few months, I was positive he loved her. It wasn't so farfetched to think he could relate to what it would feel like to lose that—to lose *love*. If something were to ever happen to either one of them, the other would be torn apart with grief.

"So, are we in agreement that you have to come back home?" he asked. "Or are you gonna make me knock down every tree in these woods?"

I'd just lowered my snout to grab the bag again, deciding to ignore his lecture and make another run for it, but then there was a sound … one that made the fur on my back stand on end.

A growl …

Instinctively, Dallas placed himself between me and whatever lurked out there. With his size and skill, there was no doubt he'd be quite the protector, but … there seemed to be too many. Of what, I wasn't exactly sure yet.

I sniffed the air, searching beneath the scent of pine and freshly fallen snow. Filling my nostrils was a familiar twinge of disgusting dark fur and razor-sharp claws that could only belong to one particular type of beast.

Mutts.

Unable to speak in this form, I opened and closed my snout two or three times, wishing I had the ability to warn Dallas. However, when he burst into flames and braced himself for impact the next instant, it became apparent I didn't need to.

So many bodies. They poured at us from all directions. There was no time to think or rationalize, just … do.

My teeth sank into the neck of one and I quickly tossed it aside, hearing its vertebrae snap against the trunk of a nearby tree. Another to my left succumbed to my claws quickly when I tore them through the tough flesh of its abdomen, spilling its intestines on the snow—black ink on a fresh canvas.

Two straight ahead squealed as flames ravished them, their

cries dying off in the night as, not too far away, Dallas had just sentenced three more to the same fate.

How many were there?

Were more waiting in the distance, set to attack in case we managed to get through the first wave?

My heart raced wildly inside my chest and I found it hard not to miss my dragon right now. In her form, I was just beginning to find myself, just beginning to feel worthy to wield her power. And now ... she was gone. No, not literally, but she may as well have been. I felt the distance, the longing and intense grief we shared.

Breathless, searching the tree line for more, Dallas panted beside me as his flames dimmed. A dozen had come at us, a dozen had fallen. Thick, black blood covered us both, as did their distinct odor. With a look of disgust, Dallas shook a layer of the filth from his arms, speckling the surrounding snow.

He glanced at me and I half-expected the look to be one filled with disdain and frustration. After all, it was because of me he was out here. But instead, he surprised me, not doing much to hide the concern behind his gaze.

He knew like I did ... this was a sign of worse to come.

CHAPTER 2

Evie

S ilent, lacking the fight and determination I bridled when Dallas first chased me down, I followed him home. If there were more mutts lurking about, I wouldn't get very far on my own, making this journey even *more* of a fool's errand.

In short, my efforts had been successfully thwarted for the night, and I was stuck.

Powerless.

The moment we walked through the door where Elise paced the foyer, it was clear she'd come undone waiting for Dallas and I to return. My fur, slick with blood, was suddenly the focus of her attention. The initial anger and frustration she aimed at me for running off was quickly washed away by concern.

"What happened?" she breathed, letting her gaze volley between Dallas and I as he traipsed in behind me.

"One guess," he sighed, glancing at the dark liquid slathered all over him.

Elise turned her questions toward me, stammering a few syllables before it came back to her remembrance that, as my wolf, I was unable to speak. She glanced toward the stairs and that regal posture—which she'd let slip for only a moment when she thought I'd been harmed—returned as she pointed.

"Get yourself cleaned up, and then I'd like to have a word with you."

Liquid glistened in her eyes as she blinked and, right away, guilt set in. I'd run off knowing it would hurt her, but ... her feelings, *anyone's* feelings, had to be a secondary concern. Liam came first.

Upstairs, I shifted back, making quick work of getting to the shower to rid myself of the mutts' stench. Beneath the stream of hot water, I breathed deep, doing what I could to block it all out.

Hopelessness.

Failure.

Inadequacy.

Tonight was yet another example of how I was so small in this great big world. A world where good didn't always defeat evil. A world where love wasn't enough to save the ones who meant the most. The proof of this theory lie in a bed across the hall—unaware of how much he was missed, needed.

Tears mingled with streaks of water and shampoo that washed down my face. My entire body ached with sadness.

What if this was how it'd be from now on—life moving forward without him?

What if I had to exist with this huge hole in my chest?

No one had said it out loud—in front of me, anyway—but I knew they were worried. He should have been awake by now.

Not only were things looking grim for Liam, there was a general sense of doom *everywhere.*

News updates had become dark and terrifying. There were sightings of strange animals in northern towns, increasing reports of missing persons. And it wasn't lost on any of us that those being taken were all able-bodied men between the ages of twenty and thirty. To the outside world, this could have easily been mistaken for a coincidence. But to those of us with knowledge of the supernatural, it was clear these men were taken with a specific purpose in mind.

Someone was building an army.

And there was no question as to who that *someone* was.

It was once explained that, in times such as these, when the Sovereign sensed a threat, he'd been known to send his lycans out in droves to turn innocent townspeople into mutts. There was no doubt the coward had something similar underway.

While other towns were dwindling, the population in Seaton Falls had exploded almost overnight, but *that* part was by design. It took the Council little time to realize the wait was nearly up. The war that had been prophesied decades ago was at our door, breathing down our necks, much like the savage at the very heart of this conflict.

Shifters from all over had come here in preparation for what lie ahead. Apartment buildings in our quaint, downtown district were now filled to capacity. To offer further aid, much of the local lycan population even opened their homes to outsiders in need of lodging. Anything to up our numbers and our chances of winning the fight.

In short, we were preparing for the worst, because the worst was upon us.

A lot had changed since the ordeal with the Sovereign. For one, the High Council ordered the construction of that insanely massive wall surrounding our property. On it, large glowing seals and sigils only visible to a supernatural, their magic keeping unwanted visitors out. It served as an added measure of protection, on top of this place now being heavily guarded with lycans and dragons hand-picked by the Council.

I understood why it was necessary, but hated being the cause of all this.

In Baz's words, no measure was too great when it came to protecting me.

But it wasn't just *my* life that needed protecting. The restorative magic that brought me back was forbidden. And while, for now, Sebastian had likely bought Liam's story about bringing me back with the aid of the *first* set of Seaton Falls witches, that lie would only hold up as long as he remained unaware that Elise was alive and well. If he laid eyes on her, on Hilda ... it wouldn't take him long to realize he'd been deceived.

After finding me in the woods that fateful day, it was obvious to him that I resided somewhere in the area, and that this was likely where I returned. Since so many of our secrets had been revealed, the Elders weren't taking any chances. For the foreseeable future, my family and I were on lockdown.

I twisted the knob and my skin chilled a bit as the last of the water swirled down the drain. I couldn't move. If I did, I might fall apart and I couldn't afford that right now.

Warm terrycloth enveloped me when I secured a robe around my waist. Stepping into my bedroom, I expected at least a moment of solitude before inevitably having to face Elise. Only, the firm stares coming from two sets of brown eyes locked on mine meant there would be no such break.

Hilda's expressionless face left me to wonder what thoughts were hidden beneath it. Whereas Elise's thoughts were painfully transparent.

"Do you have any idea how stupid you were tonight," Hilda asked, prompting Elise to move toward the door, latching it quietly.

Tension had my chest in a vice, breathing like I'd run a marathon.

"Please, Hilda," Elise intervened.

"You're chastising *me*?" Hilda snapped, placing a hand to her heart. "This girl's foolishness nearly got her *and* Dallas killed tonight. And to add to it, we can't even say for sure she didn't lure those beasts right to our doorstep."

I'd seen Hilda upset before, but tonight, she was nearly chuffing steam.

"The guards are checking the area as we speak," Elise reasoned. "And, based on Dallas' account, they took care of all the mutts. Checking is merely a precaution."

Elise was right. The brood assigned to watch over us were airtight. I was only able to escape because I'd watched them for days, kept notes until I had their schedule down, and knew precisely when their shift changed.

I already knew what Hilda was thinking. Knowing the Sovereign had most likely sent men this way to search for Nick and I—or at least me—I shouldn't have risked it. I understood that we weren't impossible to find, but she and the clan's witches certainly made it a million times harder.

I wasn't concerned about mutts finding us here, but *she* didn't seem convinced even knowing the brigade surrounding the property hadn't just been selected haphazardly. When the time came, she stepped in to ensure our safety. After discovering one of the Council's guards had been compromised and leaked information to the Sovereign, it became one-hundred-percent necessary to only employ those who'd been found trustworthy. Each had to endure a rigorous vetting process—Hilda's version of a supernatural lie detector test. From there, the two dozen she deemed to have the strongest resolve made the cut.

Upset by being quieted, Hilda glared from the seat she'd taken on my bed.

Elise took a step closer. "You've been increasingly ..."

"Stupid."

When Hilda interrupted, Elise passed a hardened glare in her direction before going on. "The word that comes to mind is reckless," she amended.

There was a depth to her wandering gaze that told of the grief she too felt when considering Liam's current state.

"No one faults you for breaking down, for ... losing yourself for a bit. Liam is important to you; important to *all* of us. But, if anything, these are times we ought to ban together, to keep our minds and hearts focused on the task at hand."

I glanced up, trying to figure out how one would go about doing such a thing—stay focused on some elusive *task at hand* while a precious life hung in the balance mere feet away.

"Are you trying to get yourself killed?" The blunt question came from my outspoken aunt—no hint of jesting in her tone whatsoever.

I suppressed an eye roll, knowing it would only provoke her further. So, instead, I muttered a halfhearted, "Of course not."

In response, she scoffed, and my blood heated to near boiling. Still, I kept my head while explaining.

"If I die, there'd be no one to save him. I'm the only one immune to magic, the only one who can find the witch and ..."

"Do you hear yourself?" Hilda interrupted. "Have you truly convinced yourself you're some half-cocked superhero?"

Elise placed a hand on Hilda's shoulder, encouraging her to ease up, but the gesture went ignored.

"Your silly antics are going to get us *all* killed."

"I never asked Dallas to follow me," I exploded. "I never asked for anyone's help." It should have been obvious I was perfectly willing to do this all on my own.

That loathsome scoff left Hilda's mouth again. "Says the girl who barely even understands what she is, how to *shift* on her own."

A stifling silence crept into the room as each of my breaths came in deep, heated gasps. Both fists clenched as I did all I could to bridle the fury building within.

"Hilda ... I think that's enough," Elise intervened. "It's been a long night. Perhaps we should leave Evangeline for now and discuss this later."

"Don't bother," I rebutted through clenched teeth. "*I'll* go."

With that, I nearly ran from my bedroom, a large space that now felt like a shrinking box with one visit from those two.

I didn't owe them an explanation for what I did tonight. I didn't owe *anyone* an explanation, nor would I apologize for my conviction. If helping Liam required me to walk through hell and battle the devil himself ... there wasn't a soul on Earth who could stop me.

I'd been with Liam the whole time. The thought that made it bearable to tear myself away and head north was that it was necessary. Deciding to make the journey was a bit of a knee-jerk reaction, but after having watched his lack of progress the past few weeks, I'd found a way to rationalize.

I guess you could say I got tired of leaving his recovery to chance. Going to the Sovereign's camp had seemed like the only thing left to do. The odds seemed promising enough that I gave it a shot. I hadn't come up with much of a plan, though.

Days earlier, I'd done a test run, stashed a bag with two changes of clothes on the outskirts of the woods and paid bus fair in advance. It would have taken me to Charlevoix, the small town near the Upper Peninsula where I would have then caught a ferry across Lake Superior. From there, I would've been on foot.

It was dangerous, yes, but he was worth it.

If Hilda thought I was stupid for that, I'd make a mental note never to put my neck on the line if *her* life was ever in danger. Wouldn't want her thinking I convinced myself I was a superhero ...

The thought of the conversation I walked out on made me tense all over again. To control it, I focused on the back of Liam's hand, traced the compass tattooed there as I held it. There was some small comfort in the warmth of his flesh. It meant he hadn't left us.

Even if he wouldn't open his eyes.

I'd done all my studying right here in his bedroom, following the hour-long tutoring sessions that had been forced on me. However, any activities I could get out of, I did—the sessions with Hilda, combat training, socializing. Nothing was more important than being with him, praying he'd be well enough to wake up soon.

Today had been just like the day before, watching as he slept through yet another beautiful sunrise and sunset. His comatose state was once magic-induced, meant to keep him comfortable until the hex was complete. It was all Hilda could do, seeing as how no witch can reverse the curse of another, but ... he should have been awake by now. The spell she cast had been lifted once he healed. Now, it was all up to him.

Nothing I'd done seemed to make a difference, because despite whatever special abilities I had, despite the wolf and dragon within, tonight I felt very ... human.

Human.

That word hit my heart like a ton of bricks. Once, being *normal* didn't seem like such a bad thing. Only now, I knew what sorts of beasts were out there, roaming the Earth, preying on the weak. Now, with my new awareness, being anything but a supernatural made a person vulnerable ... temporary. Two attributes I couldn't stomach assigning to Liam, my warrior.

My gaze drifted to the band he still wore, the one that was supposed to mean we had forever, but ... being mortal now, the possibility of keeping that promise had been stolen. Forever didn't exist for him anymore, didn't exist for *us*.

A newly-familiar feeling rose from the pit of my stomach and I had yet to master the art of suppressing it—*anger*. It'd become my default emotion.

Anger that I hadn't been able to do more to stop Sebastian and his men from taking Liam that day.

Anger that I was powerless, forced to sit idle, watching him transition.

Anger that the witch I knew to be responsible was still out there, breathing.

I'd seen her do this to him with my own two eyes. Only, at the time, I didn't know what to make of the purple powder she blew in his face; didn't realize what damage it would cause.

"She's been in there for hours. Should we check on her? Apologize maybe?"

Elise's muffled voice seeped beneath the closed door of Liam's bedroom. She did little to conceal her worry.

I pressed my cheek to the back of his hand now, aware of how long it'd been since he held mine in return.

"Let her be," Hilda replied. The fight had left her voice from our earlier conversation. Actually, listening now, it seemed she might even be remorseful.

It shouldn't have surprised me she'd be so cutthroat. That was always her way, and while I'd gotten used to it for the most part, tonight simply wasn't the night I needed her uncensored thoughts hurled at me.

A third voice approached, and with its familiar, Southern dialect, I recognized it as Dallas' right away.

"Heard from the guards. The perimeter and surrounding area are all clear now. They put down a dozen or so *additional* mutts, so

... things are definitely heating up. If I had to guess, from a military standpoint, they're hunting in a grid formation to cover the most ground in a short amount of time."

Dallas paused and I held my breath.

"Sebastian has definitely *not* decided to let bygones be bygones. He's at least partly sure Evie's still residing in the area."

"Then we should leave," Elise said resolutely.

"A pointless maneuver," Hilda interjected. "Wherever she goes, he'd hunt her down. To the edges of the Earth," she added solemnly.

My heart sank at those words, at the realization that the Sovereign would stop at nothing to end me.

"She's right," Dallas answered. "Here in Seaton Falls, we've got allies, the premises is secure, and the High Council has stuck around for more than a month now for the sole purpose of making sure Evie's safe. The last thing we should consider doing is leaving that behind."

The three outside the door were quiet again.

"Then we'll need to do more," was Elise's suggestion. "More security, more magic to conceal the house, more ... *everything*." The end of her statement was shaky, like it'd been uttered through quivering lips.

"I can't believe it's come to this," her voice came back. "Mere months ago, it felt as though we were making progress, like we might actually *win*, but ... now it just seems all our efforts are only delaying the inevitable."

I shuttered at that word—inevitable.

"I can't help thinking how different things would be if we had the boys here, how different things would be if Liam was awake."

When she said his name, I moved my cheek across his hand again, forcing myself to recite silent words I wasn't even sure I still believed.

You are *here. You haven't left me.*

"Maybe it's time we ... explored our options." I was surprised to hear such a thing leave Hilda's mouth. She'd been the one to pound in our heads how the only way to bring them back was if I miraculously lucked up on some magic. All the while, reminding us how impossible that was.

And yet ...

"I know what you're suggesting," Elise commented, "And ... a decision of that caliber would require a lengthy discussion. One I don't think any of us are prepared to have tonight."

What could be so bad, so grave as to make her shoot down an idea to bring back my brothers?

"It's been a long day. I think we're all a little delirious," Dallas sighed. "Why don't we all just get some rest and ... revisit every-thing tomorrow."

Elise agreed, but didn't move right away. "You go ahead. I'll be there in a moment."

With that, it was just her and Hilda again. Their voices picked up once more and I focused on their conversation when it came full-circle, right back to me.

"Don't you think it's time we put a stop to this? She's not doing herself any good just sitting there, watching him like that," Elise remarked. "It's all she does—day in, day out. I worry."

A short, cynical laugh left Hilda's mouth before responding. "Sitting with him seems to be the only thing that keeps her out of trouble," she joked. "But in all seriousness, if you want to try prying her away, you go right ahead. But you know as well as I do, she isn't going anywhere. As long as he's confined to that bed, Evangeline may as well be, too."

My eyes shifted toward Liam.

There was silence outside the door. I leaned my ear that way, realizing the two hadn't gone anywhere. They were either waiting for signs of life here inside the room, or they'd run out of things to argue about.

For now.

"Have you ever wondered about these two?" It was Hilda who posed the question, causing my brow to quirk when she asked.

"What do you mean?"

There was a brief pause after Elise's reply while I guessed Hilda gathered her thoughts. Meanwhile, I counted Liam's breaths, watching the steady rise and fall of his chest beneath a white blanket.

"It's just a theory I have, that souls exist long before our physical bodies. This theory extends to include the idea that some are even tied to their mates before they meet ... before they're born."

A light chuckle marked by Elise's soft, bubbly tone filtered beneath the door. "And on what have you based this theory?"

"Observation," Hilda quipped. "You've never wondered what made Noah lower his sword that day? When he journeyed to Egypt for the cleansing?"

The cleansing ... I could only guess she spoke of the mission my father and his soldiers embarked on centuries ago. They were called in to rid Egypt of feral shifters—the result of a rising epidemic at the time. Dragons had gone on a rampage, impregnating hundreds or thousands of women, only to leave them for dead when their frail bodies didn't survive giving birth. No, the children hadn't transitioned, but with there being so many, and no Elders to oversee their upbringing, it was handled in the most efficient way possible for those times.

The children were slaughtered.

Except one ... *Liam.*

Hilda's voice came back. It was softer than usual, quiet as I watched him sleep.

"So, you're suggesting that Evangeline had something to do with that? Before she was even thought of?"

I noted that some of the sarcasm had left Elise's tone, signifying the moment she maybe started thinking Hilda's theory might not be so farfetched.

"Think about it. Noah killed hundreds during that mission. I know because he came back to camp each night, silent, broken. If there'd been another option to clean up the rogue dragons' mess, he would have gladly taken it. But ... on that particular day, when he and his soldiers rode in, something was different. I knew it even *before* I noticed the small bundle in his arms."

I pictured it as Hilda spoke—my father returning that night with Liam tucked against his chest, probably confused as to why that one boy had been spared the fate the others shared.

But he couldn't bring himself to do it. That's the story I've been told.

"Their bond is special, even beyond being mated, tethered," Hilda added.

My thumb stroked his forearm as I swiped a tear with the other.

"To me, it's not so strange to think that, maybe her soul was with Noah that day. Maybe hers was that still, small voice in his subconscious, petitioning for Liam's life to be spared," Hilda concluded thoughtfully.

My mind went back to a story I'd heard a few times before, about how Liam retrieved my necklace in the woods that night. How he'd managed to find the stone that held my soul ... long after my scent was carried away with the wind, long after the first Liberator made off with what was left of my body.

Blinking away wetness from my eyes, I found myself wondering if there was truth to this theory of Hilda's. With the depth of emotion I carried in my heart for Liam, with how drawn we were to one another ... maybe it *had* been that way since time first began.

CHAPTER 3

Nick

For the fifth time in three minutes, I attempted to correctly secure my tie. And for the fifth time ... my fingers slipped awkwardly over the silky, striped pattern and I paused.

Staring at myself in the mirror, I felt stupid for going through these motions, making sure I looked presentable for a meeting I'd been called to with the Council. Silly because I wasn't entirely sure they hadn't thought better of setting me free, and had now decided to uphold their original sentencing.

Freedom hadn't been as sweet as I imagined, but it sure beat the alternative. For starters, my family—or more specifically, my *mother*—had been under the Council's watchful eye. It was clear they would have condemned her to a fate worse than mine had it not been for Evie intervening—a fact I would never forget or take lightly.

Whether my mother realized it or not, she owed Evie her life just as much as I did.

Mom's actions didn't go unpunished, though. Yes, she'd been granted permission to leave the Elders' chambers, but she was far from free. Per the Council's orders, she was forbidden to leave our home until further notice. To ensure that she abided by the rules, a small fleet of well-hidden guards were always on the premises.

So, to say we were not exactly highly favored around Seaton Falls at the moment, would have been a huge understatement. The respect and clout we once had because of my grandfather's contribution to this town were almost nonexistent now.

Angry, frustrated, I snatched the tie from my neck and dropped it to the carpet.

"What are you doing, Nick?" I asked myself, bracing the edge of the dresser as I stared at my reflection. There was this acute sense of dressing up for my own funeral. There was no telling what would happen once I descended those stairs to the chamber.

Against my better judgement, I even reached out to Evie a few times. But, each time I did, the call went straight to voicemail like expected. She'd fallen off the grid. From what Beth reported back to the rest of us, it was with good reason. Liam wasn't doing well, and on top of everything else Evie lost, she might lose him, too.

Knowing what a hard time she must be having, I should have left her alone about all this, but I thought I'd try. With her position, there was a chance she'd been let in on whatever this meeting was about, but I had a feeling she hadn't spoken to anyone she didn't have to.

The Council included.

The only thing that gave me comfort tonight was that, this time, I wouldn't be going alone. All three of my brothers had also been called in, possibly as witnesses to my behavior as of late. There wasn't a doubt in my mind the Elders' witches could pry the truth out of them one way or another. In which case, they'd be able to attest to how different I was—estranged, quiet, cut off from the world around me. While, no, this evidence wasn't damning, it would certainly alert the Council that I was changing.

I breathed deep, suddenly more confident in the decision I'd made to keep away. This, my grandfather's estate, had been my refuge, my only means of keeping these secrets. The biggest of all being that the blackouts had started again. They weren't as frequent, but for a time, they'd stopped altogether. There could have been any number of reasons for this—that I'd taken several lives on the journey I'd taken with Evie, that this evolution was just happening naturally.

But then there was another thought that kept coming up, a factor that had been eliminated.

Roz.

I hadn't laid eyes on her since before heading north to Mount Arvon. Sure, we talked and texted, but words were no replacement for seeing her face-to-face.

It was more than I was willing to admit to her out loud, but ... I *missed* her.

Now, more and more, I was beginning to believe she was the key to staving off the darkness.

On cue, my phone rang and I picked up right away, seeing it was her.

"Hey."

"How goes it?" she said with a laugh, annihilating my frustration almost immediately.

"It goes," was all I could say without being negative.

"Well, aren't you just a bucket of sunshine. All dressed and ready to go?"

Putting the call on speakerphone, I placed it on the dresser and decided to give the tie another go.

"Just about. Putting the final touches on this hunk of man-art I call a body."

She laughed, loud and hearty, bringing one out of me as well.

"Wow ... was it *that* funny?"

She settled down a bit. "It never ceases to amaze me how arrogant you can be, and somehow manage to not come across as a total douche-knuckle."

"It's a gift," I mumbled, holding my chin in the air while I eased the knot to my throat, immediately imagining the expensive silk being replaced by a noose.

"I'm sure you're looking quite dapper, Prince Nick," she exhaled, getting the last chuckle out.

I glanced up to the mirror, surprised at the broad smile she brought out of me. "There was once a time you called me that with hatred spewing from your mouth."

She laughed again. "And there was once a time you deserved every ounce of it."

I didn't bother arguing with her. Mostly because she was right.

A moment or two passed and she asked, "Nervous?"

A good question, but one I couldn't answer right away. While it was true I had no idea what this meeting was about, it was also true my brothers had seemingly been called in on the same matter. This one fact gave me hope.

"Nervous is the wrong word," I breathed. "Curious is more fitting."

"Well, either way, I still think you should have taken my advice."

I stopped with one foot partially lodged in my shoe, all too aware of what advice Roz spoke of. The moment I called to say my brothers and the rest of us had made it back safely from our field trip to provoke the Sovereign, Roz began her campaign to convince me to leave here. She had a theory that I ought to take my release from that cell as a blessing and keep going.

Her exact words were, *'The Councils' graciousness will expire as soon as you're no longer useful to them, useful to Evie. Nick, get out while you still can, before they turn on you."*

I'd be lying if I didn't admit the suggestion had a nice ring to it, but this town was still home to too many of the people I cared about.

Family.

Friends.

... Her.

Besides, I'd done enough running.

"I'll be fine," I lied, knowing there was nothing on which to base such a claim. In truth, she may have been on to something.

A deep sigh on the other end of the line did nothing to calm my nerves, but I understood her concern.

"I tell you what, if they keep me tonight, you can have first crack at my baseball card collection. Lucas might fight you over it, but just tell him I made you a promise."

She didn't laugh. Which, in turn, made my smile fade.

"Not funny."

"I guessed by your silence," I replied.

It wasn't lost on me that tonight was heavy, but I'd come to terms with this being my cross to bear—more side-effects of my less than stellar behavior in the very recent past.

"Listen," I sighed, taking a seat on the edge of Grandfather's bed. "When this is all over, when your dad finally releases you from *his* jail ... we'll hang out, act like normal teenagers who *don't* howl at the moon and have tails."

The laugh I'd been waiting on touched my ears.

"Don't get cute," she rebutted. "And don't think me laughing means I've changed my mind. I still think you should make a run for it."

I lowered my head, considering her suggestion one last time, but there was no chance of it.

With the state of things between us, with us just copping to our feelings, admitting what was really on my mind didn't feel like an option. In truth, I couldn't fathom leaving *her*.

If it was just up to us, now that we were no longer on the Council's '*Most Wanted List*', I'd consider taking off with her after graduation. Without being in hiding, we could find work, meaning we wouldn't be destitute like before. But ... it *wasn't* just up to us.

Roz hadn't divulged it yet, but her father—her pack's alpha—was pulling rank, forbidding her to leave the house without permission, especially if her goal was to come see me. I knew as much when she didn't even *attempt* to volunteer to come along to Mount Arvon. Only her pride wouldn't let her admit it.

So, we were stuck for now, but maybe it was for the best.

Instead of making *either* of us uncomfortable by saying too much, I kept my reply to a simple, "Think I'll stay put for now."

She didn't push, maybe because intuition made my reasons clear.

"Well, if you're determined to do this tonight, I suppose we'll chat later. Promise you'll call?"

It was rare for Rozalind Chadwick to be vulnerable, but she definitely was in this moment.

"Of course."

When the line went silent, I looked myself over and one thought came to mind:

Dead man walking.

I was the last of my brothers to arrive. Their cars were parked and empty, reminding me of how close I cut it. Mostly, I procrastinated for fear this might be the last taste of freedom I got for a while, maybe ever.

Think positive.

I stepped out, keeping my eyes trained on the dark windows of the library. It had long since been closed to the public for the day. Now, at this hour, there was only supernatural business to conduct.

One step was all I took before a set of headlights to my left caught my attention. Beside me, a small four-door pulled into the space and confusion rendered me speechless.

"Roz? What're you doing here?" The question left my mouth as soon as I caught sight of her dark hair just above the hood of the car.

She stood completely upright now; soft brown eyes staring back. "I couldn't just sit at home," she reasoned, shutting the door before rounding the hood.

I was set to scold her for coming out, not knowing what this meeting was about, but warmth encircling my neck made those words lodge themselves in my throat. Instead, my arms went around her too, breathing her in as we clung to one another.

How was she even here?

"Your dad let you come?" I asked, still holding on.

The warmth of her hair contrasted the chill in the air when she shook her head.

"No, I just ... came."

Leaning back, I stared at her, knowing she must have put up one heck of a fight to be standing here right now. With her dad being alpha, for her to break free would have to mean ... his hold on her was weakening.

I'd felt it, too. With Richie. Once, there was an unyielding pull to submit to him. But lately, I found it easier and easier to resist. My brothers told me once, when I first transitioned, that I would likely rise to be our pack's alpha. Maybe Roz shared that same fate.

She squeezed again. "Let's get inside before you're late."

Hand in hand, we entered and descended the dark staircase I was all too familiar with. I could hardly believe I had the balls to visit this place again, but the letter I received, requesting my presence, made it impossible to avoid.

Mysterious sounds echoed across the hollow chamber and, standing there, were my three brothers, and a surprise—my dad. Had my mother been allowed to leave the house of her own free will, I was sure she would've come, too. Although my dad hadn't been summoned, it was about solidarity.

I nodded toward my family, noting that none were quite as formal as me. But then again, they hadn't nearly been sentenced to death in this place a short time ago. I think I was allowed to go the extra mile.

"Nice duds," Kyle chuckled, tugging my tie a bit when I stood beside him.

Richie glanced over, taking note of the uninvited guest I brought along. If I had to guess, I'd be hearing about it later. However, he turned away, deciding to let it be for now.

The creaky door behind the Elders' table opened and six figures filed out—three elders, two witches, and the Chancellor. He, in particular, struck untold fear inside me. Perhaps because he seemed the most disappointed I didn't die at his feet several weeks ago.

Each seat at the table was filled and shrouded stares were cast our way. It was the Chancellor who greeted us.

"Gentlemen."

I nodded in response, as did each of my brothers. Roz simply clung to my arm, her grip tightening.

"We thank you all for joining us tonight to discuss a bit of ... delicate business," he went on. "As you are all well aware, the supernatural climate in Seaton Falls has changed quite a bit in recent weeks. Following your pursuit of the Sovereign with our queen, there were repercussions."

I couldn't have agreed more. Sightings of mutts had increased to the point that it'd been discussed whether an evacuation of the human population might be in order.

"Let it first go on record that we knew there would be a response following the attack. However, we allowed it because, quite frankly, this war is imminent. The queen's advances may have altered the timeline a bit, but we like to believe that Sebastian is now aware of something very important; that we, the lycans of Seaton Falls, are a formidable clan. We're willing to stand for the rights of our species, more than eager to bring an end to his reign." His voice trembled with delight as those words left his mouth—grave, deep.

My breaths came rapidly. For quite some time, talk of war felt like nothing more than a rumor, some half-cocked conspiracy theory conjured within the minds of the delusional and paranoid.

But now, it felt different.

Like the Chancellor said, it felt … imminent.

"As you may also know, protecting Evangeline has become a bit of a challenge," he added. "The latest report from one of the guards securing their home is that she attempted to run off several nights ago, only to have her efforts thwarted by a member of her household."

"Run off? Why?" I asked the question without thinking, forgetting to be mindful of the order that was to be kept in this chamber. It couldn't be helped, though. Several people had been worried about Evie since the incident. Myself included.

The Chancellor stared a moment, thrown by my enthusiastic interruption. "It's my understanding that she did so in an attempt to locate the Sovereign again. Apparently, she's got unfinished business with one of his witches," he explained. "It would have been a suicide mission, no doubt, so we were pleased to hear she'd been stopped and taken home."

She was doing worse than I thought, bad enough to take off in the middle of the night, headed toward certain danger. It seemed she'd become a bit … *unhinged.*

Or maybe she was just desperate.

"However, before being taken home," the Chancellor added, "there was an encounter with a band of mutts she and her companion were forced to put down. Which brings me to my next point—the need for additional, *qualified* guards to ensure the safety of Seaton Falls."

My gaze shifted left, toward my father and brothers in a row. Each stood poised, silent as the Chancellor went on, addressing only me this time.

"We've come to a decision regarding your next task on the road to atonement, Nicholas." At the sound of my name rolling off his tongue, I shuddered, recalling the last time I heard it spoken that way.

"Excuse me … *'road to atonement'*? It was my father who asked, but I knew Roz had a similar thought when her grip nearly cut off my circulation.

The Chancellor's gaze slipped to Dad. Or at least I guessed as much when his head swiveled that way. Beneath the cloak it was impossible to tell.

"It was my understanding that the death mission Nick was sent on made him square with you all," my father reasoned. "His debt is paid."

He was so sure of this that it nearly knocked the wind from him when a swift response was fired at him. This time, it was one of the Elders who spoke.

"Mr. Stokes, it's my understanding that those of us present before you today are the *only* beings in existence with the authority to decide when his debt is paid," the Elder seethed, mocking my father in conclusion. "And let us not forget that your wife's freedom hangs by a thread. We're upholding the promise we made our soon-to-be queen, but I don't believe any of us are above pulling rank should we see the need."

The threat was heard loud and clear.

"Besides ... let us also be mindful that the Stokes family name could use a little restoration as well," he added with a wicked smile.

Kyle fumed beside me, but said nothing. It was probably for the best.

The Chancellor's attention was solely on me once again.

He breathed two words at first. "A guard."

My brow quirked, but I waited for further explanation.

"We believe it would suit you. In addition, the role requires discipline, focus—two attributes you could stand to sharpen," The Elder added to the Chancellor's statement.

I could see how they'd think I could use a lesson in both.

"Doesn't he get a say in this?" It was my father who interrupted again, still pleading my case despite being put in his place once already.

I silently wished he'd stand down before he was *put* down.

"Dad ... it's fine," I stated calmly, breathing deep as I went on. "I actually think this might be good for me," I concluded.

There was so much about me that my family didn't know. I'd made it a point to keep my skeletons well-hidden for fear of judgement. So, it didn't surprise me that my father thought I needed rescuing right now. In a sense, I suppose I did, but I wasn't completely sure being trained to guard our town wouldn't be just that.

The long-awaited rescue I needed.

Dad's eyes lingered on mine for quite some time. I guess until he knew I wasn't just saying this to save my hide. When he faced forward again, the Elders and Chancellor were less than amused by yet another interruption, but ignored it since there were no further rebuttals to their decision.

"And while Nicholas' service is somewhat of an order, we would also like to make a similar offer to *you* three," the Chancellor added, gesturing toward my brothers.

"As I stated before, we're in a unique position, a shifting of roles, a shifting of authority," he added, never quite explaining what that meant, but he did the strangest things as those words left his mouth—he briefly turned his attention toward Roz. Noticing it herself, she subtly hid behind me.

"Now would be the perfect time to elevate you three within the community," he went on, "bringing you on as guards to protect our people."

The room was completely silent, all parties involved deep in thought.

"While we'd love to give you an opportunity to mull this over," the Chancellor said, sarcasm dripping from every word, "time is one thing we simply do not have. Given your recent voluntary effort to assist and guard Evangeline, we believe you three would be an excellent addition to the taskforce."

It wasn't lost on me he said '*you three*', meaning I would likely be stationed someplace far away from Evie. I was also sure they knew, like I did, what a good idea that was. Distance was key when it came to she and I.

Kyle breathed deep beside me, but then answered, sounding far more certain than I expected. "I'm in."

The Chancellor nodded in response, turning his head a few degrees toward Richie.

His reply was slightly more reluctant, but he, too, agreed to the new terms.

"I'm in," he echoed.

"Very well," The Chancellor replied. "Benjamin?"

Ben was the last to agree and I wasn't surprised. Of the four of us, he was notoriously too careful and too logical for his own good. But one positive thing came from that—he'd kept us all out of trouble more times than I could count over the years. We some-times made fun of him for not *'living in the moment'*, but respected his stance on things.

Even now.

Maybe, *especially* now.

His throat bobbed when he swallowed, bearing the weight of this decision in his expression when he finally nodded. "I'll do it."

I could practically feel the uneasiness in the room—coming from Roz, my father.

"Then it's settled," the Chancellor concluded. "We'll be in touch in the coming days."

With those words, with the four of us bending to their will, the session was over and the six retreated to their quarters behind the heavy door. It was just us now, and while there were so many things to discuss, none of us said a word.

Seemed our family had just gotten pulled even deeper into the fog of uncertainty. Only, this time, we'd sworn our allegiance.

Whatever went down in Seaton Falls, we'd all just agreed to stand on the front line.

CHAPTER 4

Evie

A heavy sigh preceded Elise's response. "You're seriously considering this? You've brought it up twice now."

Tiptoeing toward the edge of the top step, I stooped beside the rail to hide, just out of view of where Hilda and Elise were discussing their *'options'* yet again.

The first time it'd been brought up was two weeks ago—following my unsuccessful attempt to escape and capture the witch. As I sat in Liam's room that night, they exchanged thoughts outside his door. Now, tonight, they were discussing it again. Like Elise had just pointed out, bringing it up twice meant a lofty idea was slowly transitioning into a plan.

Only, I had no idea what that plan was exactly.

"We said we wouldn't bring anyone else into this. Can't we continue trying with Evangeline? Perhaps the stress of Liam being unresponsive will trigger her in some way," Elise reasoned, only to have Hilda dismiss her idea the next instant.

"If anything, Evangeline is even *less* likely to succeed while under so much pressure. Her head is foggier than ever," she expressed. "I don't even think she's connecting well with her dragon at the moment."

Elise was thoughtful before speaking. "How can you tell?"

"It's ... instinct, I suppose. Witches can sense a supernatural's identifying shifter relatively easily. For her, it was once her dragon that presented strongly. Lately? It's been her wolf—almost completely. If I had to guess, her dragon is mourning the loss of Liam's, even though the *man* is still with us, the *dragon* ... well, it was murdered. At least that's how *she* sees it. And since Evangeline and her dragon are one ... a large part of her feels like she's lost him already."

Both were silent before Hilda added, "So, like I said, she's not the one."

Elise took a step or two, maybe pacing now, but I had no way to confirm from here. "Then, if you're right, our choices are to either give up on bringing the boys back, or bring in another witch —and run the risk of exposure."

Several seconds passed and I was startled when Elise's voice came back.

"What am I even saying?" she scoffed.

This time, I was *sure* she paced.

"Worrying about exposure? Half our family has *already* been exposed," she reasoned. "The Sovereign knows Evangeline has returned, he's already looking to make heads roll because of it ..."

When Hilda replied, I imagined her smiling, because it could be heard in her voice. "And since when have we let the risk of death keep us from doing what's right?"

At those words, I imagined these two causing their share of trouble within the supernatural realm's political system. Both had stronger convictions than almost anyone I knew. Even if those convictions landed them in harm's way. They were fearless. It shouldn't have surprised me that, even now, they were preparing to make yet another bold move that could potentially get them in more trouble than they already stood to face.

"So, who do we have? Who can we *trust*?" Elise amended.

Hilda was quick with her answer. "We can trust no one. But we're beyond that now."

A sheet of paper rustled below, and I wished I had x-ray vision to read it.

"I set out to prepare a list of names, but could only come up with four," Hilda replied. "These are the most powerful, effective witches I know. And, trust me, we'll need lots of power to fill this order.

The paper was exchanged and I waited, imagining Elise skimming Hilda's suggestions. Another deep sigh made it clear she wasn't thrilled about *any* of the options.

"Ora, Elenore, Lorelai, and ... *Maisy*?"

Elise read the last with considerably more disdain than the others, which was saying something seeing as how she nearly spat the others from her mouth.

"I know you hate them all—"

"No kidding!" Elise interrupted.

"But you cannot deny they've all proven their abilities over the years."

"Yes, they absolutely have," Elise scoffed. "One for pulling off the largest heist in world history, one for helping multiple terrorist groups pull off some of the most devastating attacks the history books have ever seen, one for causing several plagues that have successfully wiped out large chunks of the human population over the years, and one who ... one who ..." she paused there, unable to blurt the last offense as freely as those mentioned before.

With the credentials of the others, I had to wonder what this one did that seemed to choke Elise up.

"I never said they ranked high on the moral scale," Hilda said calmly, an air of consolation in her tone. "I said they were effective."

"They're also fugitives," Elise added. "These witches are wanted for multiple criminal acts, with such high prices on their heads you could, literally, purchase a large island and spend less."

"Which is why three of the four may be nearly impossible to coax out of hiding," Hilda reasoned, pausing for a long time before going on. "Which is *also* why Maisy is, perhaps, our best option. She's technically a fugitive, but not nearly as sought after as the others."

A break in conversation came before the reveal of what Maisy's wrongdoing had been. And hearing it, I understood why Elise had such a hard time getting the words out.

"Whoever we call in to assist ... we'll have to invite them into our home, Hilda," she said gravely. "And Maisy? I'm not sure I can do that. Not after what she did to me, my family. What she took from us? The havoc she caused?"

There were more shuffling steps, and then silence.

"She cursed me, Hilda," Elise admitted through quiet sobs. "She's the reason our bloodline is on the verge of dying off."

"But it's *not* dead," was Hilda's thoughtful reply. "Evangeline pushed her way into existence despite Maisy's curse."

"And at what cost?" Elise scoffed. "Thanks to Maisy's magic, with Evangeline also came the Liberator."

Hilda had no response.

"And here we are again, back in the same cycle of hoping and praying history doesn't repeat itself. Praying I don't have to bear the pain of losing my daughter for a second time."

"Lower your voice," Hilda urged, but it was too late. I heard it all. Every single word.

"We must keep in mind that Maisy was not acting of her own will in those days. She was under the Sovereign's rule as his chief witch, and had no choice but to do his bidding. Even if his bidding included cursing the bloodline of his only rival—Noah, my brother."

"How can you even ask me to consider this, Hilda?" Elise's voice was strained, quiet.

"I can ask you to consider it because we want those boys back. And you know as well as I do that our backs are against the wall now. So, if you're sure you want to drop it here, forego the restoral, then I'll support that decision," Hilda reasoned. "But ... if you want to bring them back ... this is what we must do."

The air inside the house felt thick, uncomfortable. Knowing it'd come down to this, I identified with Elise's hopelessness.

"Maybe this is where we're supposed to stop." Her French accent was heaviest when her emotions were high, and now I heard it stronger than ever. "What if we're not meant to tamper with nature any more than we already have? Liam could wake up tomorrow and that alone would give us quite an advantage when things take a turn."

Hilda's silence made that strange heaviness in the air so much worse. When she spoke again, her voice was filled with remorse.

And I hated it.

"You love him like a son," she began, "and I, too, hold the same affection in my heart for him that I do for *all* my family ... but—"

My ears perked then, listening harder when she said more.

"Things are too dire to continue on like this, Elise, forsaking realism when we're both aware of the circumstances," she stated. "He should have awakened by now. I lifted the spell more than a month ago, and yet ... he hasn't moved a muscle. The longer he remains in this way, the bleaker his chance of recovery," she added. "We must accept the fact that ... he may *not* recover."

My heart sank to the floor and she pushed a knife into it with her final words.

"Elise ... Liam is gone."

No. Absolutely not.

I refused to accept that.

There was no way I'd been sitting beside a dead man all this time. Liam was in there somewhere, lost in the darkness, trying to find his way back to me. I knew he was. Whether anyone else still believed it or not.

Suddenly not caring if Hilda and Elise heard me above them, I stormed down the hall, slamming Liam's bedroom door behind me, locking it. I stood there, staring at his lifeless body, illuminated by the lamp at his bedside table.

Liam is gone.

I heard Hilda's voice echoing those words inside my head over and over again, but they simply would not stick. I wouldn't be left here alone. Even surrounded by other family, friends, without him I would most certainly be alone.

There had to be something. Something I hadn't thought of, something I hadn't tried. Searching every corner of his room with my eyes, I came up with nothing. My gaze fell on him again and I felt my heart tugging in his direction. Not the supernatural pull I'd gotten accustomed to, just the longing of a girl so beside herself with love it was almost criminal.

He looked like he was only sleeping. How could she all but pronounce him dead already?

I went to his side, swiping tears with every step.

"Why are you doing this to me?" The question left my mouth on its own, no rational thought backing it. I knew he couldn't hear me, knew my voice fell on deaf ears, but I couldn't help it.

His hand was warm when I took it, tracing the dark ink of a tattooed compass on the back of it as more tears soaked the collar of my shirt.

"This can't be how it ends, Liam. You said we had forever," I reasoned. "And I believed you."

The tears transitioned from sad to angry, washing down my face with heat and fury.

"I believed you," I whispered.

It was futile to be livid with an unconscious man, but I was. My happiness was solely wrapped up in him. It was unhealthy, I know, but it hadn't been a choice. My heart wanted what it wanted ... and my heart wanted him.

"You're not allowed to leave me," I sobbed.

In one last hopeless attempt to feel the closeness we used to share, I brought his hand to my chest, placing it over my heart, where our tether once linked me to him. The warmth of his palm made more tears swell in my eyes, spilling over my lower lids when I closed them.

Even with him resting in some distant place, I could still feel his love. That's how powerful it was. If Hilda was right, how was I ever supposed to let that go? Convince myself to keep pressing ahead without it?

At the thought, my heart beat even more wildly, causing my pulse to vibrate at the base of my neck. I was overwhelmed with grief—over what could have been, over wasted love.

Standing there, I let it all pour from me like a volcano erupting for the first time in millennia. I was so full, holding it in for fear of having to accept that things might never get better. But I wouldn't hold it in anymore.

My heart thumped against his palm—hard, wild.

I let him feel me, the pain losing him would cause. I let my guard down and stopped fighting so hard to bridle these fierce emotions that had my entire life frozen in time—pining over him, waiting.

I let him feel everything

... And that's when it happened.

That's when movement pulsed in his fingers.

My eyes sprang open only to land on hazel ones slowly blinking back in response.

I couldn't move, thinking I might wake up from the dream if I did. This had to be that, a dream. Quivering breaths breezed across my lip as I did all I could to stave off hyperventilation.

His hand at the center of my chest moved again, gently gathering the material of my shirt in his fingers as the grogginess seemed to make it hard to focus, to get his bearings.

"I'm here," I whispered, unable to speak much louder than that. "I'm here."

At the sound of my voice, a bit of awareness seemed to return and he settled down a bit.

I was ravished by so many thoughts, all at once.

Was I dreaming?

Did this mean he'd be okay?

Should I call for help?

Had this transition changed more than just his physical body?

… Would he remember me?

My first impression of him, months ago when he stepped out of my dreams, was that he, in all his beauty and intensity, was impossible. Someone like him, someone so unimaginably perfect for me, couldn't possibly exist.

Today, as my fingers slipped between his, I had that same feeling.

It'd been too long—too long since I stared at him and he actually stared back.

Too long since I felt his arms around me.

Too long since I heard his voice.

My mouth opened and shut, feeling dry all of a sudden. I was unsure what to say or do next, unsure which of my questions would be answered yes, which would be no. But … Liam did his part to relieve me of one uncertainty. And all it took to convince me was one word.

"...Evangeline."

He hadn't forgotten me.

A deep groan passed through his lips when I rushed in, squeezing him harder than I probably should have, but I was beside myself with too many emotions to identify. Drawing myself into his bed, I curled up beside him, trying to catch my breath as hot tears soaked my face.

He held me back and I wouldn't move from this spot. Not until I had to. It felt like I was owed this—the chance to soak up his undivided attention before having to share him with the others.

Inhaling deep, I breathed him in, pressing my face to the side of his neck, feeling his pulse against my mouth when I placed a kiss there. I let my eyes drift closed, fighting to keep my emotions wrangled in, but that was almost impossible. He had no idea how long he'd been out, how long I'd been suffering. No idea how much had changed. I'd get around to telling him everything eventually, but ... not right now.

Right now, I just wanted ... *this*.

CHAPTER 5

Liam

One hour changed everything. That was all it took to pry the details free from Evangeline, although I was sure she still held some back, wanting to avoid overwhelming me.

It only took an hour to understand the hell she'd been through waiting for me to come around.

An hour to realize I'd been out six weeks and Seaton Falls had practically become a military base.

An hour to realize we were weeks, maybe *days* away from the Sovereign retaliating for the clan's insubordination; for Evangeline's ambush and rescue that crippled his army.

But what *didn't* take an hour to figure out, was that *I* awakened ... but my dragon did not.

The second I opened my eyes, I sensed the emptiness swirling about with the initial confusion. It was a change that could be felt all over. I was marginally slower even with the small movements I'd attempted so far, less alert. My senses had dulled, too, and the feeling of my actions lagging behind my thoughts was disorienting.

Outside the window, water dripped from melting icicles onto the tin awning below. That coupled with sunlight beaming through the blind's slats were signs of what I guessed to be a late-arriving spring. Evangeline said March had been the coldest month so far, but as soon as April arrived, the difference in the weather was like night and day.

Closing my eyes in the dead of winter, and then waking up on the cusp of spring, made me feel that much more disconnected.

At the thought, I pulled Evangeline closer. She felt like the only constant thing that followed me over from what felt like a past life, into this one. My palm was met with the warmth of smooth skin when I touched her arm, making my heart beat faster with the contact. It seemed I couldn't get close enough, and from what I could tell, she felt the same.

"Thank you for coming back to me," she breathed against my shoulder, lifting her gaze to meet mine.

I opened my mouth, and noted the unfamiliar rasp of it—a side-effect of being down for so long.

"I wish I could say it'd been a choice," I admitted. "Feels like I've been out for a decade, dreaming," I sighed. "My sense of time is … it's all distorted. Things that happened centuries ago feel like just yesterday."

I wondered if that was where my consciousness had been—visiting memories from the past, reveling in the comfort they brought while I was away.

"Don't worry about any of that," she insisted, moving her hand across my stomach, letting it rest there as I breathed deep. "You'll catch up."

I liked to think that was true, but 'catching up' meant more than being brought up to speed on events I missed.

My eyes drifted down to evaluate my body. No, I didn't look any different, but inside? I had no idea who this person was.

"Looks like you took good care of me," I smiled, forcing myself not to dwell on the bad. The inevitable.

She smiled back. "It was mostly Hilda. She cast charms to keep your muscle mass from deteriorating, to get rid of the scars, to keep you from needing much physical care. It made it so we didn't need to disturb you," she shared, adding, "All I really did was ... sit here."

She gave another smile after that, but this time it was a bit of a shy one. Like she didn't think that'd been enough.

But to me, her presence, her devotion ... it was everything.

I placed a kiss in the soft, coiled strands on top of her head.

"How are Elise and the others?"

I didn't miss Evangeline's lack of urgency to let the rest of the household know I was awake, but I had no problem with her selfishness. I preferred when it was just us.

"They're all downstairs," she answered, lifting from my shoulder to swing a leg over the edge of the mattress the next second. "I can get them."

She'd mistaken the question for a request. Just before she stood, I stopped her, looping my fingers around her wrist before she could get too far.

"Slow down. Hang on a sec."

She turned to find me smiling and did the same.

"You're ... okay?" I knew it was an incredibly broad question, one with so many answers, but I had to ask.

Very few understood what it was like to be tethered to someone, and then have them leave you. Painful didn't even begin to describe it. It was like having your *own* soul ripped from your body. Even I felt the loss, the disconnection, but for her, it was different. She'd watched time pass, not knowing if I'd ever wake up.

That would be heavy for *anyone*. But it was especially heavy for someone who'd experienced as much loss and displacement as she had.

"I'm good," she nodded, hiding so much.

A long stare passed between us as I studied her face and posture, looked her over with the scrutiny of a protector who knew his mate like the back of his hand.

"Evangeline ..."

She dropped the act the instant it became obvious I wasn't buying it. She *wasn't* okay; no one would expect her to be. However, it was in her nature to be strong even when it wasn't required.

Like now, when it was just us.

There were several things I was sure had to be on constant repeat inside her head. For starters, now that I was human, I was vulnerable to things like broken bones, illness ... death.

No one was more aware of these things than me. Nor was it lost on me who was responsible. At the thought of Sebastian, his witches, his soldiers ... my fists clenched. Their methods of torture hadn't changed over the years; they were still just as barbaric as ever. Mostly they wanted information, wanted pieces of me to sell off, but they also just enjoyed causing pain.

I could only imagine the condition Evangeline must have found me in. Anger spiked and I pushed past it, refusing to let it take my focus off her.

She didn't rush to share her feelings, the thoughts that made water begin to pool in her eyes, so I took that as a sign not to push.

"Have you hung out with Beth?" I asked instead.

It didn't surprise me when she shook her head. "Haven't really had time, but we text."

That was a stupid question, knowing she'd been right here in this spot unless it was absolutely necessary to leave my side.

I was running out of things to say, things that weren't off limits, uncomfortable.

"We haven't talked much, but she was with me that day," Evangeline said, breaking the silence that crept between us. "When I came for you."

The incident was so foggy—a collage of images, faces, and sounds that didn't quite fit together.

"If it hadn't been for her and the others, I wouldn't have made it." Her voice quivered a bit, but she didn't falter, didn't succumb to the emotion I sensed just beneath her words.

"I owe you my life," I breathed into her ear before placing a kiss there. "*All* of you."

She was quiet again, but this time it was more reflective than anything.

"Do you ... remember?" she asked. "Remember everyone who helped?"

I would have been lying if I said yes, when all that seemed to register was that I'd seen *her* during a brief, lucid moment, and then blacked out again.

When I shook my head, she didn't offer any further explanation, which only made me curious.

"Who came?"

Big, brown eyes blinked up at me. "Dallas," she began, "Beth, Chris, Luke," she went on, adding the last names hesitantly. "There was also Nick and his brothers."

My body went rigid, only now aware of the danger she put herself in.

Because of me.

The prevailing feeling within me, since opening my eyes, had been weakness, but now the word took on a whole new meaning. It had nothing to do with the bad blood that existed between Nick and I, but had *everything* to do with the sudden reminder of all Evangeline needed protecting from.

Starting with him.

"I went to the Elders, asked them to let him go free in exchange for his help," she went on, adding to the mounting reasons for my pulse to race. It was hard to tell if she'd done all these things because she was too trusting, or ... if me being captured had simply made her desperate.

"He almost died trying to help me," she added. "Trying to help ... *you*."

There was such conviction in her tone. It was there whenever she spoke of Nick in the past, but it had faded last I remembered. With it's return, I guessed it meant this ordeal had led to her forgiving him.

Which might *also* mean she'd let her guard down with him, trusting him again when he was just as much a threat today as he always was. She couldn't afford to forget that. Especially now, with me in no position to protect her.

"I knew you wouldn't like it, but I ... there was no other way, and—"

"Don't apologize," I cut in as she stammered.

The last of what I needed to say was particularly hard to admit. Mostly because I didn't want her thinking I condoned it.

"You did what you had to do."

I wanted to add to that a reminder, something I told her once when she'd run into the woods when I'd been attacked by mutts—she was never to run toward danger. Definitely not for me. She'd broken so many rules to save me—mine, the Council's. Although, if they handed Nick over to her, she must have done this all with their blessing. Which left me with the sense that no one but me was qualified to look out for her.

She leaned in, placing a soft kiss to my lips—one that, if I'd been stronger, might have turned into more.

"Be back," she announced, standing from my bed with a dim smile. "I suppose it's time to share you with everyone else now."

It wasn't a shock that, between Elise and Hilda, Hilda was the most frank with me. Elise, emotional and unable to form words for the first several minutes, sat holding my hand on the side Evangeline hadn't taken.

"Things have mostly been calm here," Hilda began, adding, "Almost *too* calm, if you ask me."

Elise's gaze lowered at the very moment my brow tensed.

"He's fully aware of the Damascus facility," Hilda continued, "and others like it, operating without his knowledge, fully aware that a member of the Bahir Dar royal family is alive and likely residing here, and yet ... he has yet to do more in Seaton Falls territory than send in a handful of mutts. There's even been talk of evacuating the town's human population to minimize casualties."

I focused on the wall while thinking.

"Has he called a meeting with the High Council?" I asked.

Hilda shook her head and the grave expression she wore said it all. "According to what we've been told, they haven't heard a peep."

She was right ... this wasn't good.

"He hasn't been completely quiet, though," she added. "Every day, the news reports a new animal sighting, a new name to add to the list of missing persons. All men. All athletic in build."

Sebastian hadn't changed his stripes. This—creating an army of mutts—when his back was against the wall wasn't a new tactic. This was the exact move that enabled him to be the victor of the Lunar War.

This was how he slaughtered so many of my comrades, Elise's sons, her husband.

I pushed the thought from my head.

"We haven't been sitting idle either," Hilda sighed. "You'll find that Seaton Falls' population has become a bit … *shifter* heavy," she smiled.

"They brought in others?"

When she nodded, I breathed a sigh of relief. No, we weren't out of the woods, but higher numbers was a step in the right direction.

"There were clans that refused, but most showed up without the Council even requesting their involvement," Elise added.

That didn't surprise me. The lycans were tired of being ruled by a tyrant.

"He has to know by now how deep this rebellion against him has spread," Hilda stated. "And you know as well as I do, he has no tolerance for insubordination."

The man had an ego that barely fit in the solar system, so yes, I had an idea of how something like this going on right under his nose might be frowned upon.

I glanced up at Dallas where he stood at the foot of my bed, reading the heavy concern on his face.

"What are *your* thoughts?" I asked, aiming the question at him.

A deep surge of air swelled his chest and, letting it out, he answered. "I believe we're in the calm before the storm. And, historically speaking, that means any day now … all hell will break loose."

As much as I wanted to argue with his logic, I'd seen enough war in my lifetime to know he was exactly right.

CHAPTER 6

Nick

This was the closest night I'd had to a normal one in so long I couldn't even remember.

Just me, Chris, Lucas, a box of pizza, and *Madden* fired up on the Xbox.

Like old times.

Not so long ago, I didn't think I'd ever lay eyes on them again— on *anyone* I cared about. Because I was always aware of how close I came to that being my reality, I learned not to take so many things for granted. First free night I got that Roz couldn't break past her father's coercion, I invited the guys over to the estate to hang out.

"Are you freakin' kidding me?" Lucas yelled, feeling zero shame for getting emotional over an ugly loss, thanks to a well-timed, last-minute touchdown.

I tossed the controller to the floor, celebrating in his face just to piss him off.

"Now *that's* how it's done."

He shoved me aside before reaching for another slice.

"Yeah, whatever. Just keep in mind that *I'm* the one who taught you to play," was his comeback.

I shrugged, settling in my seat again with a brazen grin. "On Xbox ... maybe, I'll give you that. But I'm *definitely* the one who schooled you on the *real* field."

"Are you serious?" Lucas protested over Chris's laughter, sounding more like a howl. "Last I checked, our stats were nearly identical."

"Then you must not have checked since sixth grade, because my stats *own* yours, boy!"

Chris was nearly on the floor, out of breath as he pointed at a very irritated, very red Lucas.

"Whatever, just run it back," Lucas concluded, abandoning his food for another round.

I picked up my controller again, and happily obliged.

Beside me, my cell chirped, and Chris grabbed it before I had the chance, reading the incoming text aloud.

"I kinda miss you," he recited, doing his best impression of Roz. "But have fun with the guys and call me later," he added as I snatched the phone from his hand.

He and Lucas got a laugh out of it, of course. To them, it was still strange how Roz had gone from being my sworn enemy to ... well ... '*kinda missing me*'.

They didn't have to understand it, though. To me, to *us,* it made perfect sense. In so many ways, we were compatible. She was calm and level-headed, while I had a tendency to take things too seriously. We were opposites, but that's why we worked.

I took a sec to text back, letting her know I missed her, too, and then un-paused the game.

"Things with y'all are getting pretty serious, huh?" Lucas asked.

I shrugged, having an answer, but being very much aware of the fact that he was only asking to mock me.

"So, how's she feel about your new job?" This time it was Chris who asked, and, unlike Lucas, he wasn't aiming to get under my skin.

I shrugged and waited until completing my touchdown to answer. "I'm sure she hates it, but she hasn't said much. In her opinion, I should've ghosted when we came back from the U.P."

In my peripheral, Chris nodded. "With how things are going, she might be right," he scoffed.

We all noticed the changes—how the streets, stores, and schools were more crowded than they'd ever been. All the newcomers, the *shifters,* were hard to miss in such a small town. The Council was readying Seaton Falls for attack. Our quaint town nestled beside a waterfall, was likely soon to be marked in history as the site of one of the supernatural world's bloodiest battles.

And yet ... I hadn't run away.

Maybe I was crazier than I thought.

"Where do they have you posted?" Lucas asked, chiming in again as I intercepted another of his sloppy passes.

I laughed, giving the most accurate answer I could. "As far away from Evie as possible."

They both chuckled, understanding.

In the Council's eyes—maybe in mine, too—I was a ticking timebomb, set to detonate at some unknown hour. So, the smartest thing to do was position me far from Evie's house, with a team of experienced guards who I had no doubt would shoot me on site if I started freaking out. In fact, one had all but told me so during training.

So, there's that ...

"They've got me near the old warehouse, deep in the woods," I clarified.

"Seen any action?" Chris asked

"Not too much. We get the occasional mutt wandering in, but nothing too crazy. They've gotten to be a bit more frequent over the couple weeks they've had me out there. I'm guessing because the Sovereign is sending them in to scout, report back."

Neither spoke right away, probably thinking the same thing I was—that, soon, things here would change forever, and there wasn't much of a chance they'd ever go back to being like they were.

"I, for one, just wish we could get it all over with, take the fight to *him*," was Lucas' idea.

"You read my mind," Chris concurred.

"Nah, they have to play it cool. The guy has some pretty powerful witches." I'd seen as much with my own two eyes. "And who knows what else," I added.

All our thoughts seemed to snag on that concept—that no one had any idea what the Sovereign had planned, what he had up his sleeve. All we could do was prepare ourselves for battle.

For war.

"And that's game," I gloated, patting Lucas on his head when I stood.

He pushed my hand away and I laughed, stepping over his outstretched legs as I passed between him and my grandfather's old school TV set, which was even older than Richie, I guessed.

"Give yourself a pep talk while I'm in the bathroom," I called back over my shoulder, rubbing in the fact that I beat him.

Again.

He mumbled something under his breath that I didn't catch as I rounded the corner. Flipping the switch beside the door, I locked myself in.

... And that's when the world around me fell away, plunging me into total darkness, all that awaited was emptiness

Emptiness like none I'd ever experienced.

Gasping for air, I bolted upright, fighting through a fog of confusion, unsure where I was, how I'd gotten there, how much time had passed.

It was the feel of cold wetness beneath my hands that gave the first hint of being outdoors. Then the tall, surrounding shadows shifted into focus, suddenly becoming white pines and oaks, familiar. A heavy breath puffed from my mouth as I stood, rising from all fours, naked.

There was no doubt in my mind I'd shifted into my wolf, despite not remembering. I blinked, trying to get my bearings.

I spun slowly, but couldn't make heads or tails of which direction I was facing, where I might have been headed.

Nothing. Just trees, melting snow, and moonlight.

I breathed deep, knowing there was only one way to tap into my body's internal compass, and that was to shift back into my wolf.

So, I did, grunting and panting until each bone had moved into place and I was on paws instead of hands and feet.

I turned right and sniffed the air. East—the direction of my grandfather's estate. I aimed my body that way and walked. My steps were sluggish, which meant I'd been running at full-speed for a long time.

Why did this keep happening?

Where was I going?

What did it all mean?

My foot smashed down into a cool puddle of slush and mud

just before I heard it—a second set of steps tailing me. I stopped, but didn't turn, just listened. I heard it again, coming closer now. When I sensed whoever—or *whatever*—it was close enough that I might get a good look, I whirled around, scanning the trees for movement.

There, in the shadows ... another wolf. Too far away to catch a scent. Whoever it was, they knew to keep their distance.

We were in a stalemate. If I continued on, they'd follow, and would possibly attack me from behind. If I pursued them, it could be perceived as a threat, ending in a fight.

But ... before I could decide what to do, this wolf ... he or she took a step toward *me*.

I stiffened, wondering if it was a mistake not to take off running while I still had the chance. But that's when I caught the scent—female, familiar.

Roz.

As if she, too, just now realized I wasn't a threat, her steps quickened. When she ducked behind a tree, I paused, confused as to why she hid. It wasn't clear until her wolf, silhouetted by moonlight, shrank into the form of a woman. The only part of her visible to me was the shadow she cast in the snow.

I stepped closer on instinct, wanting to go to her, but I quickly reminded myself she might not appreciate me prying. For one thing, she hid herself behind the tree for a reason. Still, the inkling to peek was there.

"You good?" she asked, panting after her shift.

There was no way to reply like this, without being human.

She laughed from her hiding spot. "Just ... change back. I won't look. Promise," she added.

If I'd been able to, I might have smiled—despite having no idea what was going on or how I got here.

The chilled air hit my skin and I immediately missed my fur. Taking a page from Roz's book, I pressed my back to the opposite side of the tree, halfway sure I could feel her energy pulsing through it.

Or maybe I just *wanted* to feel it … wanted to be close to her.

"Chris and Lucas called me," she stated. "They said you took off and they had no clue where you were headed."

Good to know I wasn't the only one.

"I pulled away from my dad and came right out to find you."

Pulled away … I assumed she meant she somehow managed to break rank again, resisting the inclination to submit when an alpha pushed.

"When they described what happened, I assumed you'd gone dark again."

I smiled at the cutesy little way she put that, like me *going dark* didn't have sinister implications.

"I appreciate your concern, but these woods aren't safe anymore. I told you about the mutts and—"

"Which is why I came," she cut in, missing the point I was trying to make.

I breathed deep, glancing around, wishing I had the answers.

"Why didn't you tell me the episodes started again?" Her voice was soft, sympathetic.

The back of my head rested against the bark while I thought of the right words. When I found them, I answered.

"Because I didn't want you to be as disappointed as I was. Because I didn't want you to lose hope that I was getting better."

She was quiet and I didn't blame her.

There was something seriously wrong with me, and just when I thought things were beginning to turn around, *this* happened.

"You scared us all pretty bad," she added in that same somber tone.

I nodded, despite her not having a clear visual of me. Truth was, I scared myself sometimes, too.

"They stopped for a while. The blackouts," she clarified. "Do you think they're back because you had to kill again?"

I considered that. The venture north to help Evie retrieve Liam may have been a setback, but I still felt like my other theory was a better fit.

"Nick?"

I glanced up when she said my name, focusing on the moon and stars when I chose to let her inside my head.

"I think it might be a lot of things," I shared. "But, most of all, I think it's you."

She said nothing.

"Well ... I think it's a *lack* of you," I clarified.

A soft chuckle brought a smile to my face.

"*This* is new," she teased. "When'd you come up with it?"

"Mmm ... around the time I had to climb down from my grand-father's roof and had no idea how I got there."

Somehow, despite it not being a laughing matter, we laughed anyway.

I glanced left when five thin fingers wiggled beside me. I latched onto her hand, feeling relief the second we made contact.

"If I could hug you right now, I would," she sighed. "You're not alone in this. You could have told me."

I knew this before she even said it, but my original statement still held. There was this huge part of me that was dead-set against disappointing her. In *any* capacity.

"Tell you what, next time—if there *is* a next time—I'll say something."

I imagined her nodding when she replied. "I'll hold you to it."

A period of silence crept between us and the next second, her fingers untangled from mine.

"Race you back?" A broad smile touched my lips at the sound of a challenge in Roz's voice. Especially when she added, "Unless you're scared I'll win."

Before I could even reply, a commotion on the other side of the tree meant she'd gotten a head start on shifting. By the time I turned to confirm, she sprinted off into the darkness.

I smiled and followed her lead.

It wasn't lost on me that the first time we met had been because *I* saved *her*. But lately, in circumstances like the one we found ourselves in tonight ... seemed she'd been the one saving *me*.

CHAPTER 7

Evie

They were preparing for something.

Twice, Elise rushed downstairs with her phone to her ear, speaking in code about an estimated time of arrival and shielding sigils. Hilda was unusually quiet, holed up inside her room, which usually meant she was studying.

Dallas wasn't so much behaving oddly, just being a bit ... aloof. At dinner, he didn't have much to say, and whenever Elise made an attempt to pull him into the conversation, he responded with nods and head shakes instead of actual words. She'd then pass him a weary smile before turning back to her plate.

Like I said, things were just a bit strange.

And then there was Liam—shockingly normal, considering all he'd been through. Actually, he was a bit *too* normal. He hadn't said much about the changes I was sure he'd been experiencing—

physically, emotionally—but I couldn't imagine this not being a difficult time.

Every now and then, when there was no conversation or background distraction to help him hide it, I caught him zoning out, lost in thoughts he hadn't yet shared. I made it a point not to push, but I hoped to discuss it soon. Aside from those bouts of drifting, he was the same old Liam.

Attentive.

Protective.

Loving.

Thinking of him as I toweled my hair dry, I nearly attempted to wander inside his head. It only took a second to remember we were no longer connected. A flicker of sadness crept in, but I smothered it with thoughts of how grateful I was just to have him back. How grateful I was that the Sovereign and his witches hadn't taken him from me completely.

I dug around in my drawer until I found it—an oversized t-shirt I stole from Liam's laundry a few days ago. Slipping it over my head, I stepped out into the dark hallway. The house was completely quiet, which was why I nearly leapt out of my skin when I took a step and a voice pierced the silence.

"Going somewhere?"

Hilda ... I swear the woman's a freakin' ninja.

I cleared my throat, knowing she only asked because she had a knack for putting me on the spot. We *both* knew where I was going.

I sighed but didn't answer.

A soft laugh fluttered into the air, one quiet enough that no one more than a few feet away would have heard.

"Go but remember, he's not as strong as he used to be. He might not be comfortable admitting it, but he feels the difference," she added. "I've been keeping an eye on him. He gets tired easily."

Even if she hadn't said it, I knew. No one had kept a closer eye on him lately than I had.

Her statement killed some of my enthusiasm to cross his threshold. My desire to be with him hadn't lessened, but I now questioned whether it was selfish for me to disturb him tonight.

Well ... *every* night.

I suppose I was pestering him a bit, although he didn't seem bothered, but he needed more down time than before. The thought crossed my mind that I should just turn around.

Hilda let out another soft laugh. "I didn't mean to discourage you. He needs you," she reassured me. "I only meant to caution you. He may need a reminder to slow down from day to day, if he's too prideful to tell you *himself*."

I considered her suggestion—one of many she'd made lately concerning him—and nodded.

"Yes, ma'am."

Continuing toward the steps, where I assumed she was headed before I came out of my room, Hilda touched a hand to my shoulder. Alone, I stared at Liam's door, the faint outline of light between it and the frame. Hilda was right about giving him time to heal, to rest, but ... I couldn't seem to make myself stay away.

I walked in, aware of running water in his attached bathroom as I closed the door behind me. The sheets were cool when I slipped between them, snuggling beneath the comforter while I waited. His bed was now basically mine, too, seeing as how this was where I spent all my nights.

Not that he seemed to mind sharing his space.

The water stopped and my keen hearing made it easy to mark his every move—the moment his foot landed on the rug beside the shower, the rustling of fabric when he grabbed a towel, the hinges creaking when he opened the door.

Our eyes locked and I was relieved to note how his expression softened at the sight of me, making it clear he definitely preferred our new sleeping arrangement versus the old.

Feeling unbearably shy under his stare, my teeth sank into my lip as he sauntered closer. Beads of water escaped the ends of his hair, streaming wet trails down his chest, his stomach. It was impossible to decide whether he looked better coming or going. Even after seeing him from all angles, I hadn't been able to choose.

I hardly took my eyes off him this week, since he'd been awake and, once again, an active member of our household. But mostly, I hadn't been able to look away because I was drawn to him. Just like the proverbial moth to a flame. In fact, the allure seemed to be even stronger now than before.

A warm smile passed my way and my heart lurched as he lowered onto his side of the mattress, covered only by the towel wrapped around his waist.

"You're spoiling me," he said. "Having you here every night is something I could definitely get used to again." The words puffed from his lips with a deep, gentle laugh, but I was fixated on one word in particular.

Again.

He said again. As in ... like before.

Our past together was never far from his mind.

My fingers flitted through my still-damp hair, and the thoughts I tried to keep bridled got away from me. Once *that* happened, it wasn't long until a bit of doubt crept in despite myself.

Thanks to Hilda.

"Is it ... okay?" I stammered. "It wouldn't hurt my feelings if you wanted space sometimes."

And it wouldn't. The last thing I wanted was for him to feel crowded out of his own sanctuary. I understood he was dealing with a lot, and wouldn't take it personally.

His brow tensed when he glanced back, letting an incredulous laugh slip out.

"Are you joking?"

The question made a smile quirk on my lips, but I didn't respond.

"Evangeline, I'm pretty sure the decision to return to your own bed would force me to kidnap you," he chuckled. "I'd drag you back, kicking and screaming if I had to."

That smile of his widened and the bout of nervousness passed.

"Caveman-style?" I asked, relaxing against his headboard.

His thick brow jutted up when he passed another look over his massive shoulder.

"If that's how you like it," he quipped.

Those smoldering, hazel irises dragged over me, the look inducing erratic breaths before my eyes slipped from his.

Lower.

To a body corded in rigid muscle, sheathed in bronzed skin. The temptation to reach my hand toward his back was overwhelming. At the very thought, I imagined feeling the water from his shower on my palm.

He needs rest, Evangeline.

I repeated those words to myself often, in moments of weakness such as this. A few minutes ago hadn't been the first time Hilda scolded me. She issued *many* warnings, actually. All brought on by her tendency to catch me watching him, or sneaking into his room like tonight. Once, she went as far as comparing my behavior to a cat in heat, clawing at the walls, restless. I didn't argue with her, and actually laughed at the analogy because, well ... her observation wasn't too far off.

I sighed, feeling the steady thrum of my pulse throbbing in my lips as I licked them.

He needs rest.

Hilda was right; I should back off.

"So, I heard you and Dallas talking about putting that gym in the basement to good use," I inquired—anything to get my thoughts fixated on something other than ... *the physical.*

Liam nodded, using the second towel he brought with him to dry his hair a bit.

"Yeah, I think it's time. I know everyone's concerned about me taking it easy, but I won't get back to being myself by just sitting around."

Silence.

Neither of us spoke as I imagined mirrored thoughts passed between us—that no amount of working out would ever really get him back to being himself. There wasn't an exercise regimen for reviving a dragon.

"But ... that's the plan," he sighed.

I pursed my lips together as I watched him. There were certain topics I avoided. *We* avoided. Talking about how he felt was one of them, but it only seemed right to ask.

"Are you ... okay?" My voice was small, and I hated the tone of the question the instant it left my mouth. *'Defeated'* was the word that came to mind.

Broad shoulders lifted into the air with a shrug, the muscles beneath them working with each movement.

"Depends on the day," was all he said.

I didn't push.

With what seemed like a forced smile, he gazed at me. "But I hardly notice I'm not whole when you're here."

I drank in the sight of him, drowning in the emotional wells through which he stared.

He needs rest.

Giving him space was easier said than done. I understood he still needed time to completely recover, regain his strength, but ... did he really *need* strength? I mean, I had no problem doing all the work.

I discreetly palmed my forehead.

Dude ... seriously? What the heck are you saying? Just ... stop!

My cheeks burned hot as I imagined us entangled in ways I ought not to, considering he was still on the mend and all. But then he stood, our gazes locking once more, as if these unladylike thoughts of mine had been blasted from a speaker. Didn't help that I *looked* guilty—biting my own lips because I'd gotten beside myself.

He blinked and I knew he felt it, the raw, almost animalistic attraction I held for him. Usually, I was able to hide it, but not so much lately.

Maybe it was brought on by my excitement over having him back.

Maybe it was because nearly losing him made the feelings between us so much more powerful.

I loved him, yes, but ... this felt like more than love.

It was a deeply rooted need I developed—to belong to him. The only thing that made sense for me was being his.

Let the man rest.

Good ol' Hilda's voice rang inside my head again, also making me recall yet *another* of her helpful quips—*'Put it on ice, child!'*

I smiled to myself, hearing her rich dialect as though she were in the room with us. Liam—having no inkling of the madness running rampant inside my head—smiled back before disappearing for only a moment to slip into a pair of pants. On his way back, he turned out the lights. I listened to his steps as he crossed the room and then filled the space beside me.

Within seconds, I was warm and in my happy place—his arms. Solid, strong, they engulfed me. Breathing deep, the smell of him satisfied my senses—the combination of his skin's earthy aroma, blended with soap and clean linen.

I remembered waking up in his bed after I first transitioned. That same intoxicating blend had been on his sheets, the shirt he loaned me after burning my own. I didn't realize then that I'd always known it, but I did now.

We were more than a couple, more than bonded.

We were soul mates.

The vows we took centuries ago were merely a formality, I guessed, because although I had no memory of the promises exchanged, the connection was still present and strong.

Even in the absence of our tether.

"I could do this forever," he uttered, the softly spoken words moving into my hair.

He trailed my skin, arousing goosebumps down my arm that met his fingertips on contact, and now our hearts thundered in sync. Mine desperately seeking his, nearly leaping from my chest as he drew me closer by the curve of my hip. I submitted, letting my figure fuse to his beneath the blanket.

A deep, quivering breath left his mouth and I shuttered, feeling the weight of his need—an unquenchable need that plagued us both. The desperation was nearly tangible, leaving no reason to acknowledge it aloud.

Let him rest.

I heard it ... the warning ... but was lulled into a daze by a kiss. One so deep, so mind-bendingly intimate, all sense of time and space melted away, leaving nothing behind but us.

Sharing this bed was once steeped in innocence, a means of solace we both sought. However, as the temperature beneath the comforter rose, our good intentions burned away until they no longer existed.

All that remained was temptation.

Heat from Liam's lips triggered tiny explosions wherever they touched my skin—my mouth, the underside of my jaw, the hollow of my throat, my collar bone.

He was ... everywhere.

His palm moved to my thigh, pulsing more heat through the

limb as it was brought to his waist—a rough motion that shouldn't have excited me so much, but it did.

The sound of wild, rapid breaths filled the space around us. We swallowed long drags of air as though we were drowning.

Maybe we were.

Drowning in this feeling, in each other.

My hands roamed his solid frame with the greed of a woman starved for the affection of her mate, somehow aching for physical contact I'd never even had the pleasure of knowing.

Or maybe I did.

Maybe some small part of me remembered what it was like to be with Liam. Which was why it seemed so natural to decide the wait was over.

Time seemed relative—one stretch passing in short, choppy bursts; the next, a series of slow, sensual moments that took my breath away.

I pulled away only long enough to snatch the t-shirt over my head. I didn't care that the hasty maneuver told of my impatience. Liam shifted onto his back, bringing me to straddle the warmth of his smooth, toned waist between my thighs. The softness of my chest pressed against the unrelenting solidity of his. He released a breath at the feel of it, and that sound—his inability to contain himself—was intoxicating.

Centuries of bridled passion were mounting within him and I could hardly stand the tension.

His.

Mine.

The culmination of all the waiting, the careful steps we'd taken around one another ... it was bubbling to the surface now as hands wandered greedily without restriction, as kisses deepened.

It was no secret I wanted him. No secret the feeling was mutual. But what Liam nor I could have known a short time ago, was that our words and feelings were on the verge of being brought to life.

Tonight was the night the past collided with the present. In one heart-pounding, soul-stirring crescendo, two worlds never meant to exist apart, returned to their rightful state.

As it was fated from the beginning, as it was decided before we were even born, our two souls were finally as they should have always been.

... They were one.

CHAPTER 8

Liam

I t took effort not to laugh as she fussed over me, pressing a wet rag to the gash on my lip. In the heat of the moment, she lost herself, and a kiss turned into a bite.

She saw it as an injury.

I saw it as a compliment.

"This is so embarrassing," she huffed, completely unaware of her perfection as moonlight outlined her delicate features.

She dabbed the spot again, using her other hand to hold a white sheet in place over her chest. Modesty seemed like a moot point, considering what we'd just done, but I suppose she had her reasons.

To her, this experience between us was new.

Every few seconds or so, as she nursed my wound, I'd catch her gaze wandering to my chest, my stomach, and then lower before her eyes would flit back toward mine. I wasn't bothered by it. If I had been, I would've put on clothes, but it felt unnecessary. I had nothing to hide from her, and soon she'd come to the same realization.

I let her tend to me with the cloth a while longer before looping her wrist with my fingers, halting her when I smiled.

"Evangeline ... I'm fine," I promised with a laugh. "You didn't break me."

She nodded as her eyes shimmered in the silvery-blue light, smiling as I reassured her with a kiss.

I turned onto my side, keeping her close. The motion exposed my back to the air, and the broken skin where her nails left lengthy tracks stung a bit. Those would heal, too, but the pain had been worth it.

Her curls were wild, covering the pillow and my arm where she laid her head. In this state, she was at her most natural, the way I remembered. The sheet formed to her figure, leaving little to the imagination. Admiring every inch, every tempting curve, I counted myself a lucky man. There had never been a more beautiful woman. Not in *either* of her lifetimes.

Her long, slender fingers tangled with mine as she gazed thoughtfully toward the ceiling. I didn't miss the hint of a satisfied smile set on her lips—one my ego wouldn't let me *not* take credit for.

"I hope we weren't too loud," she grinned. "Well, I hope *I* wasn't," she corrected.

Bringing the back of her hand to my lips, I placed a kiss there. "So what if you were?"

The statement made her laugh and I brought it out even more when my kisses trailed up her arm.

"Stop!" she protested, not meaning it for a second. "Keep it up and Hilda's gonna be at your door."

I shrugged, mumbling my response against her skin. "Maybe she already is."

A playful slap to the shoulder wasn't truly meant to scold me. "Don't be gross."

I didn't respond because I'd gotten caught up in her all over again as I tasted her neck. Her body went still at the feel of it, like the contact left her helpless.

My appetite for her had always been insatiable and we might have spent *another* two hours holed up in my room had it not been for the commotion downstairs. My eyes were immediately drawn toward my bedroom door. Just beyond it, an otherworldly shriek forced us to abandon the bit of fantasy we managed to create, being flung violently toward reality.

"What was that?" Evangeline's voice trembled when she asked, fumbling to pull on her clothes as I searched for my own.

"Not sure, but I need you to stay here."

The request made her pause, as if the racket downstairs had stopped altogether, while it had, in fact, begun to sound more like a war zone—a cacophony of bumps and bangs, glass breaking.

"Liam ... if anything, *you* shouldn't go down there," she reasoned. The worry in her voice was hard to miss.

She didn't speak it aloud, but I was positive I seemed more fragile to her now than any other moment since I awakened.

I didn't say a word, pulling the drawstring at my waist.

This new dynamic between us—one where *she* felt the need to be the protector—it didn't sit well with me. It had nothing to do with it being some sort of hit to my masculinity. It had *everything* to do with what the end result would be: her heading straight into danger.

As if she hadn't already done that enough. For me. For others.

We reached my bedroom door at the same time, making it clear neither intended to heed the other's warning. So, instead, we went together.

Every light downstairs seemed to be on. Peering past the rail that overlooked the foyer, there was a body. Cloaked in dark, tattered clothing and a sackcloth hood, it writhed in the arms of the six guards that struggled to manage its weight.

The voice was hard to place, presenting as both female and male in unison as it howled, or more like roared. In size, the creature could have easily measured up to an Elder.

Evangeline stepped back from the rail as her eyes widened. There was fear in them—unmistakable and present for good reason. The next second, she covered her nose and mouth, retching behind her palm.

"Oh, my gosh ... that *smell!*" she nearly gagged.

I turned toward the body again, but sensed nothing, which meant the odor was only detectable to supernaturals.

"What is it?" I asked.

She closed her eyes for a long time, looking as though she might vomit if she spoke too quickly.

"Death," she said. "It smells like ... death."

My eyes left her again, shifting down to where the thing had been wrangled to the floor, and it hit me.

A witch.

And judging by the way Evangeline responded to the powerful stench, I could only guess this one was as evil as the day is long.

"Liam ... wait!"

Soft hands grasped at my arms as I rushed down the steps, but I slipped through them.

"Liam," she called out again, making it hard to miss the panic in her voice.

Her steps fell in sync with mine as we descended, my focus never leaving the creature someone thought it'd be wise to bring into our home.

Stepping down into the foyer, I crossed the few feet to the witch, but was halted by a hand pressed firmly to my chest.

"It's not a good idea to get so close, Liam." I glanced up,

meeting Elise's worried gaze. As she stood between me and our *'guest'*, the panicked expression she wore matched her daughter's.

I ignored her, feeling the roughness of the sack between my fingertips when I pulled it from the monster's head.

Putrid.

My shoulders squared as I laid eyes on the thing—skin the sickening greenish-gray of a corpse, brittle black hair that stood out in every direction. It's dry, crusted lips parted with another scream, revealing blackened teeth rotted away by a lifetime of dark magic.

Anger filled me to capacity.

"What is this?" I asked, barely getting the words out as I gritted my teeth. "You brought this thing here? Where your *daughter* lays her head at night?"

I couldn't wrap my mind around the negligence.

"We're all out of options," Elise reasoned. "We needed another witch to assist Hilda with the spell."

"Or maybe it's just time to accept things for what they are," I snapped.

The house was quiet other than the mindless screaming that came from Elise's guest.

I braced both fists at my sides. It felt like my heart would come through my chest, throbbing against my ribcage as I struggled to breathe normally.

"And *you* thought this was a good idea?" I asked, directing the question at Hilda. "Judging by the fight she's putting up, I'm guessing she's a fugitive, one with a hefty bounty on her head. Yet, it still seemed smart to endanger your niece's life bringing her here?"

Hilda glared for a long moment before making an admission. "This was *my* idea."

I'd begun to pace, but those words made me pause. She was

usually more level-headed than the rest of us, so this news was definitely a surprise.

"And to answer your question," she went on, "no, I did *not* think it was a good idea, but I can't help but to think it would be an even *worse* idea to do nothing, to pretend we don't need the boys back." She hesitated a moment, and then said more. "We're not as strong as we used to be as a unit, and it's foolish to pretend our numbers haven't decreased."

Even without her being direct, saying my name, I knew that remark was meant for me. No, not a petty jab, but Hilda's way of explaining why I was in no position to fight this decision.

"Hilda, please," Elise cut in, interpreting the comment just as I had.

"We're not in the business of coddling one another or sparing each other's feelings!" Hilda's voice boomed above that of the outsider. "Not with all that's at stake."

"No, but we *are* supposed to behave like a family." Hilda and Elise's attention shifted toward Evangeline when she spoke up. Dallas', too, from his position against the far wall. I hadn't noticed him standing there before now, but the look on his face made it apparent he wasn't a part of this. He *looked* almost as angry as I *felt*.

Evangeline stepped forward and, instinctively, I stretched an arm in front of her, blocking her from getting too close to the witch.

"Liam's more than just a '*number*'," Evangeline said in defense of me, rendering her aunt speechless with her tone. "We *all* are. Or at least we *should* be."

Typically, Hilda had been revered in this home, allowed to speak her mind freely because her years and knowledge surpassed us all, but today ... she'd been challenged.

To my surprise, she had no rebuttal.

"Listen, we're all a bit ... emotionally charged at the moment,"

Elise intervened, pushing a hand through her hair as tension marked her expression. "Guards, please escort Maisy to the designated area."

The way she spoke, it was clear this was a well-thought-out operation, one Evangeline and I had conveniently been left out of.

With the witch gone, I could actually hear myself think, but no longer wanted to discuss the matter. The more time that passed since awakening, the more I realized I was powerless, the more I realized the others saw me in the same light.

Evangeline followed as I took the steps by two, and I let her in before slamming my bedroom door shut behind me.

My chest heaved as I paced, and I became lightheaded.

"You can't stay here. In this house. Not while that *thing* is here," I seethed, finding it hard to focus.

What on Earth would possess them to do something so stupid?

"Liam ... I think you should calm down."

I ignored the plea and continued to pace. My own heavy breaths rushing from my nostrils was all I focused on—the sound of my rage peaking with nowhere to go but outward, like an explosion.

"Check with Beth to see if you can stay there for a while," I ordered. "I'll help you pack."

"No," she rebutted, crossing her arms over her chest.

If I'd been in my right mind, I would've known demanding that she do something would result in her direct refusal, but now wasn't the time for treading lightly. *She* might not understand how dangerous it was to be here, but I did.

"And what about you?"

Her question made me halt. "What *about* me?"

The concern in her eyes bled through her expression—another reminder of my vulnerability and her awareness of it. I walked away, going to stand near the window instead. Seeing the concern that riddled her face had become a struggle.

She rested against the door, letting out a heavy sigh.

"I'll be fine here," she reasoned. "Her magic can't hurt me, remember?"

I didn't answer right away, still trying to grasp how I got to this place. It wasn't that I'd forgotten her immunity, but the idea of her sleeping here, under the same roof with something that vile ... I couldn't grasp it.

Soft footsteps came closer, and then hands circled my waist, warming my stomach at the same time her cheek warmed my back.

"I agree this is crazy, and I also agree it sucks," she sighed, "But ... I kinda trust Elise and Hilda on this one."

I breathed in, readying myself to argue my own point, but she continued on before I got the chance.

"Granted, they should have told us, but I'm sure they had their reasons for going over our heads."

"Reasons like not wanting me to stop them?"

I felt her cheek tighten against my back and I knew she was smiling. How or *why* she was smiling, I had no idea.

"Or maybe because they know you've been through a lot," she reasoned. "Because they know I was a mess a short time ago, waiting for your eyes to open."

My thoughts lingered there, on imagery of Evangeline sitting beside my bed all those weeks, hopeless, wondering if I'd ever wake up.

"I trust them," she finally breathed, the warm air drifting over my skin as she explained. "I trust that they took whatever precautions are necessary to keep us all safe, trust that Hilda wouldn't have suggested it if she didn't believe we were all out of options."

That didn't make me feel any better, knowing we'd reached the point on our rope where we had to decide whether to tie a knot or let go. The disadvantages seemed to be mounting against us, and I'd seen enough of war to know good didn't always triumph over evil.

"You need a breather." Her voice was sweet, calm.

She cinched her arms tighter around my waist.

"How about, if I agree to go to Beth's til' morning, you agree to get out of here for a while, too?" she suggested. "At least for a couple hours."

I considered her offer and realized how desperate I was to know she'd be safe tonight. It became clearer when I nodded, agreeing to those terms.

She took a breath. "Okay. I'll pack my things and you get dressed."

I glanced toward the clock; it was well past eleven. Normally, that wouldn't have been a big deal, but lately, it'd been a struggle keeping my eyes open past midnight.

Still, because she agreed to take off for tonight, I had to keep up my end of the bargain.

At the sound of my door latching and Evangeline heading into her own room, I exhaled the tension mounting in my gut. Not even the strength and determination I had *before* proved to be enough to save her.

I could only imagine how inept I'd be if something—or *someone*—was to come for her now.

I couldn't keep living like this.

Something had to give.

CHAPTER 9

Nick

'Can't. Exhausted.'

Yawning, I set my phone aside after declining Kyle's invitation to hang out. Before his text came through, I received nearly identical ones from Ben and Richie. Their shifts ended shortly before mine, so what they saw as an opportunity to blow off some steam, I saw as an opportunity to catch up on some much-needed sleep.

Burning the wick at both ends left me drained and not much fun to speak of. Struggling to balance my new guard duties *and* school had proven to be more difficult than expected. While it would have been nice for the Council to cut me some slack, maybe by allowing me to serve a *couple* days a week as opposed to five, I knew I was in no position to ask for favors.

They made sure I didn't forget I was forever indebted to them, made sure I understood my mother's status as a free woman could easily change.

The dark, uniform jacket I'd worn slipped off the back of the couch where I placed it, but I was too tired to even care. My body had functioned on auto-pilot all day, craving the moment I'd get to drop down onto the bed, or even the floor at this point. Deciding to forego dinner, I turned off the last light and touched a foot to the bottom step, intending to head up where I'd hibernate until morning.

But someone had other plans.

A brassy bell rang throughout the house, which meant it was likely my brothers hadn't taken my rejection seriously. If I had to guess which of the three was currently standing outside on the front porch, I would've put money on Kyle.

However, when I pulled the door to, and stared at an innocent face framed in brown hair, a smile touched my lips.

Tired as I was.

Roz lifted a brown paper bag into the air, as if she needed a peace offering for stopping by so late. Meanwhile, I would've gladly dragged myself out of bed for her no matter the time.

"I come bearing food," she grinned, crossing the threshold when I stepped aside.

"Thanks."

I accepted the bag, wanting to just be grateful she thought enough of me to stop by, but more came out. A prompt eye roll let me know she was expecting as much.

"You really shouldn't be out here so late on your own," I added. "It's not safe anymore." I knew she hadn't forgotten, but her actions made me think she may need a reminder.

She did a quick twirl, all while wearing a smile that made me worry she didn't really grasp the seriousness of the situation.

"See? All in one piece," she beamed. "Besides, it's not like I *walked* over," she reasoned.

My weight dropped down onto the cushion of one of four armchairs in the living room and I dug down into the bag while responding.

"Yeah, but to an army of mutts, you being in a vehicle only makes the challenge of attacking you more fun, but it wouldn't stop them."

And it wouldn't. We witnessed firsthand how vicious these things were. If *I* was capable of stopping a moving truck, surely they could, too. Then, from there, they would tear the thing apart until there was nothing left but scraps.

A chill scurried down my spine at the thought of something like that happening to Roz, all because she wanted to stop by.

"I'll escort you home," I offered, biting into one of three burgers she brought me.

When she didn't answer, I glanced up, meeting the self-conscious stare of a girl who was almost *always* fearless. The look made me pause after swallowing, unsure of what I missed.

Her shoulder touched the wall beside her when she leaned into it.

"Actually ..."

A thought danced on the tip of her tongue, but she still hadn't quite found the way to say it from the looks of things.

"I thought I might just ... stay? If that's okay," she revealed, wearing her heart on her sleeve in that vulnerable moment.

A moment where she didn't care how apparent it was that I knew she wanted to be close.

A moment where I, too, reveled in the idea of having her here for the entire night.

We hadn't had much time to spend together since finally owning our feelings. Between her father's disapproval of whatever our friendship was transforming into, and my newly swamped schedule, there was little to no time to see each other. No time to just be Nick and Roz.

But ... together.

I was suddenly less focused on the food in hand and more focused on her—how her dark hair cascaded over the shoulder of a leather jacket that fit her form like a glove; how tempted we'd been in the woods not too long ago. That night, she'd gotten away from me, but I wasn't so sure she'd be so lucky tonight.

A distracted nod from me brought her smile out more. "I think that sounds like a good idea," I replied, forcing myself not to expect anything other than her company.

But maybe secretly hoping for more.

"Good. Cool," she said, sinking down into the seat across from me. I watched as she tucked both feet beneath her on the cushion.

As much as I looked forward to her staying, it wasn't lost on me that her father, technically, still hated my guts. There was no way she told him the truth about where she'd be tonight, so I had to ask.

"Where does your dad think you ran off to?"

Her dark eyes danced up to meet mine, and she smiled. "I didn't tell him," she beamed, seemingly proud of this newfound freedom she carved out for herself.

If I had to guess, it was driving her father insane that he could no longer control her with a glare. I knew this because I'd seen the same look of frustration bleed through Richie's expression every time I defied him as well.

But still, this was bigger than some random act of defiance. No, Officer Chadwick and I weren't exactly on great terms, but as someone who'd put his parents through quite a bit lately, I didn't want Roz to be guilty of the same.

She'd never accept me telling her what to do, so I left it alone for now.

"So," she began, that one word so loaded, "... has it happened again?"

My ears perked at the question, taking a moment to understand fully. When I did, I set the half-eaten burger aside.

She was referring to the blackouts.

I shook my head. "Not since the one you know about."

"If there *had* been another, would you really tell me?" There was curiosity behind her gaze, but not distrust.

I nodded. "I gave you my word." Hopefully, she knew that meant something, wasn't just an empty promise I made that night just to get her off my back.

Her gaze slipped from mine and I wondered what she was thinking when she focused on her hands, twiddling her fingers together as she seemed to daydream.

"What you said the other night, about *me* being the thing that stops you from having episodes ... do you really believe that?"

This was another of those rare, vulnerable moments when she couldn't hide from me, couldn't keep it locked inside that she felt the pull toward me like I felt it toward her.

"I do," I admitted, trying to pin down the words to explain. "The darkness is there. Always," I clarified, "But I can see my way through it when you're around. It's like ... something about you makes it so I'm able to fight harder; makes it so I'm able to just be ... *me*."

That was the easiest way to break it down. Mostly because I didn't fully understand how it worked myself.

She was thoughtful for a bit, but then shared something she hadn't before.

"These moments when I'm able to break rank, it feels like more than just ... defiance," was the word she settled on. An uncertain stare landed on me. "I feel more powerful than him. Like, I can sense his weakness. Like, if I wanted to, I could force *him* to submit."

She blinked and I referenced my tie to Richie, noting I hadn't quite felt what Roz had—so much power. While, yeah, I could break free from Richie and do my own thing, I hadn't felt his weakness yet. I guessed it was coming, but to me, this meant Roz was progressing more quickly than I was. Soon, her father would become her beta.

A long, dragging sigh left her mouth and she raked a hand through her hair.

"But I don't want to talk about that. It's weird and only hints at even *more* change," she shared. "And I don't know about you, but I'd love for two freakin' weeks to pass and things stay the same."

A small smile broke free and I smiled back, agreeing with her wholeheartedly.

"How's your mom?" she asked, leaning forward to pick up the half-eaten burger I set aside.

I shrugged and thought of the many different ways to answer that question.

"She's ... managing," was the best I could do.

In truth, she was going stir-crazy, which was driving my *dad* crazy, but none of us made a huge fuss about it because we knew what the alternative was.

Imprisonment.

Exile.

Death.

"She's trying on new hobbies to make time pass faster," I grinned, thinking about the too-small hat she knitted Richie just last week.

"Any word on how long they intend to keep her on lockdown? I mean, I know she's got it better than a lot of people, being afforded the luxury of serving her sentence at home, but ... still. It must suck," Roz concluded.

I nodded agreeing. It *did* suck.

"The Council has stayed pretty tight-lipped about it," I sighed. "I'm guessing that's strategic; their way of keeping me on a short leash."

I hated that they still owned me, but ... I brought all of this on myself.

Including the part where I screwed things up so bad that my mom thought the only feasible solution was to bring the Sovereign into this.

"If they *did* try something like that, couldn't Evie just override them?"

My thoughts drifted back to the last meeting I had with the Council, how clear they made it that they only honored Evie's wishes as a courtesy, stating that they were under no obligation to do so again. Not as long as she hadn't, technically, been named queen.

So, to answer Roz's question, I shook my head again, stating what I knew to be a fact. "No. Not this time."

There was a solemn silence that weighed heavy on us both. I wondered if she was thinking the same thing I was—that I should have taken her advice and ran while I had the chance, while I wouldn't have been punished for doing so.

I glanced down at the uniform I still wore—dark shirt, pants tucked into military-grade boots. No, I hadn't signed a contract or pledged my allegiance.

But this clan, the Council, still owned me.

"You're quiet," she observed. "Work stuff?"

There was a *lot* going through my head, but 'work' stuff was definitely part of it. During my shift, something big had gone down. Something above my paygrade. From what I gathered, a few of the guards had smuggled someone into town tonight. I had no clue if this was something the Council arranged or not, but it crossed my mind that I should speak up. Then again, my failing reputation had damaged my credibility to the point that I was certain no one would have listened anyway.

So, I kept quiet, even when I caught a glimpse of a huge, cloaked creature wearing sackcloth over its head being hoisted from the bed of a truck. Kept quiet even when I caught a whiff of the foul smell it emitted.

My guess? A witch—and not one of the good ones.

Failing to see the point in worrying Roz with bits and pieces of a much larger story, I never answered her question. At the sight of me yawning, she didn't press.

"You look exhausted." She stood, stretching her hand toward me. I wasn't sure what her plan was, but stood, anyway.

"Go up and change," she suggested. "Then, meet me back here on the couch so the TV can watch *us* while we doze."

I smiled and it amazed me how she did that. How she somehow made sitting up on the couch with her all night sound more appealing than spending the night in bed.

Then again, I guess it shouldn't have been that big a surprise.

After all, I was no longer fighting the truth—that Roz was kind of it for me.

CHAPTER 10

Liam

Astrange turn of events took me from lying beside my mate, my weakness, to sitting in a crowded bar with a burly, southern dragon with an appetite for cheap beer and chicken wings.

Agreeing to leave the house for a bit tonight was the only way I managed to convince Evangeline to do the same. Only, she wouldn't return until morning.

Dallas knocked back another mug, bringing his total to five. I, on the other hand, settled for water per his request. Apparently, Evangeline wasn't the only one who noticed I hadn't quite bounced back yet. A night of drinking and a hangover in the morning wouldn't help the matter any.

I'd been here a few times before. Most notably, to meet Evangeline face-to-face again, for the first time in ages. We didn't make it inside, but did collide just beyond the front entrance, in an alley off Handler Street. At the sight of me, she'd nearly taken off running, but after tonight, I was certain I'd completely changed her mind.

About me.

About us.

I lowered my head as thoughts crept in—thoughts of her in my bed, thoughts of my name seeping from between her lips in a whisper ...

I smiled to myself. Despite the chaos that followed, the time we managed to steal, the time we managed to feel like a normal couple those two hours ... it was incredible.

I zoned out to the sound of murmuring voices, clanking glasses, and low-playing country music. It wasn't exactly how I wanted to spend the remainder of the evening, but my coming here was the only bargaining chip I had, the one thing I could do that finally swayed Evangeline to call Beth about crashing at her place.

I both loved and hated her stubbornness.

Another smile broke free as I scanned the crowd, thinking of her. The place was packed. With the town being so small, there was no need for more than a couple bars, but with the sudden shifter population boom, Dallas and I had been lucky to get a booth.

A plate of bones sat at the center of our table. He dropped another onto the pile and started in on the next.

"Lay it on me," he prompted in between bites. His distinct drawl rose above the volume in the bar and I glanced his way.

"Not sure what you mean," I said, sipping from my glass right after, wishing it was something stronger.

He lifted a brow, sucking the last morsel of meat from the wing. "Don't give me that," he rebutted. "Man-to-man, I can see it," he reasoned. "All over your face. Something's bugging you and you need to set it free 'fore it eats you alive."

I didn't readily respond, which made him go on again.

"You won't talk to Evie, because that's your woman," he broke down. "You won't open up to Elise because she's been distracted lately, and you don't wanna feel like you're bothering her. So, you've got me. And I'll listen to whatever it is with no judgment. I'll even cut you a deal; first time's free," he joked.

We hadn't known one another long, and my trust in him was kind of grandfathered in, thanks to Elise, but I wasn't itching to tell the guy my feelings.

"I can sit here all night," he uttered, pausing mid-chew. When I still didn't speak, he raised an eyebrow defiantly while glancing up, as if to say he wouldn't take no for an answer.

I breathed deep and eyed the crowd, unnerved by the fact that I could no longer tell a supernatural from a human. Being like this made it impossible to know when, and from where, a threat was coming.

"I'm no good to her like this."

It pained me to let those words leave my mouth, but they were the truth. Nearly biting a hole through my lip, I gazed around the room, at nothing in particular while I thought.

"She's a nervous wreck all the time. She tries to hide it, because she's used to being brave, but I know what she sees when she looks at me."

Wiping sauce from his fingers, Dallas looked up. "And what's that?"

"Weakness," I answered, adding, "someone who's gonna die on her one day. Even if not by the hand of a supernatural—which is a very strong possibility—it'll be something. Someday."

I never feared death, but leaving Evangeline to grieve was one of the hardest things I ever had to imagine. When Sebastian captured me, the only thing that made laying down my life an easy decision was considering the alternative—which was losing her. My only comfort was knowing she had Elise to look after her. But still, there wasn't a soul on this planet I trusted to put everything into taking care of her that *I* would. She had to survive.

With or without me.

Dallas sat back, shoving his plate aside. "Hmm ... that's interesting," he stated. "I guess you and I have two totally different vantage points then."

I didn't reply.

"I won't lie and say that girl isn't probably scared out of her head, thinking you're not as durable as you used to be, but if you ask what *I* think she sees when she looks at you ... I'd say she sees a man who'd give up his life for her." His brow quirked, and he smiled a bit. "Partly because that's exactly what you did."

My eyes drifted to the glass in my hand as I twisted it aimlessly across the tabletop.

"I haven't known Evie or Elise as long as you," he breathed, sipping from the fresh mug the waitress brought over. "But from what I can tell, you and me have ourselves two of the toughest women this side of heaven. You've gotta learn to rely on that strength a little bit, learn to trust she won't shatter into pieces the second you turn your back."

I heard him, but he hadn't seen it before, hadn't seen with his own eyes that Evangeline *wasn't* indestructible.

"My purpose has always been to protect her," I admitted. "Now that I can't, I'm painfully aware of the fact that I'm more of a liability than an asset."

Hilda had all but said it just a little while ago.

"Nah, man. That's where you're wrong," Dallas reasoned. "Your *assignment* was to protect her. Your *purpose* ... that's only ever been to *love* her. And that has nothing to do with what you are."

All sound left the room when I zoned out, thinking on his words. This body I was in, it was mine and yet, still felt foreign.

The aches and pains of recovery were an everyday reminder of how finite this life was.

"Take my advice," he went on, belching into his fist before continuing. "The main thing Evie needs from you right now is reassurance. Let her know you're okay."

Let her know I'm okay.

It seemed like a lie, but I saw the logic in it.

Our conversation came to a sudden halt when Dallas stood from his seat, eying the door when he spoke.

"Hold that thought."

My eyes followed his and I watched as he crossed the bar, headed in the direction of the three who just entered—the Stokes boys, minus Nick. The dark uniforms they wore, similar to those that had been issued at the Damascus facility, were those of guards. The Council had most likely appointed them, or it was possible they volunteered.

My first encounter with this many members from their pack had been with mutts outside my home. Apparently, since then, there'd been another run-in I couldn't recall. Evangeline named them among those who traveled to confront the Sovereign's army alongside her. They risked their lives just like she had. All for the sake of rescuing me. Whether I liked it or not, it wasn't lost on me that I was only here because of them.

Wasn't lost on me that the same held true for Evangeline; they were the reason she was still alive.

As I watched from my seat, Dallas had begun making his way back to our booth, but not alone. The three who shadowed him all stared with weary expressions. There was no doubt they hadn't forgotten the discord between their brother and I, and I could only guess they were leery about approaching the table.

"Thought it'd be cool if the fellas joined," Dallas said, sliding into the half-circle booth we once occupied alone to make room for the others.

They hadn't stopped eyeing me, and probably noted the difference in my scent. For all I knew, they were already aware of my … situation.

"Good to see you on your feet again," the one with the glasses said, extending his hand. "Name's Ben. Not sure if we ever got to meet properly."

I stared at his hand lingering there a moment, maybe a little caught off guard by the kind gesture. After all … I was kinda responsible for their brother running off months ago. I'd also threatened his life so many times I lost count, but from what I could tell, the air between us was clear.

Except with the big, broody one, because his expression gave nothing away. I guessed he was their alpha.

"This is Richie," Ben went on as he slid into the seat, "and Kyle."

I nodded toward the two he introduced, keeping my eyes on Richie longer than the other.

"So … how're you feeling. You know … with all the changes?" It was Ben who asked, but Kyle stared with the same curiosity. Surprisingly enough, there didn't seem to be any malice behind the question.

I cleared my throat before answering. "As good as can be expected, I suppose."

They nodded, seeming to understand it was kind of difficult to put into words. On the one hand, yes, I was happy to be alive. However, on the other, I was pissed my dragon, my true self, had been stolen from me.

"Well, it's good to see you're out and about," Ben jumped in again with kind of a nervous energy, like he wanted to fill the dead air that nearly crept in.

"I'm guessing y'all are attending the meeting tomorrow night?" I turned toward Dallas when he asked. This was the first I heard of it.

The others nodded.

"Can't afford to pass on the opportunity to be better informed," Richie reasoned. "With things heating up like they are, it's no wonder talk of evacuating the humans has gone from a far-off suggestion to something they're thinking of bringing to a vote soon."

My fist clinched, but I hid the tension as well as I could. Things were getting worse and it was likely all we knew was what the Council *wanted* us to know. The big picture was probably far grimmer than any of us realized.

"Between us, our patrols have gotten a lot more interesting."

Dallas perked up when Kyle offered this new information. "How so?"

"Witches are being brought in from all over. Just the other day, I was sent to escort fifteen of them safely to the Elders' chamber."

"And, from what I overheard, communication has been cut off from the Council's Canadian division because it's rumored they've chosen to align with the Sovereign's army," Richie added. "Rumor *also* has it, many of the clans in that region are organizing to defect."

It was insane to even fathom someone fighting in support of Sebastian's continued reign. But, if I had to guess, those who aimed to uphold it were likely on the receiving end of some sort of shady backend deal—access to money and power the rest of the Council were denied.

After a brief lull in conversation, Ben spoke again. "Evie's doing all right? I imagine she's tired of people making a fuss over her by this point," he chuckled.

"She's learning to deal with it," I answered, knowing he was right to assume she was sick of the special treatment, sick of the pressure her eventual title had placed on her head already.

That silence came again and I took it as a sign I was supposed to speak up, saying what I knew the guys at this table were owed.

"Thank you. *All* of you," I stated. "Evangeline made it clear she couldn't have gotten to me without your help."

Each one nodded.

"No problem," Kyle grinned. "Gave us a chance to give the Sovereign a taste of what he's got coming to him."

Kyle's confidence was admirable, but a sneak attack on Sebastian was one thing, facing an army of bloodthirsty mutts with an order to kill ... that was another.

"We mostly just distracted the soldiers," Ben added modestly.

"Well, either way, I appreciate it. She wouldn't have even gotten close if it hadn't been for you all being there to help," was the last I planned to say about it.

But then, something else came forth. Something that made the world stop spinning the moment it was uttered.

"Can't believe she tried to go back."

It was Ben again, thinking what he just shared was common knowledge, but when I glared at him across the table, I was pretty sure he knew that wasn't the case.

"She tried to go back? When?" My hands quaked with rage.

A curious gaze around the table and I guessed Ben realized he shouldn't have said so much.

Dallas scrubbed a hand down his face with a sigh. "Don't get yourself worked up," he stated, so calm it only pissed me off more.

"Why wasn't I told?"

Dallas sighed again. "Because it was before you were awake, and it seemed like a moot point after that. Besides, I'm pretty sure it wasn't Evie's proudest moment. Hilda and Elise ripped her a new one once I brought her back."

I tried to steady the rapid breaths that puffed from my lungs.

"Why was she going back?" I couldn't fathom a reason she'd put herself in harm's way for a *second* time, and in this instance, she intended to set out without anyone's help.

The blank expressions around the table nearly drove me crazy.

When my fist slammed down on the hard surface, some of the peripheral chatter ceased, meaning I had the attention of a few patrons, but I didn't care. I wanted answers.

"Because she thought it might help."

I shot Dallas a look, one I would've followed up with a choke-hold to squeeze the answer out of him. Good thing for him I didn't forget I no longer had the upper hand—my strength compared to his was almost laughable.

"She thought it might help what?" I seethed, hearing the question escape my gritted teeth.

Dallas wore a pleading look, like he wished I hadn't backed him into a corner, but I needed to know. What reason did she possibly have for putting herself in danger?

"She did it to save you," he finally explained, making my thoughts go singular when he did. "She thought she might be able to find and capture the witch who ... *changed* you ... and fix it."

Fix *me*.

That's what he really meant.

I said nothing, just let this new information sink in. Outbursts like this were exactly what I was afraid of. There was no telling how many times in the coming years she'd go on these excursions, all in the name of saving me.

I suddenly felt like I needed air.

No one followed when I stood from our table, keeping my eyes fixed on the door. I burst out into the night and knew I couldn't continue on like this, as a human.

What no one seemed to realize was, with me stuck in this form, the Sovereign was no longer the biggest threat to Evangeline's safety.

... *I* was.

CHAPTER 11

Evie

The sky dimmed to the perfect shade of royal blue. Soon, stars would dot the heavens and another beautiful evening would be ruined by clan drama.

Tonight's event, a meeting with the Council to update us on the latest tidbits they saw fit to share. I believed, deep down, we all knew the details were being spoon-fed to us, but I could attest to their being a marginal increase when it came to trusting them. Yes, a bit more transparency would have been nice; however, I no longer doubted their intentions. They truly did have the clan's best interest at heart, but simply didn't trust their ability to process or apply deeper knowledge than what had been given.

Proving that, perhaps, the trust issue lie with the Council itself.

"Will it just be us tonight?" Elise asked, doing her best to pretend things were normal, when things were nowhere near that.

As I sat on the steps gazing out the front window, a witch howled just beneath the foyer, locked in a basement room I hadn't even known existed just a day ago. It'd been built behind a false wall, some sort of safe room I guessed.

I did my best to ignore the wailing.

"Dallas said he'd be down in a bit," I answered, leaving it at that.

Elise stared, but I wouldn't dare meet her gaze. I knew what she was thinking, that I forgot to mention one other member of this household. Hilda would be staying behind to babysit our house-guest, but we definitely expected Liam to attend.

I couldn't say for sure he didn't plan to, but we barely said two words to one another when I came in from Beth's. He greeted me, said he wasn't feeling well, and then went to lie down. The one time I tried to check on him, he simply stated that he was fine, but never invited me in.

Elise gazed up the stairs, tension in her brow evident, although she tried masking it.

"Well, I suppose we'll just bring him up to speed when we return." She forced a smile and pivoted quickly, most likely to hide what I already knew.

She was worried about him.

After the drama with the witch the night before, he'd been different—quiet, distant. Toward us all. I was being patient, giving him space, but it wasn't easy. I hated seeing him like this, hated knowing he didn't feel whole. I wanted nothing more than to make it all go away, but as I found out on my failed attempt back to the U.P., this problem was bigger than me.

I followed Elise to the car and Dallas joined us shortly after. The ride to the library was mostly silent as two SUVs trailed us. I felt ridiculous having guards present wherever I went, especially having three stationed outside Beth's when I stayed over. I wanted to protest, wanted to make a fuss about it being over the top ... but I'd seen enough lately to know that wasn't the case.

The dangers around us were real, and they were only closing in with each passing day.

The lot was full. Even more than usual. With all the new shifters, the chamber was sure to be packed to capacity, too. Looking around at how our numbers had increased, I stepped out and trailed behind Elise and Dallas. We entered through the back as usual and descended the long, stone staircase to the meeting hall.

I was right. There were bodies everywhere. Nearing a thousand, maybe surpassing it. What I always perceived to be wasted square footage had been put to good use tonight.

Even with so many in the space, it was still almost silent. That must have been protocol. Dragons, wolves, witches—every faction was represented, and from what I observed so far, all came in peace. I suppose in times like these, it's easy for people to put their differences aside, putting their energy toward fighting their common enemy.

An enemy he certainly was.

The door behind the Elders' table opened and the ritualistic entrance began—witches first, our local Elders next, followed by the visiting members of the Council. All filed in in a single line before dispersing to either their designated seats, or their posts against the back wall.

There was a moment of silence before anyone spoke. Baz stood after setting down a paper he glanced at when first entering the room.

"Good evening," he began, the crowd echoing the greeting before he continued. "I would like to first state that I, as well as the other members of our sacred Council, have been quite pleased with the reception of our visiting shifters. You all have been quite gracious to make accommodations in your homes, in your businesses, and it goes without saying that your loyalty to Seaton Falls is greatly appreciated."

There were a few muffled responses, all positive from what I could hear.

"Tonight's meeting was called simply to keep you all abreast of the latest information." He lowered his head for a moment, and although his face was hidden, I imagined a trace of remorse might have been found there with what he said next.

"We are aware that our lack of forthrightness in the recent past created more confusion and distress than we realized. For that reason, we are doing our best to share the knowledge we've been given, as we've been given it."

That came as a surprise to me, and probably to everyone else as well. Especially if their impression of the governmental system of the lycan populace aligned with mine. I initially thought of them as being shady as heck, and probably corrupt to the core. However, as I stood here today, I realized I'd been wrong. They operated in secret for the most part, but only because that had been their way for so long. Now, as Baz prepared to share the latest news, it seemed a new day was dawning.

"Some of you may have already been informed that our Canadian constituents have decided it would not be in their best interest to stand against the Sovereign," he expressed.

The crowd murmured amongst themselves, a blend of concerned whispers and contempt.

"However, it has been brought to our attention that the opinions held by many of the clan members are incongruent with their representative Council members," he amended. "In which case, it would be ideal to offer asylum to these members in exchange for their willingness to contribute to our war efforts."

I half expected to hear mumbling and complaints—about how crowded the city had already become, about how those who opened their homes wouldn't put themselves out even more than they already had. But the clan surprised me. All around me, hands shot into the air, volunteers who still had additional space to offer, even if the additional space was their living room couch.

Their hearts were willing, and it spoke volumes about the heart of this community.

"Your kindness is admirable," Baz said in response to the people's eagerness. "While we *will* need your assistance, we've been exploring another option," he went on. "It's been discussed whether the time has come to evacuate the human populace from Seaton Falls, given our current status. In which case, those empty homes would serve as temporary residences for those in need."

There was a hush over the crowd.

"This is *our* fight," he explained bravely. "It would be remiss of us to put their lives in undue peril while it is within our power to ensure their safety."

My heart raced as I listened, thinking of my parents, all too aware of how their living in this town had made them just as vulnerable as all the others. The Council's decision to get them to safety was one I appreciated.

"While, ideally, this issue would be put to a vote, the Council has chosen to act on our own authority. So, it is official; within seven days, the humans of Seaton Falls will be evacuated, sent to nearby cities under the guise of our dam being deemed unsafe. As far as they will know, the structure was found in violation of several safety codes, and is considered a threat to our residents per a recent inspection. Military barricades and qualified personnel will seal all roads leading into and out of Seaton Falls."

Beside me, Elise and Dallas exchanged glances, and I crossed my arms over my chest, wishing Liam had been there. Having him close always made me feel safe, even when the world around me was shifting, changing ... falling apart.

Baz took his seat again and the Chancellor closed out the

meeting. There was a brief question and answer segment at the end, which the shifters seemed to appreciate, but the message was already quite clear.

War was upon us.

The meeting adjourned with so many feeling unsettled. Chilled air swept my face as Elise, Dallas, and I neared the car, neared the security detail we'd been assigned. Tired and anxious to get home to check on Liam, I only stopped because my name was called in a deep, familiar voice. One I hadn't heard in weeks because I successfully avoided his calls.

I turned to find Nick headed my way, and he wasn't alone. Roz stood beside him, her lips pressed into a tense smile. She still didn't seem quite comfortable around me. I returned the gesture, making sure my smile was more natural than hers, warmer. She'd come around eventually.

Elise and Dallas had stopped as well, eyeing Nick as he approached.

"I'll catch up in a sec," I said dismissively, prompting them to continue on without me.

Just as Nick came close, I faced him again, noting how he and Roz had seemingly settled into their new status—their interlocked fingers telling me as much.

"What's up?"

His question was so general, which I appreciated. It wouldn't require me to go into detail about how my life felt like it'd been turned upside down recently.

I nodded, pretending to be okay. "Everything's good," I lied.

In truth, things were the opposite of good. Things were … hard. Scary. Confusing.

These were all the reasons I avoided his calls, his texts just to check in after we made it home from our run-in with the Sovereign. I knew he only wanted to know I was okay—and, actually, to know *Liam* was okay—but I shut everyone out while I tried to cope with it all. Even calls to Beth were few and far between. As I stood before him today, Nick seemed to understand my recent detachment hadn't been anything personal.

His lips parted to speak, but halted when Roz's name was called from across the lot. Waving her in his direction, wearing a less-than-happy expression, was Officer Chadwick.

A breath puffed from Roz's lips and it was clear she would have preferred to stay with Nick, but alas.

"Guess that's my cue," she sighed, glancing up toward Nick.

He nodded. "It's cool. I'll call you later."

She reached up to loop her arms around his neck, and after a brief embrace, she jogged toward her father.

It was just Nick and I.

"I was going to say I'm glad to see you out. Beth said you've had a lot going on."

I nodded, confirming. "Yeah, that's one way of putting it."

My thoughts immediately went back to Liam, to the strange mood I returned to find him in today. It honestly put me in a funk, too, bringing out a depth of sadness I wasn't sure most people were able to feel for another.

But I felt it for him.

His emotions, like always, were mine.

"Crazy stuff they're talking about, right?" Nick aimed a thumb over his shoulder, gesturing toward the building where we'd just been informed Seaton Falls would soon be a town strictly composed of shifters. At least temporarily.

"It's insane," I concurred. At first, he smiled, but then it faded.

Quickly.

What was left behind was a tense brow and closed lids that hid Nick's eyes from me.

I was just about to ask if something was wrong, but he spoke again, forcing the words from his throat.

"I'm sure it's mostly a precaution, but still. It makes it all feel real, like it's actually happening."

He flinched a bit when he finished speaking, and I no longer had to guess if he was in pain.

My concern for him grew.

"Nick ..." I stepped closer.

Maybe it was a headache, one of the ones that came on suddenly. This one seemed to have stolen whatever words he would have said next as he gripped his temples.

I stepped a little closer, and this time, I instinctively placed a hand on his shoulder, opening my mouth to ask if he was okay.

I didn't get the chance. At my touch, he shrugged away like I had the plague. Like I had been the cause of all this.

I didn't understand.

"Are you ... okay?" It seemed like a dumb question as he began to recoil, inching away from me.

"You don't ... you don't hear that?"

The question made me glance around, thinking I'd missed something. I paused, listened harder, and then looked him over again—the redness in his face, tension in his jaw.

"No," I breathed, suddenly aware of a chill in the air. "I don't hear anything."

He stepped back even further, and instinctively, so did I. It wasn't that I was afraid of him, but I'd be lying if I didn't admit my concern.

Considering our history, mine with his grandfather.

"It's like ... buzzing or ... electricity," he tried to explain. "And it's louder than your heartbeat."

That was something we'd *both* gotten used to—his ability to hear my pulse racing like it was now. This new sound, the one that seemed to overshadow all others, driving him mad ... I was as clueless as Nick was as to what caused it.

The hairs on my arms stood on end and I shuddered. This

time it had nothing to do with the trace of cold air winter had left behind.

It was fear. I knew that feeling well.

My eyes shifted left and then right, taking note of who was still around, who might be able to help if things suddenly turned ugly. I accepted the fact that the event we both dreaded may finally be upon us.

Maybe this was it—the moment he could no longer fight his nature.

"I have to go," he huffed, forcing the words out through clenched teeth.

He took several more steps back and I stared at his feet. The distance between us grew and I couldn't explain why I felt relieved by that, relieved that someone I considered a friend was getting as far away from me as possible.

Shouts from the left drew my attention there. They were the voices of his brothers calling him in the direction of what I guessed to be his ride. Only, he wasn't answering. Instead, he took off in a full sprint toward the woods. Richie turned to me, looking about as confused as I *felt*. When I shrugged, letting him know I didn't have an answer for the question in his stare, his gaze followed Nick into the trees where he disappeared.

Screeching tires caused every head to turn, including Elise's from where she and Dallas watched discreetly from the car. I turned to where I'd just watched Nick run off and couldn't help but to wonder what was happening.

Was he changing again? Going deeper into the darkness.

My heart raced as yet another threat was apparently beginning to surface. Deep down in my gut I knew whatever had just happened was a sign.

The Sovereign was easy to spot as an adversary. He made it clear it was my head he wanted served to him on a platter.

However, there was another, one I regarded as a friend. One I'd underestimated once before.

Friend or not, it was time to accept something I'd fought for quite some time now.

Nick was beginning to lose control, and when he did ... he'd come for me.

CHAPTER 12

Evie

I was distracted and grateful I wasn't expected to take part in the spell. While I'd been at Beth's, Hilda coerced Maisy into assisting with the first portion—a preliminary *'seasoning'* as she called it—and now they were delving into phase two.

Liam would have blown a gasket if he knew I was even in the vicinity of the beast Hilda and Elise brought into the house. However, in order to blow a gasket, he would have to know I was even down here.

When we came in from the meeting, I didn't bother heading upstairs to check in. There were many reasons. For one, I knew for a fact he preferred to be alone right now and there was also the strange incident with Nick. I was confused and wanted to sort through my thoughts before jumping to conclusions, before telling Liam what I suspected.

So, here I sat, perched in a chair just outside the false wall in the basement where, beyond it, the sound of undecipherable chants grew louder. Through the sliver where Elise left it cracked when she went in, bright green light filtered through, swirling a peculiar pattern on the wall beside me.

There was a real chance of the spell working this time. If it did, things around here would undergo yet another significant change. My brothers would be back, for one. Meaning, Hilda and Elise would get their wish; our precious numbers would be up.

The volume rose even higher, the sounds coming forth making my skin crawl. I could only imagine what was taking place in there, but dared not venture inside. While I was positive Maisy's magic couldn't affect me, and I was equally sure Hilda took extra precautions, I still wanted nothing to do with that disgusting witch. Laying eyes on her as the guards held her down ... I was sure I'd have nightmares for years to come.

Eventually, things went quiet. The commotion that had nearly shaken the house only moments before ceased completely. The silence was eerie.

A door crept open, and then the seam in the wall widened as Elise emerged, clutching a violet-colored stone too large to close her fingers around it. There was no missing the nervous excitement in her expression. She bore the look of the skeptically hopeful.

I smiled at her. It was tense and reserved, but it was the best I could offer.

"So?" I breathed. "How'd it go?"

She took slow steps as her eyes danced across the floor, still doing all she could to bridle her enthusiasm.

"Better than expected," she stated. "Maisy cooperated, thanks to Hilda being quite skilled at persuading others to bend to her will."

I found myself not wanting to know what that entailed. Maisy didn't strike me as the 'bend to another's will' kind of witch.

"Did it ... *work?*"

The question left my mouth quietly, my own nervousness getting in the way.

It took a moment, but Elise finally flashed a smile.

"It's a bit early to tell, but I believe so. All that's left to do is wait," she concluded, placing a hand on my shoulder as she sauntered toward the steps. I didn't linger in the basement long either, mostly because I was still kinda creeped out by Maisy.

I ascended and then crossed the foyer, heading up another flight of stairs. When I got there, I stood in the hall, hesitating in the space between my bedroom and Liam's, wondering if it'd be okay to knock. It didn't take long to realize I didn't yet have the nerve. So, I changed first, sat on my bed a while to stall, and even stared over the balcony thinking the fresh air would help.

It didn't.

It seemed strange there was so much distance right now, considering what had transpired between us a mere twenty-four hours ago. A girl could get insecure being blown off so soon after giving herself to a guy. Only, I knew better than to let my mind wander in that direction. The one thing I knew for sure, period, was that Liam's love for me was the fiercest I ever experienced. There was never a question of whether last night meant as much to him as it meant to me.

It was the rationalizing I did on the balcony that brought me to my senses. Liam could have his space, but only after I made sure to let him know I cared. After that, I had no problem leaving him to his own devices while I slept alone in my own bed.

But he did need to know.

I crossed the hall quickly before I lost the nerve. Movement on the other side of the door after I knocked had me running a hand through my hair, straightening my hoodie over the waistband of my shorts.

There was music—low enough someone with normal hearing

wouldn't have even heard unless they were within a foot or two of the radio, but I picked up on it right away. The earthy tone of an acoustic guitar and a soulful male voice accompanied Liam's footsteps as he neared the door.

He answered and the sight of him still made me lose my breath. My chest heaved when I laid eyes on this living, breathing work of art. Even broody and sad, he was impossibly perfect—his dark hair pulled back into a disheveled bun, his torso lacking a shirt as a pair of tattered jeans rode low on his hips.

I blinked and lifted my gaze, trying to focus on his greenish-brown eyes.

"Ca—can I come in?" I stammered, fidgeting with my nails while I struggled to concentrate on only his face, trying to distract myself from ... well ... all the rest.

He nodded, stepping aside to let me pass. He still hadn't said actual words, which was strange.

Behind me, the door latched gently. He took a few steps and then stopped, crossing both arms over his chest as his gaze lowered to the carpet. I was left with the impression it was difficult to look at me.

I breathed, let my hands fall to my sides, breathed some more as I searched for words. I didn't really have a game plan beyond coming to see about him. Only, now that I was here and sensed a strange, cold vibe, I found myself wishing I'd thought this through a bit more.

My eyes wandered behind me, to his bed.

"Can I sit?" It seemed strange to ask, but I felt awkward here, like maybe I *should* have stayed away.

Again, only a nod.

I crossed the room and dropped down onto the mattress. Things had gotten so hot and heavy last I touched it, but you would have never guessed as much now.

I gathered the nerve to look at him again, to ask a question I hoped would break the mile-thick ice between us.

"Did I do something?"

In a perfect world, he would have answered right away, but that wasn't the case. He made me stew in my own anxiousness as I watched him nearly gnaw a hole through his lip.

His tone cutting deep with its sharp edges when he finally answered, "Nothing I didn't already expect."

My brow twitched and I felt an inward recoiling, as some small part of me reacted to the brashness in his voice that'd never been aimed at me before.

"I'm not really sure what's going on," I breathed, feeling how my lungs quivered with every syllable. "But whatever it is, I'm sure we can just talk about it," I suggested.

However, when he didn't readily respond, doubt crept in.

"Can't we?" The smile I tried to brave slipped from my lips with the question.

His broad shoulders rose and fell with a deep breath. The rims of his nostrils flared, making it abundantly clear he was pissed, but had yet to brief me on the cause. All I knew was, somehow, I was at fault.

With anyone else, I might have let the awkwardness get to me, would have stormed off to let them figure it out on their own, but I couldn't bring myself to walk out on him. So, I stayed.

Stayed and waited.

When his lips moved, I focused intently.

"Found out something interesting last night," he said, taunting me with the lighthearted cynicism that dripped from the statement.

I watched him, all too aware of this being a new experience. He'd never been angry with me. Not like this, anyway.

"What'd you find out?" I did my best to hide how much this got to me, how much it hurt to feel distance like this between us.

He let his back rest against the door before going on, folding thick arms across his chest.

"You went after him," he seethed, adding more for clarity. "The Sovereign."

My stomach sank and I didn't immediately know what to say. I wouldn't lie to him, so denial was off the table.

"Who ... told you?" I stammered. "Dallas?"

Liam shook his head, still not meeting my gaze. "No. One of the *other* hundred people who knows," he answered bitterly. "One of Nick's brothers."

My teeth sank into my lip.

I had every reason to keep what I'd done from Liam. Namely ... this reaction. Granted it might have gone over better had he heard it straight from me, but there still would've been hell to pay.

"I would have told you, but—"

"But you knew how reckless it was? But you knew I'd tell you how that monster would have ripped you apart the moment he laid eyes on you?"

Those shoulders were heaving again, muscle rolling beneath skin as he stared. The disappointment in his gaze was impossible to miss.

"Evangeline, I can't ..."

He stopped and began pacing in front of the door while searching for the right words to scold me.

"I can't protect you," he admitted.

Watching him, my warrior, I knew those words burned like venom as they left his mouth.

I lowered my head.

"And if you keep doing things like this, if you keep—"

This time, I was the one who cut *him* off.

"It won't happen again," I promised, knowing I only gave my word to make that look he wore go away. To describe it as heart-breaking would be an understatement.

A response didn't come immediately, and I knew that meant he was still thinking, knew it meant the conversation was nowhere near over.

"I'd like to believe that, but every time I turn around, you're running straight into the eye of the storm," he fumed as desperation rivaled anger for dominance. The frustration within him was bubbling over.

More pain in his voice. More hopelessness.

I heard him. Really, I did, but also felt so misunderstood. It wasn't lost on me how stupid I'd been. No, it wasn't okay that what I did caused him distress, but in my eyes my actions were justified. As much as I hated to admit this after I'd just given him my word, I'd go out there into the darkness, the uncertainty, all over again if I had to.

For him.

"I'm not ashamed of what I did," I spoke up, knowing he heard the boldness in my voice, knowing he likely resented it under these circumstances. "You would have done the same for me."

He didn't argue with that because we both knew I was right. The difference was, in his eyes, my life had more value. However, I begged to differ. The same resolve he felt when it came to putting his life on the line for me, I felt for him.

I stood when my blood heated in my veins.

"What was I supposed to do?" I asked, lifting my hands into the air before they fell to my sides again.

"You asked me to do something a while back," he interjected, ignoring my question. "You asked me to always tell you the truth. Even when it was hard. Even when it felt like the wrong thing to do."

The conversation was still fresh in my mind. "I remember."

"Then you should also remember that I agreed to this, gave you my word."

I nodded, feeling a breath hitch in my throat when he took

steps closer, so close I felt his energy pulsing in tandem with mine, even in the absence of his dragon.

"I remember," I repeated, distracted by the pull of his soul as it lassoed mine closer.

"Do you also remember the one and only thing I *ever* asked you to promise me in return?"

The question sobered me, made me focus again. When I didn't answer quickly enough, he answered for me.

"I asked that you never run toward danger. No matter what. Not even for me, and you gave me your word," he huffed, each syllable leaving his mouth more laboriously than the last.

"Liam, I—"

I lost my thought when he came closer, a mass of bronze skin and intense emotion as he stood before me.

"Our word to one another has always been everything."

I blinked, I breathed, but words wouldn't come.

We were nearly toe-to-toe now, staring into one another's eyes as our every thought and feeling came bursting from within like fireworks. I couldn't even pinpoint when he took my hand, when his fingers interlaced with mine, but they had.

"Nothing in this world is more important than you breathing your next breath." There was so much conviction in that one statement, it rendered me speechless. Maybe that had been his point.

My heart throbbed inside my chest, heavy as it pounded my ribs. A confession was brewing within me, one that both frightened and freed me all at once. I inhaled a mouthful of air, and exhaled words my soul demanded I speak out loud.

"Without you, I'll die."

I knew how weak and desperate that sounded, but also knew how much lighter I felt now that it was out.

A bitter tear slipped down my cheek and I was surprised by the anger that followed. I was angry forever was no longer on the table for us. Angry at how I failed to prevent this all from happening.

The side of my face warmed against Liam's palm when he pulled me to his shoulder, embracing me at the exact moment I was about to explode—with rage, sadness, everything.

Hot tears slipped from my cheek and onto his flesh.

"I'm sorry," I finally said.

No, I wasn't sorry for running off on my own, but I *was* sorry I made him worry for what I might do in the future. I may have even been sorry I knew I loved him enough to cause him this same hurt again if it came down to it.

He sighed and his air breezed through my hair, but a response never came. Instead, I was moved from his shoulder and a kiss just beside my eye melted away some of the tension. Then another to the corner of my mouth nearly made me forget.

My lips moved with his when he captured them, as his hands blazed a heated trail, moving the material of my shirt up my torso, my chest, so slowly. He knew he didn't need to ask permission. The confidence in his touch made that clear.

We both knew I belonged to him.

The rest of my clothing followed, and then those jeans that rode low on his hips were on the floor, too. Stripped bare—physically, emotionally—we felt more like us.

A set of broad hands lifted me from the floor and taut skin met my calves when they encircled his waist. At the feel of being laid on his bed, when he stared down on me with unmatched adoration, there was no doubt I'd been forgiven.

Forgiven for the one and only crime I'd ever been guilty of.

Loving him.

We stayed close as the high we'd just ridden leveled off. There was no space between us. Where his skin ended, mine began. The world could have been decimated outside his window and we wouldn't have moved from this place.

A soft kiss to the back of my shoulder made me draw a deep breath at the feel of it.

"I'm sorry I missed the meeting," he sighed. "I should have been there."

Shaking my head required strength I no longer had, thanks to him, so the movement was halfhearted, lazy.

"It's fine. You needed space. I get it." When I finished speaking, I pulled his arm tighter around my waist, pushing my hips back toward him a bit more.

"There's no excuse. Things are too unstable right now," he rebutted. "Did they share anything important?"

I shrugged, again giving the action only half my effort. "They reiterated a few things we already brought you up to speed on. Something about Canada's sect of the Council not cooperating, but the clan members are aiding our side anyway."

My eyes drifted closed when I shared more. "And they're firm on evacuating the humans in the coming days."

Liam's body went unnaturally still, and I could guess why.

My parents.

"And you're ... okay with all this?" he asked.

"I am, because it's best for them."

Another kiss to my shoulder, lending me comfort right when I needed it. "You're right. It is."

I had come to terms with the way things were. Their safety was now my only concern. So, with the Council deciding to move them far away from the potential danger zone, that concern would no longer exist.

"You've changed so much." The statement was sort of vague,

but the pride that swelled in Liam's voice when he said those words made it clear what he meant.

I smiled a bit, thanking him, but he didn't stop there.

"From where you started, to where you are … you're almost a completely new version of yourself. Your strength," he commented, "your bravery."

I couldn't recall the last time I'd been so flattered, but right after making heat blossom in my cheeks, a loaded pause lingered between us.

"I know what you attempted to do—searching for the witch—was a direct result of the traits I just admitted to loving about you, but …"

He fell silent, maybe weighing his words, or feeling the contradiction in them before they left his mouth.

"Sometimes you scare me."

The way he phrased that made me smile. "I scare you?"

Stubble from his chin tickled my shoulder when he nodded. "In all the best ways," he shared. "And all the worst."

Hearing the genuine concern in his tone was sobering.

"It'd be nice to think I can just put you in a box and hide you away from everything," he said, chuckling a bit right after. "But I can't. And it terrifies me. Especially knowing you have no regard for your own safety when it comes to mine."

I had no response, because he was right. It would only cause him more distress to hear me confirm that theory.

"I've accepted the fact that I can't stop you," he sighed, sounding just as defeated as I imagined he was. "But I think it's only fair you have to make the same promise you asked of me."

I knew exactly what he was asking—that I promise to never withhold information, that he never have to hear of something reckless I did from anyone other than me.

I nodded. "That's fair. You have my word."

He seemed to relax once I agreed.

"So, is there anything else? Anything you haven't told me?"

I smiled at how light his tone sounded now. Not quite like the weight of the world had lifted off him, but our understanding seemed to bring with it some semblance of peace.

I racked my brain for anything I hadn't shared. "Um ... the spell seems to have worked," I beamed, knowing the potential return of my brothers was news he'd want to hear. "Elise says we should know something soon. A day or two, I'm guessing."

He sighed and I didn't miss the hint of relief that seemed to come with it. "That's ... really good to hear."

I imagined it must have been.

A warrior by nature, he didn't show much emotion outside the depth of our connection, but I knew he missed them. There were a lifetime of stories and experiences that bonded them, and I was excited for him to have that back.

To have *them* back.

He was quiet again, like he was waiting for me to continue on my own. But when I didn't, he asked the same question as before.

"Is there anything else?"

I shook my head. "No, there's nothing."

The silence returned and I wondered if that meant he didn't believe me. But then, he asked a more pointed question that accounted for the momentary silence.

"Nothing new with Nick?"

There was no malice infused in the question from what I could tell. Only concern.

Just as I fixed my mouth to, again, tell him there was nothing, I recalled the strange exchange between us tonight after the meeting. Thinking about it now, I shifted a bit, still feeling uneasy.

"Well ... I'm not even sure it's worth mentioning, but ... things got kind of weird when I saw him at the library."

Even before speaking, I sensed Liam's tension.

"Weird how?"

That question wasn't exactly easy to answer, seeing as how I had no idea what happened.

"We were talking for a bit, and then he just ... started being strange, saying something about a noise, but there *was* no noise. No one else seemed to notice anything, so I think it was just him."

Liam was like a statue behind me.

"And this noise, he didn't hear it until he got close to you?"

All traces of fatigue had slipped away. I stared at silhouetted branches outside his window when answering.

"Seemed to. Not right away, but it got worse the longer he stood there. And then he ran off before I, or *anyone,* could ask if he was okay."

Liam's heart thundered against my back as he held me.

"Does that mean something's changed?" I asked, trying not to let my voice quiver like I feared it might.

"It could, but ... what?" He was just as baffled as I was. "Maybe this is something we need to run past Hilda."

A rush of cold air swept over my naked flesh when he lifted the cover. "Wait ... now?" I protested, his urgent reaction making it hard not to smile. "I'm sure she's still in the basement with Maisy, and besides ... whatever the answer is, it won't change if we talk to her in the morning."

He sat on the edge of the bed for several seconds, leaving me to guess what he'd do next—rush downstairs like a madman, demanding answers; or let it be for now, and continue to lie with me.

My back warmed when he took his place beside me once again. There was more static in the air than before—a sign he was a bit on edge—but at least he wasn't being hasty.

He'd never get to sleep like this, though. On edge. Worried.

I turned to face him, staring as his beautiful eyes glistened in moonlight.

"You haven't finished forgiving me," I said, touching my lips to his right after.

He seemed confused, which I expected.

"When you told me the story about us, about how you finally helped me see you," I explained. "You said I ... *forgave* you three times that night, right?"

It only took him a few seconds to catch on when I finally smiled, giving him a hint as to what I had in mind, showing him further when my kisses moved to his chin, his neck.

"I think it was something like that," he teased, growing more distracted by the second.

I smiled, pressing my lips to his throat, tasting his skin again.

"Then, if my math is right ... our count is off by two."

At those words, his pulse raced faster where my mouth covered it, and when I pulled him on top of me I knew he was no longer thinking about the drama. It could wait because it would still be there to greet us in the morning.

It always was.

CHAPTER 13

Liam

"Stop pacing. It's bad for your nerves," Hilda sighed, clearing the remains of a cleansing spell from her work table. The recipe was one of the few I knew off the top of my head.

I guessed she felt the need to rid the house of whatever dark residue the ghoulish witch might have left behind. She'd gotten her out of here sometime before dawn. I knew because I was lying awake when the guards escorted her out. She certainly left quieter than she came in.

"Well, if you won't stop pacing for the sake of your *own* nerves, please stop pacing to spare *mine*."

My feet halted, but I didn't like that she had no explanation for what Evangeline shared about Nick, about the sound so impossible to withstand he had to run off.

When I finally caught up with his grandfather, my thoughts

weren't on extracting answers from him—things like why he'd done it, why he'd taken the one thing that mattered right out of my arms. My thoughts were singular.

I wanted him to suffer.

Had I realized there was a chance Evangeline would one day return, had I known another Liberator would show up as well, I might have done things differently. It could have been useful to understand what he experienced leading up to the day he crept through our bedroom window.

"It has to mean something."

"Or, it could mean nothing at all," Hilda countered.

"But the sound intensified when he got near her. This morning, when we discussed it again, she said he described it like a buzzing in his ear."

She sat back in her seat, dusting the remains of sage ash from her lap. Her eyes landed on mine and I guessed she saw the desperation in them.

With a sigh, she jumped in to help me brainstorm. "Buzzing," she said to herself. "Vibration. Spiritual frequency," she rambled.

None of that made sense to me, but I listened anyway. She knew more about these things than I did.

"Perhaps it's because her dragon has left her," Hilda suggested, catching me off guard with the statement.

My brow tensed with confusion. "What do you mean?"

Her brown hand lifted into the air, a cluster of metal bracelets clanking together when she gave a dismissive wave.

"You must have known," she went on. "Her dragon has withdrawn from her, leaving her to solely rely on her wolf. It's been that way since ... well, I'm sure you can guess." Her eyes flitted toward the window as her fingers laced in her lap.

I lowered my head, imagining the loss Evangeline must feel. It wasn't difficult to do because I, too, felt incomplete in the absence of my dragon. I dismissed the thought, focusing on Hilda's last point.

"You think that's it? He senses her dragon is gone?"

She tipped her head from side to side as she considered my theory. "Not exactly, but it's possible that with her wolf so strong, she's vibrating on a different frequency and this was his body's response to it."

I was lost. Hilda noticed as much and rolled her eyes with a laugh before explaining.

"Life is energy and this energy has a detectable frequency, although most are unable to pick up on it, it may be that Nick can. At least when it comes to Evangeline," she explained. "I'm of the mind that altering the state of matter changes its frequency. So, in theory, if Evie's no longer meshing with her dragon as she once was, it's possible her frequency has changed."

"But why would that matter to him? Why would that be something he's able to detect?"

I looked at Nick differently than most. From my vantage point, he was far from being an innocent, teenage kid. Even though I now believed he was on a mission to meet those expectations. However, in reality, he was one thing and one thing only ... a killing machine. Everything about him made him a more efficient killer as his destiny related to Evangeline's.

He hears her heart because it makes it impossible for her to hide.

He's a half step quicker than she is so she can never outrun him.

He would eventually be the strongest wolf to exist since his grandfather, only so he'd be a formidable match for the hybrid queen.

These traits, these *abilities,* made sense. They served a purpose, but what Hilda explained ... it felt like a stab in the dark. Unless Evangeline being estranged from her dragon made her weaker. In which case, being aware of this would put Nick at an advantage.

"I'll look into it," Hilda concluded, letting her gaze land on me again. "Is there something else you want to know?"

A thought crossed my mind for a second and she picked up on it right away. Maybe the result of magic, or maybe it was just intuition.

"I can't fix you," she breathed, boring a hole through me with her dark eyes.

"I didn't ask you to."

"No, maybe not out loud, but it's crossed your mind."

Again, I wasn't sure if she'd purposely dug around inside my head or if this was just one of those cases where women know what you're thinking before *you* even know what you're thinking.

I dropped down into the seat across from her, staring at nothing while my mind raced.

"You know I can't undo this," she reiterated.

"I know," I said before she could finish.

"Then ... why are you still lending your thoughts to the matter?"

I glanced up.

"Because I can't shake the feeling she'll die because of me." The words fell from my mouth without thought, because if I'd been aware of what was coming, I wouldn't have uttered such a thing out loud.

And that's when I *knew* this was Hilda's doing.

"A spell," I sighed.

She smiled, shaking her head. "I've done nothing to you. It's the furniture. Anyone who sits in these chairs must speak only truth," she revealed. "But if it makes you feel any better, there's another side to this. Whatever you say while under the spell's power, I'm also bound to secrecy."

Bracing my hands on my knees, I prepared myself to stand,

was free to do so, but stopped. It'd been a long time since I said exactly what I was thinking, feeling. Maybe I'd come here for a reason, and this was it.

When I settled in again, a curious grin crossed Hilda's face. Those bracelets sounded into the air again when she shifted to cross her legs, never letting her gaze leave mine.

"So, I see the loss of your dragon hasn't made you a coward," she smiled, knowing I'd chosen to stay, had decided to see just what truths her spell would bring out.

I took a breath and waited for the questions to begin.

"You're afraid of Evangeline's untimely death, but ..." Her eyes narrowed into suspicious slits. "Something scares you even more," she observed. "What is it?"

"That being mortal will rob me of an eternity with her. It's going to rob me of what I'm owed."

My eyelids twitched with the emotion the admission brought with it, at the feel of these deeply rooted fears being ripped from my body.

"What you're owed," she repeated, never breaking her gaze. "Explain that to me."

The answer came pouring out. "I fought for this," I seethed. "I fought to survive all this time ... to get *here!* Maybe knowing that someway, somehow, she'd come back, because ... I felt her even when she was gone. And now that it's happened, now that, by some small miracle, she's whole again ... my days are numbered."

My throat burned with rage I'd held in for weeks.

"So, what are you going to do about it?" Hilda asked, her tone far calmer than mine.

For the first time since I agreed to participate in this parlor trick of hers, I was at a loss for words. Her brow quirked.

"Perhaps I should rephrase," she amended. "What are you *willing* to do about it."

Again, the response was fluid.

"Anything."

She stopped there, staring so intensely it was like she looked *through* me.

"I want Elise to do it," I went on, unable to stop myself now. "I want her to turn me. I know the process, the pain. I know the risk, but it's the only way."

The once stoic look on Hilda's face was now teeming with emotion—pity, hopelessness.

"She'll never agree to it and neither will Evangeline," she countered.

"I don't need Evangeline's approval," I blurted, adding, "Only her forgiveness once it's done."

A hypocrite.

That's what this spell had proven me to be as it drew my truth out into the open. Just yesterday, I'd come down on Evangeline for being in the same self-sacrificing frame of mind. But, when it came to making these sacrifices with her best interest in mind, I felt justified.

And so did she.

We were two sides of the same coin. Our only flaw being our weakness for, and dependence on, one another. Historically speaking, it made us reckless, cruel to anyone who threatened to tear us apart. Our love for one another turned us into our own worst nightmares—a threat to the other's survival.

I said very little as this realization set in.

Said even less as I accepted the fact that, out of nowhere, a new idea had just been birthed in my subconscious. One that bore dire consequences that, somehow, didn't even register with me.

All I saw was possibility.

"I won't endorse this decision," Hilda said with conviction. "I will not be involved in an act I'm sure will break my niece's heart. She's been through enough," she added, speaking of Evangeline.

"There's no guarantee in what you're thinking Liam. Elise hasn't turned anyone using that method in ... *centuries*."

There was a reason the dragon population paled in comparison to that of the lycans. It went beyond the death tolls racked up by war. It was a matter of logistics. There were limited options for becoming a dragon—you were either born to at least one other dragon, turned by magic, or you were turned by the original.

Seeing as how magic was off the table because it went against the rules that governed it, my only option was to petition Elise, to ask that she consider an attempt sure to be as painful as it was dangerous.

"It's what has to be done," I replied, hearing the resolve from the spell laced in my tone. "I'm damned if I do, damned if I don't."

Hilda rose from her seat and my gaze followed as she moved toward the door.

"Just know, I'd speak of this if I weren't bound to secrecy by magic," she huffed, bearing a look of frustration at my willingness to risk so much.

"You were right," she said with her hand on the knob. "Your love for her truly has made you her worst nightmare. She fears nothing more than losing you, and in your anguish, you've become your own biggest threat to survival—her nightmare in the flesh."

The declaration pierced my heart like I was sure it was meant to.

Hilda's eyes deadpanned to mine and she left me with her final plea. "I beg of you, if you really love that girl ... reconsider."

CHAPTER 14

Evie

"These things take time. We put in a tall order," Hilda explained, doing her best to help Elise relax.

"It should have worked by now. The spell should have brought them here within a few days. It's been a week," she pointed out. "We've left the room sealed like we were supposed to, the spell itself went off without a hitch, and we even took extra precautions." The crease at the center of her brow deepened. "Something should have happened by now."

Her eyes shifted to the hunk of violet-colored stone—amethyst. I hadn't seen her without it since the ritual. According to Hilda, she used it to create a beacon of sorts, one that would alert us the moment my brothers had returned and awakened. I understood its purpose, but it'd mostly served as a distraction when it came to Elise. Even now, her eyes were glued anxiously to where it sat beside her plate.

In a week's time, certain areas of our home had been transformed to accommodate our expected guests—the brothers I was equally excited and nervous to meet. Excited because, growing up an only child, I always wondered what it'd be like to have siblings. Now, I was getting my wish.

But then there were the nerves—a trivial concern that resided at the back of my mind. A fear that, somehow, the *new* me wouldn't meet their expectations. I knew I was different in so many ways, and from what I'd been told, my brothers would return with their memories intact, their abilities as refined as the day they died.

So, yeah ... I was a bit concerned what their perception of me would be, which made me kind of grateful things were taking longer than we anticipated. The two empty bedrooms were now furnished and sprinkled with personal touches Elise handpicked for the six. Daily, I'd catch her in there, straightening a slouched pillow or picture frame, doing all she could to dispel her nervous energy. This, the waiting, it was beginning to wear on her.

"It will take as long as it will take," Hilda concluded, her tone conveying her confidence in the process.

She stood after that, opening and closing her hand in a quick flash that instantly cleared the dining room table of our dishes. When I smiled at the cool trick, she winked at me before disappearing in the kitchen. When she returned, she carried a crystal dish in hand and the sight of it made my mouth water. I knew it held the cake I smelled being prepared earlier in the day. It'd been made with real, tangible ingredients, no conjuring involved, so the entire house smelled of vanilla, butter, and cinnamon for the better part of the afternoon. Another quick flash of the hand and a stack of plates previously displayed in the china cabinet a second before were now in a stack beside the cake dish. Being a hybrid had its perks, but having magic would've been cool, too.

I guess a girl can't have it all, though.

All our eyes were glued on her as dessert was sliced and served. This wasn't a special occasion, but it *was* Hilda's way of trying to lessen the tension that seemed to swell within the walls of the house as time passed. Everyone had their own source of contention—Elise's anxiety concerning the spell, Dallas as the guards reported an increasing number of mutts, Liam and his ever-present concern for me, and my now mirrored concern for him. While I'm sure Hilda knew cake wouldn't fix our problems, it would certainly make them seem a bit further away for a moment.

A slice was placed in front of me, and then the rest was served counterclockwise with Elise being next. Finally, when Hilda came to Liam, his plate hit the tabletop with an aggressive clank. She shot a cold look his way right after, one he returned.

There'd been something odd between them this week, something neither spoke of, but I'm sure the others felt it, too. When I asked Liam about it, he dismissed the question almost as soon as I brought it up. I dropped the subject, but knew this wasn't something I imagined, the strain on their otherwise cordial relationship.

I'd seen it in the daggered glances from Hilda, the lack of conversation and acknowledgement between the two. Even now, I noted how her jaw flexed while taking her seat, all the while sporting a glare she aimed right at Liam.

"It's nice spring has finally decided to grace us with its presence," Elise said, maybe desperate to break the awkward silence.

Her comment made me glance out the window beside me, at the damp grass that still lacked its usual vibrant green. But at least the snow was gone.

"Any day now, the flowers will bloom and these woods will be coming back to life," she added.

I nodded with a smile, but my very next thought was of carnage and blood staining the petals of the very flowers Elise had just mentioned. Yes, spring was indeed upon us, but so was war.

No one spoke. Maybe I wasn't the only one having a hard time suspending reality for extended periods of time. Cake or no cake, our stressors were real, and they were still here.

Even if no one wanted to talk about them.

We finished and did our best to remain just as upbeat as when we first came to the table, but the amount of effort it took was exhausting.

"Well, I suppose I'll turn in," Elise announced, reaching to remove her plate from the table, only to have it poof into thin air while Hilda sat smiling. Elise returned the gesture, but the expression never reached her eyes. Only worry resided there as she left the table, headed for the stairs.

"Be up in a sec," Dallas said with a gentle nod toward Elise. It was his nightly routine to check in with the guards for a briefing before the shift change in a few hours. When he stood and walked toward the front door, I assumed that to be his destination.

With no table to clear or dishes to wash, the rest of us retreated to our rooms as well. It was still too early for sleep, but here in Liam's bed was the only place I felt relaxed, untouchable.

His broad hand moved down the length of my spine and up again. My cheek to his abdomen, I lay there hypnotized by the steady rise and fall as he breathed. The house was silent. Even with the door to his bedroom wide open, we could have easily pretended it was just us here.

The aroma of Hilda's homecooked meal still wafted in from the dark hallway. The longer we were here, in this massive estate Elise chose with us all in mind, the more it felt like a home. An idea I was afraid to fully embrace. The possibility it could all be taken away was too great. So much so, it made my stomach ache every time I thought about it.

"We used to play a game," Liam spoke up, piquing my curiosity right away.

"What type of game?" I smiled against the fabric of his shirt, imagining a thousand different ways this conversation could go.

His fingers traveled to my hair, their tips lightly caressing my scalp.

"It was kind of a word association thing. I'd say a word and you'd say whatever came to mind next."

My smile grew and I nodded. "Okay, go for it."

He took a deep breath, thinking for a moment before blurting, "Dog."

"Bite."

"Candy."

"Sweet," I answered, letting my eyes drift closed as his fingers continued to work their magic beneath my hair.

"Ugly."

"Maisy," I frowned, remembering the hideous face that matched her smell.

"Fun."

My first thought was of my parents and our Friday night ritual. "Movies," I smiled.

"Happiness."

"... This."

His stomach flinched beneath my cheek when he chuckled. "Hate."

"Love."

"What about ... money."

"Elise." My answer came swiftly as I gazed around the expanse of Liam's bedroom.

He laughed. "Water."

"Mermaids."

"Fruit."

"Salad."

"Pleasure."

I smiled again, answering, "You."

He was quiet for a moment. "Mmm ... rain."

"Thunder."

"Bed."

"... You," I repeated, feeling heat blossom in my cheeks. The sum I arrived at when adding Liam plus a bed could definitely do that to a girl.

I turned to find a loaded stare already set on me. The corner of his mouth curved up into a half smile, one I knew the meaning of before he nodded toward the door, suggesting that I close it.

We'd been insatiable lately, unable to get within two feet of one another without things taking a turn toward the *physical*. Listening to music or reading together on the living room sofa always ended with a race toward the stairs, peeling one another's clothes off as soon as the lock engaged. Hilda once threatened to take a hose to us if we couldn't get through a meal without what we *thought* were discreet innuendos. In short, it was nearly impossible to keep our hands, and everything else, off one another.

I scooted toward the edge of the mattress, impatient to lock us inside, but barely stood to my feet when Elise came charging from her room. My mouth was fixed to ask what was wrong. However, I never got the chance because a brightly lit hunk of amethyst said it all.

"They're awake," she stammered.

CHAPTER 15

Evie

Hilda came bounding into the hall from her room.

Elise's eyes danced excitedly, finally finding mine as we faced one another in the doorway.

"I should go to them," she said as a smile ghosted on her lips.

"Of course!" I nodded, feeling her excitement leap onto me. This was what she'd been waiting for, the moment her family would be more complete than it had been in centuries.

Yet, her feet were glued in place.

Just beneath the surface of her excitement was a twinge of fear. Maybe that something hadn't gone right. Maybe even a smidge of doubt that she'd done the right thing bringing them back. Maybe fear that she'd disturbed them to bring them into chaos.

I'd considered that last possibility. We were definitely inviting them to stand knee-deep in our madness. Yes, because we desired that they be present with us in general, but we also needed their help. However, every time I allowed myself to feel guilty about that, I remembered how Liam described them to me—fearless, loyal, and they had a passion for battle.

"They'll need these," Hilda said in a rush, taking charge when Elise froze.

A stack of folded clothing was placed in Elise's hands and next, Hilda guided her to the stairs by her shoulders.

"This way," she sing-songed.

When the bed stirred behind me, I glanced toward Liam, feeling my pulse throb behind my ears. This moment was what we'd been working toward for so long. And now, it was here.

"Ready?" he asked, our previous plans now completely gone out the window as this news was brought to us.

I wanted to just say yes, wanted to share his enthusiasm, but ... I just shrugged, hating that I felt so uncertain about all this, but I did.

My fingers warmed with his touch and I was led from his room with a gentle tug. The journey from the second floor to the basement seemed like a lifetime. Mostly because I experienced such a wide range of emotions. By the time we reached the false partition, I felt inebriated.

I glanced left, toward Liam, and it was hard to miss how anxious he was. In all this, I'd focused so much on what having them back meant for Elise, I'd nearly forgotten what it meant to *him*. My brothers were practically *his* brothers.

For so long, he'd roamed the Earth alone. It was hard to imagine what it would feel like to have almost everyone he loved back again.

I squeezed his hand, finally feeling some of that eagerness transfer to me.

This would only be a good thing.

Slowly, the partition was eased back. It was Hilda who stepped out, and much to my relief, she was smiling. Smiling meant everything went fine and all six were alive and well. Smiling meant that, on the other side of the wall, Elise wasn't heartbroken.

My own heart thundered and I squeezed Liam even tighter.

"It was a success," Hilda confirmed.

It was no secret she was a hard nut to crack. There was no question of her love nor her loyalty, but she'd never been one to deal in emotions.

However, as I stared at her mouth stretched broad, bringing out deep-set dimples I didn't even realized she had, there was no missing the fact that she was elated right now.

"Come," she beckoned. "They'll want to see you. Last they remember, you were no longer with us."

She couldn't have known this, but the very thing she just pointed out was perhaps my biggest source of anxiety when it came to facing them. They'd be expecting their sister, and would instead get … me.

My feet didn't move and Liam didn't miss a thing—not my stiff posture, not the terrified look I'm sure I had.

He glanced toward Hilda. "Mind giving us a sec?"

She nodded quickly. "I'm headed upstairs anyway. Elise has asked that I prepare a meal for the boys."

Her jovial tone made it clear she had no problem doing so, even at this late hour.

Alone, Liam turned to me, his gentle gaze steadying my heart just a little.

"What is it?"

That one question had so many answers. "What if I'm too different?" I started. "What if it weirds them out that I don't remember? What if …"

"It won't be like that," he interjected, shortening my rant. That tall, foreboding frame of his stepped between me and the doorway. I glanced up when he went on.

"They'll think the same of you that they did before," he assured me. "That you're their sister, the one their father named his heir, and above all else ... they'll love you."

I breathed deep, letting his words sink in, praying he was right. When I nodded, he smiled, taking my hand again as he led the way.

I hadn't ventured this far. The first I even knew of this space existing was when Hilda and Elise used Maisy to complete the spell. Needless to say, I steered clear ever since. Cinderblock walls lined the hallway and, just at the end, a brightly lit room where the others waited. We drew closer, and with each step, my pulse raced.

All the way to the door.

And there they were, six massive bodies, each with his back to me. Down their spines, tattoos that were so familiar—phases of the moon that stretched the entire length.

The tattoos ... I didn't expect to see them. Theirs were still present despite having been resurrected, while my own from the past were not. All having to do with the fact that, for the spell that brought *me* to life for a second time, Elise only had half the magic she needed. This lack was the reason I'd been forced to start over from birth, the reason I had no memory of the past.

The six who stood before me today, they were as whole as the day they breathed their last breaths.

Each was so different, and yet so similar to the one standing beside him. Skin varying in shade from nearly the same fair tone as Elise, to warm toffee. Three sported curls as tightly coiled as mine —one whose hung to his shoulders, another with his cropped close to his head, the last with close-shaven sides and a dark mohawk down the center. The fourth in line had inherited Elise's bone-straight texture, while the fifth and sixth kept theirs so closely shaven it was impossible to observe any detail other than the dark shadow of its color.

I stood in silence while Elise addressed them, doing her best to explain where they were, how they were here, and what era this was. It was more information than they'd ever be able to take in at one time, but she was trying.

Each seemed groggy as I evaluated their stances, even *before* Elise confused them with words like 'talisman' and 'restorative magic'. It made sense that they'd be out of it. Two swayed a bit with dizziness, another rubbed the back of his own neck as he struggled to focus on her speech. One on the end braced himself against the stone wall. One leaned with his elbow propped on the shoulder of the brother beside him who stood strong, both arms folded over his chest.

Only some even had enough strength to put on the pants Elise brought down for them, so they still sported white towels secured around their waists. I tried to imagine how confused they must be by all this—their surroundings, seeing the faces of brothers some had witnessed being slain in battle, the modern surroundings, even Elise's sleek, fashionable attire. At the thought of how disoriented they had to have been, I felt sorry for them.

Our experiences being brought back were different, but similar in that we hadn't asked for any of this. While, yes, being given a second chance was a blessing, we were still here by someone else's doing.

I stepped forward. Just a few inches, but quietly enough that they still hadn't noticed me.

Which was how I wanted to keep it for now.

"I'm ... I'm still not sure this is even real."

My eyes stretched wide at the depth of that voice. The one who spoke ran a hand down his stubble-covered head. A heavy accent distorted the words considerably, but I understood him. His large arm flexed when he gripped the back of his neck, making his frustration apparent. Each matched Liam in height and stature, and I imagined that, in their day, the brood must have stricken fear in all those whose paths they crossed.

Elise passed a sympathetic glance toward her son, revealing his name.

"Caleb, it will take time, but I assure you this is all quite real," she smiled.

In an unforeseen display of emotion, his gaze shifted to the right and I was grateful the shadows hid me as he stared at our brother. The one who, from here, seemed to most closely resemble Elise. Caleb stretched a hand toward his shoulder, but didn't speak right away, just let his eyes linger for so long I thought he might not speak at all.

But then he did, and my chest felt tight at his words.

"The last time I laid eyes on you," Caleb began, "I was carrying your body to the woods for a proper burial."

My gaze went to Elise and it didn't surprise me to see her eyes glisten with unshed tears.

The two embraced so tight it would have likely broken the bones of a *normal* person, but these six were far from normal. They were the first lycan/dragon hybrids I'd ever met. The first beings I'd come across who were just like me.

My chest did that squeezy thing again and I swallowed. Liam's hand was still in mine when Elise's gaze shifted toward us. Suddenly aware it was not only her and her boys in the room, her eyes lit up.

"Where is my head?" she smiled, elation lifting her voice an octave when she gestured behind her sons, right toward Liam.

And me.

At the movement, my brothers all turned, all six sets of eyes landing on mine in tandem.

My heart stopped. I froze.

"Declan, Josiah, Ivan ... you asked about Evangeline, and I said I would explain," Elise beamed, not needing to add more than that.

The three she called out by name all stepped forward first, the others moving right behind them. I was swept up into tight hugs, much like the one I'd seen Caleb give. But I wasn't the only one being attacked. They had Liam, too—another of their long-lost brothers they could hardly believe was here.

There was so much going on—phrases being tossed about in a language I wasn't familiar with; others in French, which I *still* didn't understand. It was almost sensory overload, but the best kind.

No, I didn't recognize or remember *any* of them, but couldn't deny I felt a lingering connection I imagined one only shared with siblings.

I, Evangeline Callahan, had siblings.

A sloppy kiss landed on my cheek, followed by a laugh. They were fawning over me like a child, but I guessed that was normal, the way older brothers treated their baby sister. Still, all the attention made me a little shy.

"Boys, settle down," Elise said with a laugh as she stepped forward. It amazed me how they obeyed, these large men immediately falling back at the sound of her voice.

She came to me, placed both hands on my cheeks, holding my stare as she addressed them.

"Be gentle with your sister," she encouraged. "I know seeing her is, perhaps, the biggest miracle of all, but ... Evangeline will need a bit of patience from all of you."

The room grew silent and I felt the weight of her statement before she even finished. It also resonated with me that I was referred to as '*the biggest miracle of all*', reminding me they'd all been alive when my life was taken. They'd all felt the brunt of the grief right alongside Elise and Liam.

"Evangeline wasn't brought back in quite the same manner as the rest of you," she began, turning from me to face them. "Hilda and I had to operate in secret even more so than we do now. So, with only half the magic required for the spell ... I was unable to bring Evangeline back with her memories of the past intact," she revealed. "She was restored as an infant, starting fresh, with no knowledge of her past."

Those six pairs of eyes were on me again, mostly passing confused glances in my direction as I'm sure question after question bombarded them. However, only one spoke up as he gestured toward Liam and I.

"She remembers nothing?" Caleb asked.

Elise nodded. "That's right."

The confusion in his expression spread like wildfire and it only took Elise a moment to understand why.

She turned her attention to my hand linked with Liam's, gesturing toward it when she spoke.

"This," she began with a smile, "has nothing to do with memory. This is the result of a lot of hard work on Liam's part."

There was a quiet moment while they stared at me like an exhibit in a museum, but then a voice cut through the silence. And with a joke, no less.

It came from Josiah, spoken in a still-raspy baritone. "If she's anywhere as stubborn as I remember," he quipped, "that must also mean Liam's patience hasn't thinned."

The others laughed a bit—one shaking Liam by the shoulder, another rustling his hair. I simply smiled, because it was true on *both* accounts—my stubbornness and Liam's patience.

"But Evangeline has come a long way," Elise continued on. "Perhaps the six of you could do your part to help her fill in some of the blanks."

Their expressions were all so warm toward me. I felt it when they nodded or agreed out loud.

"Good then," Elise smiled, glancing at my brothers once again.

"It smells like Hilda's finished preparing your meal. You'll eat, and then we'll talk more after that."

She leveled a knowing stare toward Liam and I when adding more, a coded message only he and I understood concerning our current plight.

"There's much to discuss," she concluded.

If only our new arrivals understood what that really meant.

CHAPTER 16

Evie

I was pretty good with names and had memorized each one long before today. Only now, there were faces to match.

Declan, the oldest, was almost the spitting image of Elise —mirroring her slight facial features and straight, dark hair. Since we settled in the living room, he'd been posted by the stereo in a daze. From the looks of it, he was pleasantly surprised by the evolution of music, appreciating how it had transformed from his time to now.

Josiah and Caleb had finished their meal, but were still snacking on a tray of fruit Hilda brought in. Tobias and Ethan were getting to know Dallas. He made it a point to stay away for a while, giving Elise space to get reacquainted with her sons before stepping in, I guessed.

And then there was Ivan.

He hadn't gone far from Liam since first realizing he was here.

I recalled Liam sharing that, of all my brothers, he and Ivan were the closest.

I smiled to myself from where I rested on the couch, watching the two chat about … probably *everything*. It'd been a while since I'd seen Liam behave so normally, so much like who he was *before* the last several weeks altered his life in so many ways. There had been such a strain on him lately, a struggle to deal with what'd been done to him. The guys noticed pretty quickly he was human, which forced him to explain why. Doing so *then* led to a brief explanation to our current predicament with the Sovereign and his army, but we had yet to get into the meat of the issue.

However, when Elise stood and all eyes shifted toward her, I knew it was time to do just that.

In the center of the living room, she was poised and elegant like always. Her gaze passed over us all—her family. There was a look of pride that couldn't be concealed. I was sure she would have preferred for tonight to be about nothing more than spending time with her boys, enjoying their company after so many years apart. In a perfect world, it would have gone *exactly* like that, but in *our* world, we weren't fortunate enough to suspend reality for so long.

Some of the light went out behind her eyes the exact moment the air in the room thickened with tension.

"Let me start by saying how incredible it is to lay eyes on all of you again," she smiled, emotion riddling every syllable. "You have no idea how long I've dreamed of this."

Some of my brothers lowered their heads as Elise's feelings transferred to them.

"As you all know, the magic used to bring you here comes with grave consequences," she went on. "Consequences dire enough that I swore I would only put the talismans to use if one of two things happened. One: if the Sovereign were overthrown and there was no longer a stigma attached to restorative magic. Or two: the survival of the people he's ruled with an iron fist depended on it."

Her watery stare panned around the entire room.

"Unfortunately, the latter came to pass first."

We were all silent, listening as she explained to the newcomers.

"The Oracles prophesied that Evangeline would take the throne following a great war," she went on. "As you all know, it was your father's desire that she be the one to wear the crown should the day ever come. So, with Hilda's help, and a special blessing from the Oracles, we brought her back eighteen years ago. She went most of her life having no idea who she really is. Which is why I asked you all to be patient with her. We've done our best to fill her in on her past, to teach her how to hone her abilities, but this is all brand new to her."

I caught several of the guys passing curious glances my way. A sudden spike of insecurity had me turning straight ahead, focusing only on Elise when she went on.

"But Hilda and I pulled some strings to get you all back at full strength, with your memories intact, because, well, in addition to wanting our family to be whole again ... we also need your help."

She swallowed deeply, and then forced the next part out.

"In short, the war the Oracles predicted is upon us and things are not as they were in your day—shifters have forgotten their strength, their purpose," she explained. "Those who have recently transitioned are just now coming into the knowledge of what they are, what they're capable of. So, we've been on a mission to educate them, to help them fully realize their potential." Her gaze dropped to the floor before adding. "However, as unfortunate as it may be, we were unable to complete that task, and now, the hour is upon us where we must face our greatest adversary."

"Ready or not," Hilda added.

The room was silent again, and I glanced around at them all. The guys were deep in thought, taking in the breadth of what Elise had just shared, maybe feeling overwhelmed by it all, or maybe—

"You need us to fight and that's what we do."

It was Declan's deep booming voice that made the declaration, bringing some of the life back to Elise's expression.

"It would be our pleasure to bring Sebastian's reign to an end like someone should have done centuries ago," Tobias chimed in.

There was the unmistakable gleam of excitement filling their eyes. It was as if they actually *wanted* this fight. I compared their reaction to my own—timid, frail, always imagining this whole thing would just blow over for lack of attention. Then there were my brothers—brave, ready, thirsty for war.

"We'll need weapons," Josiah said, standing as he went on. "With Hilda's help, we can lace our blades with magic."

Dallas nodded, joining in on the conversation when it switched to a topic he was well-versed in—combat.

"And keep in mind, a lot of time has passed since the six of you were in battle. A lot's changed. Weaponry and tactics have all evolved quite a bit. I'll spend a couple days bringing you all up to speed on what I can," he offered.

The guys nodded and I was painfully aware of one who had strategically dismissed himself from the conversation.

Liam.

Instead of giving input and sharing his knowledge, he was completely silent. No one else seemed to notice, but I did.

Making my way to the other side of the room, I went to him. Giving a smile, I pretended not to notice how his mood had shifted. Mostly because I knew him well enough to know he would prefer it that way. So, I didn't say a word, just settled in front of him on the floor, letting my back warm against his chest as his arms enveloped me.

"How do our numbers compare to theirs?" Ethan inquired.

Elise turned to Dallas to interject.

"There's no way of telling for sure, but I'd bet he's been multiplying his army pretty rapidly," he answered.

"Yes, we can imagine," was Declan's solemn response. "I'm sure he's turned several hundred innocents to mutts by now."

"It's his favorite tactic," Josiah added.

"A *coward's* tactic," was Ivan's take on it.

I agreed wholeheartedly.

"So, this is where we are, boys," Elise sighed. She'd given them the condensed version of our plight, but even *that* was weighty. "Are there any questions?"

Some shook their heads, some mumbled responses, but the general consensus was that they understood.

I could have been wrong about this, but ... they definitely seemed to be looking forward to what was to come.

Declan stood to his feet, and the rest of us were silent as he went to stand before Elise. He pulled her into his arms, and amidst a long embrace, spoke to her with such conviction, it mattered very little that I didn't understand what the words meant.

"Du côté de mon frère, je vivrai ou mourrai. Mais ce dont je suis certain, c'est que je me battrai."

I was only at a loss until Liam whispered the meaning in my ear, broadening my perspective of the six who joined us today.

"At my brothers' side I will either live or I will die. But what I'm certain of, is that I'll fight."

Among the many other traits and strengths I observed among them today, one stood out above them all.

Loyalty.

CHAPTER 17

Evie

C oming up as an only child, I'd never awakened to so
much noise.

Ever.

Boisterous conversation and laughter startled me conscious,
only to find Liam smiling at me from his side of the bed—bright-
eyed, seeming to love all the commotion. I, on the other hand, felt
like my head had just hit the pillow. This must have been the norm
to him, having grown up in such a full home.

What sounded like a stampede thundered through the house
and I guessed there was some sort of roughhousing going on down
there. With a groan, I buried myself beneath the comforter.

"Rise and shine, beautiful."

The sweet words only made me marginally less aggravated
when the blanket was snatched away, letting sunlight beam across
my face again.

"Just ten more minutes," I whined, smiling when a kiss was placed on the corner of my mouth.

He always knew how to get to me.

"In ten minutes there won't be anything left to eat," he warned with a laugh. "Trust me."

I opened my eyes some, remembering that there were six more his exact size downstairs. He was probably right about that.

I hopped up, hoping the aroma of pancakes and bacon weren't only a tease, a trace memory of the breakfast my brothers had already devoured.

I finger-combed my hair as best as I could, but it was a mess and all over the place. It would have taken more time than I had to fix it correctly, and like Liam said, breakfast was no longer an unlimited resource around here.

We took the stairs by two, racing to the bottom where I was swept up into his arms and braced against a broad chest as he carried me into the kitchen. There was so much going on—so much noise, so much laughter, so much life.

A kiss to the cheek and my feet were lowered to the tile again where I fidgeted with my hair for a second time, noting how it doubled in size after my shower last night. It was no use, so I left it for now.

Seated around the island counter and at the table beside the sliding glass doors, the guys shoveled forkfuls of food into their mouths, showing no signs of stopping.

I glanced up at Liam and he gave a knowing smile. He was right to get me up and downstairs when he did.

Hilda and Dallas seemed to blend right into the craziness. With a wave of her hand, Elise ushered us over, her expression revealing how much she was enjoying the chaos. She grabbed two plates from the cabinet and began filling them for Liam and I.

"Find a seat where you can," she laughed, "and I'll be whipping up more while you all eat, so bear with me."

I accepted my plate and thanked her before turning to search for a seat. Preferably *two* seats, so Liam could sit with me.

I still hadn't quite warmed up to them yet—to my brothers who seemed so close to one another while I still felt like an outsider. Standing there, holding my plate, it was like the first day of school all over again. It was like that dreaded moment when lunchtime finally came and it was thrown in your face that you didn't quite fit in.

Only, it didn't go quite like that.

From the table, a large hand lifted into the air, waving Liam and I over. He went right away, but I was slower to move. *Nervous* to move.

Ivan grinned big as he brought a half-full glass of orange juice to his lips. When he lowered it, the grin only grew. We approached, and before Liam had the chance to pull my seat out, it was nudged from beneath the table by Ivan's foot. On the one hand, it was sweet he bothered, but on the other it was totally something a sibling would do—a halfhearted gesture I still considered kind.

Yeah, I was a girl, but to him I was mostly just a sister.

Sensing how comfortable he felt around me, I smiled. Seemed I was the only one nervous about interacting.

I sat and he promptly zeroed back in on his pancakes.

"Did you sleep well?" he asked in a deep, booming tenor, a voice wrapped in the rich undertones of an accent that didn't sound so peculiar anymore. "I hope we didn't disturb you."

He was so polite, almost proper. I imagined Liam used to speak with the same old-timey quality to his voice, but it had likely faded with time, with how much he traveled and experienced. At the thought of what it would have been like to know him in his prime, I smiled.

"I slept okay," I said, answering Ivan's question. I sounded so timid. Hopefully, he didn't notice.

"Things can get somewhat rambunctious when we're left to our own devices," he added, still chewing. "It didn't help that Mother shared quite the story about you while she prepared this meal."

I paused with my fork halfway to my lips. "About ... me? What kind of story?"

In my head, I imagined the many faux pas I had over the months and wondered how embarrassed I should be.

Had she told them I had to be taught how to fly again?

Or how I nearly passed out from the pain of shifting into my wolf for the first time?

I was certain she hadn't shared any of these experiences for the purpose of humiliating me, but what was cute and entertaining to Elise, was potentially devastating for me.

My stare was glued to Ivan while he swallowed another load of food he'd stuffed in his mouth.

"Well," he sighed with a coy grin, wiping his mouth before continuing. "According to our mother, you went up against the Sovereign and his men on your own."

My stomach sank when I realized the inkling of fear wasn't warranted. *This* was the information Elise divulged.

Ivan's gaze lifted to Liam for a moment before coming back to me.

"To save *him,*" Ivan added.

I swallowed before answering. "He would've done the same for me," I said, amending the statement right after. "Actually, he *did* do the same for me. The Sovereign only captured him because he offered his life in exchange for mine." I glanced toward Liam while still responding to Ivan. "If he hadn't acted to save me, I never would've gotten away."

It was still difficult to talk about, especially seeing as how Liam was still suffering the consequences.

I lowered my eyes to my plate, suddenly less hungry than a moment ago.

"She's as fearless as ever," Liam cut in, placing his hand discreetly on my thigh. His touch always comforted me.

"Fearless," Ivan echoed, wearing a smile when he addressed Liam again. "Still against your will, I assume?"

Liam didn't hesitate to nod. "As if you even have to ask."

Clearly, my brothers remembered me as being defiant. Perhaps much hadn't changed in that respect.

Ivan's brow quirked when he remembered something and looked to me. "And your training is tonight, correct?"

I came *this* close to lying, for fear of where this conversation might lead.

"... Yeah," I answered reluctantly.

"A few of us will likely be attending as well," he shared, having no idea how much I *didn't* want that.

I had nothing against them being present. It's just that training was my place to learn, to mess up without fear of being judged. But it was one thing messing up in front of others who didn't quite have their footing either, others who only knew me as the inexperienced girl who shifted at the same time as everyone else.

It was another to look like a buffoon in front of those who vividly recalled me at the height of power.

I hadn't realized how awkward I was behaving until Ivan stopped eating, lowering his fork a bit.

"Unless ... that's not what you want," he amended, his tone coming across as sympathetic and, right away, I felt like a douchebag for making him feel bad.

Liam must've seen me floundering and interjected. "That'd be perfect. I was thinking about hanging back to discuss something with Hilda and Elise later anyway."

I glanced toward Liam. This was the first I heard of him

needing to speak with them in private, but then I focused again, responding to Ivan.

"No, it's fine if you come," I rambled. "It's not that I don't want you all there. It's just that ..."

I couldn't get the truth to come out—that I was afraid they might laugh or think I was about as graceful as a fawn on ice. However, I didn't *have* to say it, because Ivan took the words right out my mouth.

"Is it because you're different?" he asked.

I stared at the glass of orange juice Hilda set down in front of me before making her way back to the stove where she now helped Elise.

"I um—"

My eyes shifted toward Liam when I couldn't put into words how I felt. He passed a gentle smile my way, similar to the one he used to flash when I was just getting to know Elise. It was a smile that let me know it was okay to open up, okay to trust.

A warm hand to my shoulder turned my attention toward Ivan at the feel of it. Facing him, I found it so strange how similar his features were to my own. His, perhaps, more than the others. Staring at him was like staring into the eyes of a male replica of myself—from his dark, coiled hair, to the mellow brown of his skin and eyes. I relaxed a bit, aware of our being related even if I didn't remember him.

"Mother explained everything last night. Your dilemma," he clarified, reminding me. "We'd actually like to help if we can."

The offer was sweet, and I appreciated it, but I had this image in my head of getting knocked onto the mat over and over again while shifters like Beth made combat look easy.

But I said nothing.

He set his fork down completely and I had his full attention. "Evangeline, from what we were told about your journey to face

Sebastian, everyone here has one feeling and one feeling only toward you," he said, holding my gaze. "We respect you."

That word resonated within me, causing me to breathe in as it echoed in my thoughts.

Respect.

They respected me.

"You went up against an entire army, knowing you aren't as capable as you used to be," he went on. "But you did it to save Liam."

I blinked, remembering how little I thought about my actions that day.

"I've known you all my life, Evangeline," he said with a smile. "And *that* was the most courageous thing you've ever done."

Warmth blossomed in my cheeks and I smiled again. "Thank you."

He smiled back before shoveling another heap of pancakes into his mouth.

Beside me, Liam had seemingly zoned out listening to my conversation with Ivan. I imagined it was still hard for him to be reminded of the danger I put myself in on his behalf.

But ... as treacherous as that journey was, I'd do it all over again if I had to.

Liam

The house was eerily quiet since the others left, making the conversation at hand feel that much more sinister. Evangeline's training would last an hour or two, finally providing the opening I'd been waiting for. I'd put off speaking to Elise and Hilda regarding my plan, but we were nearly out of time now.

Hilda had already made it clear over the past week that she said all she needed to concerning the matter. She was dead-set against it, believing I would only end up breaking Evangeline's heart in the end. What she failed to realize was, that was the exact outcome I hoped to avoid. If there was some way to do that without the risky transformation back into a dragon, then I was open to hearing it.

However, Hilda knew like I did, there was no other option.

I prepared myself ahead of time, knowing this wouldn't go over well with Elise either. But with my thoughts toward this option—the only one I had—becoming more solid with each passing day, I couldn't put it off any longer.

I paced, struggling to gather thoughts and words I thought I'd already sorted hours ago. But here in the thick of it, nothing came to me, nothing that captured my true feelings.

The last thing I wanted was for my intentions to be misinterpreted. This decision wasn't some half-cocked plan conjured by an inflated ego and testosterone. This had nothing to do with me being a man, but had *everything* to do with one woman—*mine*.

I was desperate and could only hope they saw through to the heart of the matter. Me being human put Evangeline in more danger than any other threats we faced combined. It only added to the list of pros that I would, once again, be in a position to protect her, protect our *family,* if I was my true self again.

Just as I opened my mouth to speak, Hilda shot me another look, one that conveyed exactly how displeased she was that I hadn't let this go since our talk. I ignored the icy glare, though; had to if I was ever going to get my point across.

"I've come up with a partial solution to our dilemma," I sighed, piquing Elise's interest right away. "I'm aware of how vulnerable we are, and there's something I'd like you to consider."

That's where I stopped.

The words got stuck and when I faltered a bit, Hilda did nothing to hide the grin on her face. I looked away, focusing on Elise again.

Breathing deep, I went on. "I'm no good to anyone like this. I'm weak, a liability instead of an asset," I explained.

My thoughts flickered to all the times me being like this had put Evangeline in harm's way over the past couple months. I could only guess what the future would hold. If any of us were being honest, we knew it would only get worse.

Elise's eyes softened. "I don't like when you speak of yourself in this way. You're as much an asset as anyone else."

Her attempt toward changing my mind was kind, but ... it was wrong. I was sure that, if it came down to it, Evangeline wouldn't be the only member of this household who would endanger their own life to save mine. I couldn't live that way.

I needed to just say it, blurt my suggestion before I lost the nerve. So, that's exactly what I did.

"I want you to help me," I said in a rush. "Magic isn't an option, so I need you to ... turn me."

Agony.

That's essentially what I was asking of Elise. In order for her to turn me like she'd turned the children of *Ars-en-Ré*, I would have to be burned alive before she could bring me back. It was unthinkable, yes.

But it was the only way.

"Are you ... are you serious?" she shrieked, standing from her seat at the dining room table. My feet stopped when she stood in front of me.

"Absolutely not." The words left her mouth with such conviction.

"Elise, we're—"

"Ab-so-lute-ly not," she repeated, this time breaking the statement down to syllables, like I was a child. "Do you have any idea what that would require?"

I breathed deep, nodding. "Of course I do."

"Then why on *Earth* would you even—"

"Because it's the only way!" A breath hitched in Elise's throat when my voice thundered through the room.

She froze, staring as we both heaved, short of breath and rattled for two very different reasons. The cause of her distress: the thought of losing *me*. Mine: the thought of losing her daughter.

Suppressing a frustrated grunt, I tightened my fists.

"Tell me you don't see it coming from a mile away," I pleaded. "Tell me you don't see Evangeline, the daughter you love and fought so hard to bring back, eventually diving straight off a cliff thinking it's what she has to do in order to save me," I seethed. "Make me that promise and I'll drop the whole thing."

Elise's otherwise pale cheeks flushed red, the rims of her nostrils flaring at the thought.

"Liam, I am many things, but before *any* of them I'm a mother. And despite my blood not coursing through your veins, you're my son. Whether you like it or not at the moment. You cannot ask me to choose to endanger your life, all with lofty hopes that you'll survive it." She was nearly panting with frustration when she stepped closer.

"And let's say you *do* survive the transformation. Liam ... you were born dragon," she reasoned. "The children I turned were only human. Who's to say that doesn't matter? Who's to say the dragon DNA already within you won't somehow make you different? Uncontrollable even," she suggested.

Her eyes softened when she took another step in my direction, placing a hand on my cheek when she said more. "Your sole purpose for even *considering* this is to protect Evangeline. Why can't you see that this ... '*plan*' of yours has the potential to do exactly the opposite?"

I sighed, knowing everything she said had some semblance of truth within it, but—

"The answer is no."

There was no questioning if her conclusion was final. Even with her gaze full of compassion, she was firm on this decision.

Her steps echoed through the foyer as she traipsed toward the stairs. I stood there, feeling like my heart had been ripped from my chest, my only hope shot down in an instant.

The sound of Hilda's chair moving across the wood grated my nerves, causing my fists to tighten again. I was fully prepared for her to gloat after Elise had all but sided with her, but she didn't. Maybe she knew how badly this stung, how hopeless I felt, because she simply retreated to her own room.

I was left standing there. Alone, powerless—both feelings weighing down on me more than they ever had in my entire life.

The flicker of hope I managed to cling to these past few weeks had just been snuffed out.

And there was absolutely nothing I could do about it.

CHAPTER 18

Evie

They watched from the sidelines. All six of my brothers, not just Ivan.

My heart thundered inside my chest and I hadn't even started training yet. I'd gotten worked up just at the idea of them coming tonight. Especially seeing as how this was the first session I'd been to in a while. Sitting with Liam through his recovery had been priority number one. Now, as a result, they'd all get to watch me make a huge idiot of myself.

Not even the danger of someone figuring out they didn't belong could keep them home. It was Hilda who reminded them over and over that they should stay in, keep a low profile, but they wouldn't hear of it. She warned that, if their identities were somehow revealed, if it became apparent that they were hybrids brought back using restorative magic ... there would be hell to pay.

However, with a bit of encouragement from Dallas, and a

timely reminder that this town was jam packed with tons of new shifters *anyway*, the decision was made.

And now, a brood resembling the defensive line of a pro football team stood behind me as I walked to the mat where we would be paired up, where I'd make a fool of myself shortly.

Yup ... good times.

To my left, a blonde ponytail bobbed as Beth rushed in, breathing like she'd run the whole way. My face lit up, knowing her presence would quell at least *some* of my nervous energy.

She smiled and posted beside me when Dallas leveled a glare her way for just barely slipping in on time.

"Where were you?" I whispered, nudging her when I leaned in.

She took a breath first, glancing toward Dallas again before answering, "Clan stuff. My mom and I had to see the Elders today."

The only time I'd known anyone to meet with the Elders was either when someone had done something wrong, or when they, or the entire clan, faced danger.

"Why'd they send for you?"

She shook her head. "They didn't. My mom actually arranged it."

Tuning Dallas' instructions out, I focused on Beth when she said more.

"Things have been ... weird lately. My mom's our pack alpha, but the balance has been off at home since we got back," she shared. "Usually, I can feel that she's ranked above me. I know that sounds weird, but that's the only way I can explain it. But she says the same thing's been going on with my uncle and Roz."

'*Weird*' was a relative phrase these days. And plus, without a pack of my own, I couldn't have related.

"Has that ever happened before?" I said close to her ear.

Her head shook. "No. Never. Which was why we went to see the Elders."

We paused our quiet conversation a moment when Dallas passed a warning glare our way. However, as soon as he turned to address the crowd again, we finished.

"Apparently, there have been other reports of what the Elders referred to as '*stratum deviation*'."

I stared. She said that like I actually knew what it meant.

With a quiet laugh, she broke it down for those of us who *weren't* privy to the knowledge her parents passed down to her.

"In short, she's no longer my alpha, but I'm not hers either," she stated, adding, "... yet."

"Yet?"

Beth nodded. "First, there's kind of a period of limbo, where her authority within our pack will continue to diminish while mine is strengthening. The Elder explained others have had a sense of the shift in power as well—kids being able to override their alpha's commands most notably—but they have a feeling it's happening on a much larger scale than what's been reported."

I didn't respond, unsure what the long-term implications might be of something like this happening. Especially right now, with there being so many other moving pieces to factor in.

Beth and I partnered up when the time came and took to a mat deep in a corner. One I made sure was far, far away from my brothers. Even with the effort I made to convince them to stay behind at the house, they insisted on coming to support me.

The few weak punches I threw were easy for Beth to block as my gaze volleyed between her and the guys. They were definitely watching. When I faced forward again, my very patient best friend followed my gaze.

"You know them or something?" she asked, making my stomach drop.

Hilda would kill me if I told the whole truth, so I answered as honestly as I could without saying too much.

"Sorta-kinda."

Her brow quirked when our eyes locked again. "Is that even an answer?" she smiled.

"It is. I just met them yesterday," I added.

"Are they some of the shifters who came to help?" Her tone wasn't suspicious at all, just curious.

"Yeah." I was happy these questions were easy to get around without lying.

Beth gave a shrug and then took her stance again when I did. I had to relax, pretend they weren't here, because if I couldn't, there would surely be more questions.

We exchanged a few hits and settled into a good rhythm when a shadow darkening the entrance caught our attention. My punches slowed again as I watched Nick saunter toward the center of the room in sweats. He seemed ... bothered. Maybe it was his tense posture or that uncomfortable look on his face that gave it away.

He exchanged a few words with Dallas before being assigned to alternate partners with a team that had already been paired near the bleachers. Nick sat with both elbows perched on his knees while watching the two spar, awaiting his turn. His gaze drifted around the room, observing until, eventually, it landed on me.

I forced a smile, feeling the same awkward tension resurface that lingered between us the last time we saw one another. I couldn't help but to wonder if he heard it even now—that sound, the one he described as a persistent buzzing ... the one that made him take off into the woods like it might drive him to do something drastic if he didn't.

I focused on training again, doing my best to ignore the questions that all seemed to pop into my head at once.

Eventually, things settled down and I nearly forgot about all the outside distractions. We were winded and sweating already—the result of keeping up with our partners' otherworldly speed and agility.

"You've gotten so much faster," Beth panted, pausing to catch her breath.

"Finally," I joked, making her smile. It wasn't lost on me that I hadn't regressed from not being able to attend. Somehow, things were easier, more natural.

Her eyes drifted to the clock on the wall, prompting mine to do the same. "Ten more minutes," I acknowledged.

Soon, I'd be headed home for a shower and dinner, which sounded like music to my ears. No, it wouldn't make for the most exciting Friday night, but neither did my *old* routine with my parents—our ritual of kicking our weekend off with a movie. I suppose I was simple because, tonight, I mostly looked forward to lazing around in Liam's bed, listening to music or just talking about whatever randomness popped into our heads.

It was as close as we got to normal and being with him took my mind off things, which was a miracle in and of itself.

A few combat exercises later and Dallas blew his whistle, signaling all of us to gather in the center of the room. Not too far on my left, Nick shifted from one foot to the other, giving off so much nervous energy I could feel it from where I stood. With his eyes so focused on Dallas, I got the impression he was intentionally trying to avoid making eye contact with me. And then, when he popped an earbud into one ear—the ear that would have been most susceptible to the buzzing—I guessed all my assumptions were spot on.

He still heard it.

I faced forward again.

"Good work today," Dallas announced, glancing around the room at us all. "It's obvious we have a ton of new faces, but from what I've seen today, even the newcomers pulled their weight."

There was only a hint of a smile on his face. In this role, he was all about military precision and order.

"We'll be meeting again in a couple days," he went on. "Same place, same time. In the meantime, anyone got questions?"

A couple hands shot into the air and Dallas cleared up confusion about what one kid needed to work on before the next session, and another inquiry about what shoes he thought it was best to train in. Both questions seemed to annoy him with their simplicity, but he answered politely.

"Anything else?" he asked with an eye roll.

When no one spoke, we were dismissed.

Beth and I chatted a bit while going to retrieve our bags from the bleachers. When we got there, Nick was getting his things, too. We were standing too close not to acknowledge one another, which I'm guessing was the only reason he did.

His hand lifted into the air with a quick wave. "Hey, how's it going?" His tone was dry and impatient, like he couldn't wait to get away.

That same anxious energy I sensed before made electricity scatter across my skin.

"Everything's good," I answered, trying to imagine what this noise must have sounded like, what it could have meant.

"Where's Roz?" I forced out, needing to fill the dead air. "I noticed she's not here."

He seemed distracted as he shoved a towel inside his bag. "Yeah, um ... she had a ... thing with her dad, the Elders," he explained vaguely.

Had it not been for the conversation I just had with Beth, I wouldn't have had a clue what the meeting was about.

I nodded and had just decided to make small-talk so this conversation wouldn't be such a fail, but he hiked his bag up his shoulder and spoke before I had the chance.

"Uh ... listen, I have to take off. Richie just texted to say he's waiting outside, but I'll catch up with you in a bit," he said, flashing a weak smile. No, it was a *pained* smile.

I felt concern spread in my expression and was certain he could see it.

"Sure. Yeah ... okay."

As soon as the words left my mouth, he started in the opposite direction of where I stood.

"What's up with him?" Beth asked, popping a stick of gum into her mouth.

I shrugged, unsure of how to explain the little bit I knew.

She didn't press for more info, just followed as I started toward my brothers, feeling a little nervous knowing they most likely watched and scrutinized my every move tonight.

But then ... my feet stopped dead in their tracks. The lights that hung above flickered in tandem with a thunderous tremor, one that vibrated deep beneath our feet.

My gaze darted in Dallas' direction and I grabbed Beth's hand before rushing toward him. Even Nick halted, just shy of making a clean exit. His head swiveled as the building reverberated with energy from the loud blast.

I reached Dallas, my brothers.

"What was that?" It was a stupid question, seeing as how they'd been blocked off from the outside world for the last hour and a half just like I had.

"We'll go check it out," Declan offered.

I wasn't surprised when the others and Dallas followed him, moving toward the exit like a living wall. Beth and I trailed them, too, but slowed when our names were called. Chris and Lucas approached from the left.

"Hang on. We're coming with you," Chris announced as their steps synced with ours.

Naturally, when we made it to Nick, he fell in step as well. It seemed that, with his concern focused on what went on beyond these walls, he hardly noticed the sound I was convinced he now heard whenever I was around.

The five of us walked the dark hallway just beyond the gym's double doors, leading toward the exit of the Athletic Building. Outside, the moment we tasted night air, there was no missing the plume of smoke that billowed against the inky sky.

"Looks like it's coming from somewhere north. Somewhere near the falls," Dallas explained, finding me in the small crowd that gathered in the lot.

I felt my chest expanding at record speed as my breaths came faster. "What about Liam? Elise and Hilda? We have to get to them."

Dallas pointed to a phone pressed to his ear I hadn't noticed before. "I've got Elise on the line now. They're all fine, just wondering what's going on. She's checking in with the guards."

With his reassurance, I only settled a little.

The door of a truck slamming brought my attention to Richie as he approached. He, too, was on a call, asking someone on the line for an update. The grave look on his face, the urgency in his steps as he moved toward Nick, made fear spike in me once more, like it never left. When his expression turned grim as the person responded in his ear, my stomach did a somersault.

Three words left his mouth and the crowd fell silent when he uttered them. "It's the dam."

The dam ...

"Everyone needs to get to higher ground!" Richie's voice boomed to the crowd, prompting those who once stood observing to rush toward their vehicles.

It was Nick who turned to his brother to ask the hard question amidst the sound of screeching tires, with the glare of headlights whizzing past.

"What about everyone else?"

That dark look was still plastered on Richie's face when he

answered. "The authorities are working on evacuating those they can."

I frowned, asking, "What do you mean *'those they can'*?"

Richie leveled a solemn look my way. "Whoever did this, whoever caused the explosion," he said, as if we didn't already know who was behind it "... they must've severed communication to landlines beforehand."

It became clear the Sovereign wanted this town to suffer, experience devastation at its worst—a lesson to never cross him, I guessed.

"We're spreading the word as quickly as we can via cell phone while we're able, hoping people are notified quickly enough," Richie added.

I couldn't even form a single thought. The fate of this town rested solely on civilians starting phone chains or going door to door. There was no way to contact the owners of large establishments unless someone present happened to get the call in time to warn everyone else.

Chaos.

That's what was ahead of us. We were a matter of minutes away from it, actually.

My head reeled when Dallas sprang into action, his military experience already proving to be more useful in a crisis than my tendency to panic.

"You seven to the truck," his voice boomed, addressing my brothers and I when he gestured toward Liam's pickup we borrowed to get here.

I didn't miss the nervous glance Dallas aimed in the general direction of the falls as the guys filed in, lowering the truck's bed beneath their weight.

What was happening?

What was the Sovereign's plan?

A tight hug squeezed my neck when Beth grabbed me. "I'm

gonna go check on my parents and then I'll call. If I can't get through, I'll be by later to check on you."

I nodded aimlessly, in shock. I stood there, watching as Beth sprinted to her car, watching as Chris and Lucas followed in a jeep, likely planning to make sure she got home okay.

"Don't panic."

I turned toward Nick's voice, only now realizing he hadn't moved yet. The solemn look on his face surprised me for two reasons. One, because he was probably the calmest out of everyone. Two, because it helped me focus a bit.

"Your place is at a high enough elevation and far enough away from the river that you all shouldn't be affected if this thing breaks. Same with Beth," he added, knowing I was just as concerned about her, the others.

He added to his statement, and it was then that my thoughts aligned. "And your parents will be fine, too."

My parents ...

When my gaze wandered up from the pavement to meet his, he couldn't have understood the look I gave—a mixture of dread, fear, and sadness flooded in all at once.

"But they're ... they're not at home," I stammered, adding more dribble I'm sure seemed random to Nick. "It's Friday."

His brow knitted together with confusion. "What does that mean?"

I pushed my fingers through my hair and held them there, trying to think, trying to decide what to do next, how to fix this.

"It's ... it's our ... *their* movie night. They never miss," I explained frantically, hoping it made sense.

The theater, just like this school, was nestled in the valley right at the foot of one of many rolling hills. They made the landscape of Seaton Falls the most picturesque I ever laid eyes on. However, in this instance, they made it a death trap. The heart of town would be the epicenter, the destination of the rushing water when the dam inevitably gave way, succumbing to the river behind its gate.

A loud, blaring horn followed by a very irritated, "Evangeline, let's get a move on!" shouted from the truck by Dallas made me feel like I was stuck between a rock and a hard place.

Another quick press of the horn from the other direction was Nick's warning from Richie.

The blood ran cold in my veins as it suddenly became clear what I needed to do. Turning to Nick, I stammered a quick statement, one I didn't have time to fully explain.

"I have to go," I forced out. "Tell Dallas he has to keep him there—Liam. He has to do whatever it takes to keep him there at the house. He can't come looking for me," I urged, feeling wetness touch my cheeks.

There were so many things wrong with this decision, starting with me breaking my promise not to run toward danger, but I had no choice. My parents would be defenseless if the dam broke. At least I'd have a chance.

And I was willing to risk my life to give them one, too.

"Nick," I pleaded. "You have to tell him to make sure Liam doesn't come after me." Yes, I was begging, but I didn't care how pathetic it made me look.

A quick nod came before an agreement that set me on my way right after. "I'll tell him," he promised.

And, with that, Nick giving me his word, I took off in the opposite direction of home, deeper into the valley.

Liam might never forgive me for defying him yet again, but I was willing to accept that it might take him time to come around. He would have to understand.

I had no choice.

CHAPTER 19

Nick

"Nick! Truck ... now!"

With Richie yelling at the back of my head, I trudged toward Dallas when he stepped out, his eyes scanning the lot when he noticed Evie no longer stood with me.

I promised I'd deliver her message and would make good on it, despite the nagging burn in my chest when Richie pulled rank. He was urging me to submit, but fighting it had become so easy, training myself to quench the burn.

I continued ahead meeting Dallas at the bed of the truck where six brutes—all strangers to me—hopped out one-by-one. Concern marked their expressions as they, too, scanned for Evie.

"She doesn't want anyone to follow her," I announced, putting my life on the line judging by the death-stares the strangers and Dallas leveled my way.

I put my hands up in surrender, adding, "Don't shoot the messenger."

Dallas braced both hands on his waist, releasing a frustrated sigh as his face reddened.

"I swear that girl can never just … follow directions," he seethed, which made it clear this wasn't new behavior for Evie.

"She also wanted me to tell you that Liam can't come looking for her."

I hadn't said so at the time, but I knew she meant to protect him.

"Where'd she go?"

At the question, I nearly let her destination slip, but knew what would happen if I did. Dallas would ignore Evie's wishes and chase after her. If he did, he'd never make it home to deter Liam.

I said the only thing I knew to say.

"Not sure, but I'm going after her."

I hadn't noticed Richie standing behind me until he spoke up.

"Over my dead body," he growled. "Get in the truck. I'm taking you home."

The burn returned and I extinguished it yet again. There was no missing the deep rumble in my brother's throat.

"I'll go," I reiterated, looking Dallas square in the eyes.

He had no reason to trust me. He knew everything there was to know about me, including the fact that I could hear Evie's heart, knew the reason why. But under these circumstances, I was his best bet.

With a deep sigh full of regret, he nodded, grabbing my bicep when I turned to walk away. The threatening action set Richie on edge and I felt his wolf stepping forward.

"You bring her back," Dallas warned through clenched teeth, practically daring me to make a false move.

She was loved. I got it. So, instead of taking offense to his tone, the gesture, I simply nodded. "I won't let you down."

As risky as it was to answer with such certainty, I did it anyway, praying I hadn't just made a promise I didn't have the power to keep.

It wouldn't have surprised me if Dallas had ordered the six from the truck to escort me. But what *did* catch me off guard was that he didn't have to. As soon as I mentioned going after Evie, they volunteered. I was positive they knew what potential danger lie ahead, but none seemed to care.

I knew as much because ... here they were.

They still hadn't shared much info about themselves, like ... who they were, or why they willingly followed me, but one thing was clear; they had to have cared about Evie.

Enough to risk their lives.

As we made our way through town, they spoke, but only to one another. I heard traces of French, but another language that muddled it a bit. However, they merged both into their dialogue seamlessly. I would've liked to have known what they said, mostly so I knew I wasn't in danger traveling with them, but I just had to extend my trust to them by association. If they knew and cared about Evie, they couldn't have been all that bad.

Despite their size and varying degrees of dark expressions.

After talking Richie out of tagging along, insisting that he go check in on our parents instead, I was off to a running start. Roz had been on my mind since leaving the school lot, so I dialed her while we rushed through the woods at top speed.

She picked up right away and I wasn't ashamed of how happy I was to hear her voice.

"You're okay," I panted.

"I am. Are you?" The quick response was an indication of fear.

I didn't want to lie, so a vague, "I'm okay right now," was true and made no promises I may later have to break.

"Where are you?"

At her question, I breathed into the phone, weighing my response before saying it aloud. "Doing what I can to help. It's insane out here."

"Which is why you need to get inside, Nick. You need to get to higher ground," she urged. Her voice was nearly frantic now.

"Just ... promise me you'll stay in the house," I practically begged, preparing to do just that if it came down to it.

"Promise me, Roz."

She was still quiet, failing to say the words I so desperately needed to hear.

But then, her voice came back and I sighed with relief at the sound of it. "I promise, but you have to do the same. As soon as you can," she added.

I nodded despite her not standing before me in the flesh. "I'll do everything I can to get home." And that was the honest truth. I *would* fight hard, do all I could to stay safe while also keeping those I cared about out of harm's way.

However, as the world seemed to fall apart around me, I wasn't sure that was a choice I even had anymore.

I ended the call and our small group moved through the streets quickly, but in silence, contrasting the sudden panic that seemed to have spread like wildfire. Anxious faces hurried past as bodies flooded from buildings, as the emergency sirens wailed. Doors to many of the shops and restaurants had been left wide open as those inside bolted with one thing on their minds—escape.

As we ran, a second blast cracked through the air like lightning. An outcry of horrified screams followed. I turned toward the falls. From this distance, it was out of view, but there was no mistaking how the cloud of smoke that rose had thickened, blotting out a swatch of stars in the otherwise clear sky.

"We have to hurry," I said in a rush, doubling our pace as we fought our way down the crowded sidewalk. While most were rushing toward higher ground, safety, we were headed straight into the mouth of madness.

The theater came into view and I crossed the street haphazardly, narrowly scraping past a delivery truck that hadn't seen me.

At the sight of the thin crowd straggling out, my heart sank.

What if she found them and already left?

What if they were never here to begin with and she was wrong?

When my feet stopped on the pavement, one of the guys spoke —one with a clean-shaven head and permanent scowl set on his face, like angry was his default emotion.

"Why aren't we moving?" his voice boomed in a deep tenor, one woven with a heavy accent. I glanced his way, only now really giving any of them a hard look. With their size exceeding mine and their scents throwing me off, I kept my guard up.

There was the telltale smoke of a dragon, but ... lycan, too. It only took a moment to realize I'd been traveling with hybrids. I gave the one who spoke another look before replying.

"I ... I need to hear," I explained vaguely.

An audible growl resonated from his chest—a threat meant for me, no doubt. It took one of the others placing a hand on his shoulder, and then calling him by name, to disperse some of the fury in his eyes.

"Easy, Tobias," the one with the mohawk urged. His gaze drifted to mine, almost apologetically. "Forgive my brother. He's just concerned ... and somewhat impatient," he added kindly before giving his own name. "I'm Ivan."

It was quick as far as introductions were concerned, but under these circumstances, it was enough.

With Tobias settling down per his brother's request, I gave my name and then focused again, listening for Evie's heart.

The roar of an engine threw me off when a car passed.

Breathing deep, I closed my eyes. The crisp night air of an incoming spring moved over my skin and I let myself feel the waves of energy within it.

And that's when I heard it. Or rather *felt* it, her heart pulsing through the air.

"She's still inside," I blurted, taking off toward the theater as soon as I was positive.

The others followed, but not without their doubts.

"How can you be sure?" Tobias questioned.

Knowing I couldn't exactly explain that, I turned and said the only thing I could.

"I just know."

There were stares, some only curious, but most distrusting.

We burst through the heavy, brass-framed doors of the entrance. The place was a dead zone. Bags of popcorn had been dropped right where patrons stood when news about the dam reached them. There were things all over—a jacket on the ground near a poster, a cell phone on the counter.

"We're wasting time," Tobias grumbled, staring me down with fury swimming in his eyes. The look reminded me of the one Liam often gave. And, like Liam, this guy gave off the air of being feral … a savage.

"She's clearly not here," he added. "We need to move on."

However, the rapid thump of a frantic heart said otherwise.

Again, I didn't bother explaining how I knew we needed to venture further in, I simply went. Their steps were hesitant behind me, but they followed.

"Evie!"

I called out and then listened, going down the wide, dark corridor lined with theaters, most of which still had movies blaring inside them. In other words, there was no way she'd hear over the noise.

"We'll have to split up," I sighed, knowing that was about the worst possible idea, but it would increase our odds of finding her. I got us to the general area, but we needed to search.

We scattered and I started in the screening room on the right. Pushing the door open, I rushed inside, did a quick scan, and then came out to head into the next.

This felt like déjà vu, reminiscent of another time I set out to find her amidst a disaster. Only, then, I'd been searching for the girl I loved. Now, I was desperate to find the friend who'd saved my life little more than a month ago when the Council would have preferred to end me.

"Evie!" I tried calling out again.

Still no answer.

I pushed through another door, set to yell her name once more, but didn't have to—the buzzing, an electric hum I now associated with being near her …

A set of bewildered eyes found mine. Beside her was another familiar face, that of the mother who no longer remembered her, and lying on the ground … her father.

I rushed over, assessing the situation as I went to them.

"What's wrong? What happened?"

Evie pushed fresh tears from her eyes, saying things I was sure her mother found strange considering she had no idea who we were, no idea that the girl who'd just put herself in harm's way to find them was in fact her daughter.

"I got here about a minute ago, as soon as word reached them about the dam. Everyone was rushing out in a stampede," she choked out. "Some guy panicked and … he pushed him down," she added, staring at the deep gash on her father's head.

She was in shock. Otherwise, she would've been thinking clearer and made quick work of getting her folks out of here.

"Evie, listen to me," I said gently, feeling the sense of urgency creeping further up my spine as the door opened behind me—one of the guys, I guessed. He called out to the others to come this way.

"We have to get out of here. We'll get him help," I promised. "But we have to go."

She swiped a tear, racked with so much emotion as her mother did her best to wake her husband.

Taking Evie's hand, I pulled her to her feet. I offered her mom the other.

"Ma'am?" Mrs. Callahan's gaze met mine—hers confused and tearful.

A massive body breezed past me—Tobias again, the dick-ish one. Evie watched as he lifted her father from the ground and tossed him over his shoulder. The motion caused Mr. Callahan to groan, which visibly relieved his wife. It was a sign of life, and possibly returning consciousness after having been unresponsive for a couple minutes.

We moved quickly, the ten of us. Our group had swelled in size and I tried to ignore how that could become a handicap if things got hectic. We cleared the door, moving quickly through the lobby, but what met our vision when we finally reached the exit … it sent us all staggering back.

"Grab on to something!" After yelling out to the others, I scrambled for a nearby pillar to latch on to. A wall of churning water highlighted in moonlight raced toward us, sweeping stragglers off the street who hadn't gotten out in time. Cars parked against the curb were shoved out of the flood's path.

Evie's heart hammered tenfold now, that high-pitched buzz holding steady.

"Tobias!" she called out, gaining his attention. "Don't let him go."

She was still fighting her emotions while clinging to a pillar with her mom.

Amidst the chaos, Mrs. Callahan must not have thought it strange that Evie's hand made its way into hers, that she held it tight like they weren't strangers at all, but I knew there was real emotion behind the gesture. As a moment of silence mocked what would follow, Evie was just a girl clinging to her mother as we took what might have been our last breath.

The floor-to-ceiling window exploded and cool mist hit my skin a millisecond before a powerful surge that tugged my body away from the beam, filling the building in one mighty rush. My fingers locked tight, struggling not to pull free from the force. Water covered my head and I held my breath, not knowing how long it would be before I got air again. All sound muffled around me except the liquid gurgling in my ears. My heart raced with uncertainty. Not only for my own fate, but for those here in the trenches with me.

Slowly, I felt my mass lowering, and my head was again above water. Spurting some from my mouth as I gasped, squeezing my eyes to clear my vision, I took a look around at the swimming pool that was once the theatre. One by one, others surfaced, but not Evie, not her mother. Even Tobias had managed to keep a grip on her dad, thanks to the wave pinning them both to the wall behind the concession stand. Had it not been there, they would have been carried away.

"Evie!" There was no missing the desperation in my voice, the panic as I called out to her.

Water still rushed in, but nothing like the first wave. With the current calmer now, I could at least swim through it, to the spot where I'd last seen her. Holding my breath, I went under only to find that the beam she and Mrs. Callahan clung to was missing its bottom half, an indication that something large had passed through and took a large chunk with it, and ...

"Evie!" Her name quaked from my lips.

No trace of them anywhere.

I listened for her heart, hoping and praying, but ... that prayer came back void. It was impossible to hear over the sound of falling debris, the building groaning, and the cries for help that now filled the streets of Seaton Falls.

General chaos.

I turned to the guys, these men who followed me into this mess all to find her.

"She's not down there. And something wiped out the beam," I added, trying to keep a cool head.

"Evangeline!" one called out, and then another once he caught his breath, pushing long hair behind his ears to see.

We all dove deep again and that's when I spotted something as it floated past. Evie's bracelet. An ancient-looking, leather band she had on every time I'd seen her lately. I grabbed it, tucking it deep inside my back pocket so it wouldn't get lost. I looked around, doing another scan.

Had it not been for keen vision, I would have missed it … would have missed the tips of thin fingers moving frantically, barely breaking the surface.

"Over here!" At the sound of my voice, the others followed.

I took in a swell of air and went under again, unsure of what I'd find. However, the sight before me was one I never would have imagined. The hand I glimpsed belonged to Mrs. Callahan. Her strength was fading as she pointed desperately at her leg, which seeped blood from an injury. It'd been pinned to the wall by a vehicle—the one responsible for the damage to the pillar when it burst through the building with the river.

A weakening heartbeat pulsed through the water, as did the newly present hum, which was much stronger. Had it not been for that, I might not have even peered down, deeper in the murky water. When my eyes focused, I spotted Evie—lifeless as she lie beneath the wheel, unable to move with the weight of the vehicle locking her down by the shoulder.

I had the guys' attention and two gripped the rear bumper, while me and the long-haired one took the front. Our strength was limited without being able to get traction, but it budged. Right away, Ivan, who stood by waiting, took Evie over his shoulder and moved toward the surface. With my aid, Mrs. Callahan swam to the top, favoring the hurt leg a little.

A collective gasp filled the space when we were finally able to breathe.

"I need to help them," I said in a rush, knowing Mrs. Callahan needed medical attention, too, but her circumstances were nowhere near as dire as Evie's.

"Go," she urged, glancing toward Evie's lifeless body—the girl who had undoubtedly saved her life. "I'm okay. I don't think it's broken. Just ... help her," she urged. "Please."

I nodded and moved away, pushing random debris and people's personal effects aside as I swam over.

"Is she breathing?" I asked, trying to keep calm. Her heart was still beating, I knew, but I wasn't sure of much else.

Close by, Tobias was nearly beside himself with frustration that his promise to look after Evie's father had rendered him useless. Mr. Callahan had come to, but was still too groggy to support his own weight.

The brothers spoke their native tongue again, leaving me to feel even more at a disadvantage as I listened for a morsel of discernible information. All I wanted to do was help.

Blood oozed from a broad gash on Evie's shoulder surrounded by a fast-spreading, purple bruise. However, I knew the physical injuries would heal. My main concern was whether she'd been under too long? Had I gotten there too late?

They talked over me again and the frustration got to be more than I could stand.

"Tell me what's going on!" My voice echoed and a few of their gazes shifted to me, but only one responded.

"Pain," Ivan blurted. "Pain is the only way to bring her out of it. She's slipping away."

Confused and *beyond* skeptical, I intervened.

"What are you talking about? She's *already* in pain," I pointed out, gesturing toward her injured shoulder.

He shook his head and his expression made it clear he didn't think I'd understand.

So, instead, he showed me.

His hand emerged from beneath the water where it'd been supporting half Evie's body. I stared at it, still just as confused as a moment ago, but then the pieces started to fit together when the tip of his finger lit with a bluish-green flame like nothing I'd ever seen before. The strange light spread to his palm and eventually engulfed his entire hand.

"No ... *real* pain," he clarified, a grave and yet sympathetic look overtaking his expression.

I breathed deep, bracing myself for whatever this meant, bracing myself for however Evie would respond to it.

My gaze shifted to Mrs. Callahan, her wide eyes, when I remembered she was present. She stared at the otherworldly blue light that blazed from Ivan's hand, speechless, in shock, but not frightened.

Among the clans many rules was one stating that we were to conceal our identities at all times, but ... these were extenuating circumstances. There was no time to help her understand or go to her to ensure she didn't flee out of fear.

I'd forgotten this woman had raised one of the most fearless people I'd ever met in my life. Some portion of that had to have been because she, herself, was braver than most.

As if to prove this exact point, instead of cowering in a corner at the sight of something I'm sure she would never understand, she came closer to help. Her hands replaced Ivan's to support Evie while he acted quickly to save her.

Mrs. Callahan's eyes went to Evie's shoulder, the wound that had already shrank to half the size it was a moment ago. Where

Evie's shirt was torn, shredded muscle and severed tendons slowly mended themselves together right before her mother's eyes. Fresh skin formed over the laceration and it was nearly gone. In some spots, the only indicator anything had ever been wrong was the blood left behind.

The hand engulfed in turquoise-tinted fire moved through the air in a brilliant streak, making contact with the nearly-healed wound at Evie's shoulder. The sound of searing skin was sickening, as was the sight of her flesh tearing open once again. I was nearly at my breaking point being a bystander while they tortured and maimed her on a whim that it *might* help.

But then ... she twitched, coughed a bit, prompting us to shift her onto her side as we tread water. The liquid that had blocked her airway spilled from her mouth as she choked it out, a blood-curdling scream bursting from within right after. It pained me to see her like this, but Ivan was right. It worked.

I glanced at her mother again, and to my surprise, she still didn't show signs of running.

Only concern.

I braced Evie's head to my shoulder while she caught her breath, and as if Mrs. Callahan's actions hadn't already stunned me enough ... she reached for her daughter's hand.

Some might have assumed it was a knee-jerk reaction, that people in crisis situations sometimes form strange bonds, but I wasn't that close-minded. I believed that, on some level, despite the spell that had been cast on her, Mrs. Callahan knew. She knew the brave young girl who risked her life to get her and her husband out of harm's way was no mere stranger.

"Thank you," she said just above a whisper as she continued to clutch Evie's hand. "I don't know why you did this for us today, but ... thank you."

Still not quite herself, Evie nodded and squeezed the hand she held. "I had to," she rasped. "I had to make sure you were okay."

Not even that made her mother flinch, confirming what I suspected—that on some level she felt the connection with the only daughter she'd ever known.

Somehow, we all made it through alive, despite the Sovereign's best efforts. Today's attack was a clear sign. A sign I, and the rest of the clan heard loud and clear.

He wanted a war ... and we would give him one.

CHAPTER 20

Evie

Ten minutes outside the valley—the section of town most hard hit by the flood waters—we crossed paths with the first emergency vehicle we'd seen. They'd come to Seaton Falls from the neighboring city of Smithstone and were a sight for sore eyes. Both my parents needed medical attention, now I was certain they'd get it.

The paramedics made quick work of getting my dad on a stretcher and into the ambulance. They covered my mom's leg with a temporary bandage for now, until doctors could get a better look at it once they reached Smithstone General.

Her eyes were locked on mine as she sat beside my father, letting the medics fuss over her. I did my best not to cry. She wouldn't understand if I did. I didn't want to let them go, but the most important thing was that they would be safe.

The door on one side of the ambulance was slammed shut and

I held my breath watching the medic grip the other to close it as well. I prepared myself to let them go. For good this time, because there was no telling where they'd relocate once the town was officially evacuated.

But then, before that door closed, my mother's hand shot out, pushing against it.

"Wait ... Evie!"

At the sound of my name being called, a breath hitched in my throat. Her lingering stare filled with awareness, displaced emotion I wasn't sure she understood.

But *I* did.

What she felt were lingering traces of love. Love a mother once carried for her perfectly imperfect daughter. I knew because I felt it, too.

I stepped closer when she motioned for me to do so.

As I approached, leaving Nick and my brothers to wait by the side of the road, she had a short conversation with the female medic. When the woman disappeared out of sight, I was confused. She came back with a pen and paper in hand, passing both to my mother.

Closing the last few feet that separated us, I watched her scribble something on the sheet.

"Keep this," she insisted, pressing the paper into my palm. "It's the number of a close friend in Chicago. Once my husband is well enough to travel, that's most likely where we'll settle until we sort things out."

My brow tensed and those tears threatened again. Especially when she gripped my hand.

"I don't ... understand why you came into that theater to help us, but ... thank you," she breathed, emotion causing the words to leave her throat strained. "I don't want to lose touch," she explained, a look in her eyes that gave me hope. Hope that, maybe, somewhere deep down inside her, she knew. Or at least felt the same connection I did.

"Me either," I shared freely, hearing my voice break a bit.

She smiled with a familiar kindness in her eyes. "I'll look forward to hearing from you," were her parting words, but not before bringing me close, embracing me the way she'd done so many times in the past.

My eyes closed and I reveled in the feel of it.

She couldn't have known how important this was to me, how significant, but it was. I'd been pining for the love of my parents for so many months. And now, although they still didn't remember, I had closure.

Or perhaps a new beginning.

I watched that ambulance until the taillights faded into the distance, grateful we hadn't failed today. I needed that, to win for once.

The guys and I continued on, the next stop in our trek home being the entrance to Nick's neighborhood. He paused a moment before walking off, staring as though there was so much he wanted to say. However, before he had the chance, I said it all with a tight embrace.

He and my brothers had been brave. Each blindly walked into danger, and all on a whim that they *might* find me.

Might.

I released Nick and no words were exchanged because they weren't necessary. An understanding existed between us; one where it went without question that we were on the same side and, hopefully, always would be.

We watched him walk away and I was reminded of how he'd gone above and beyond for me today. Especially when I glanced down toward my wrist, at the priceless bracelet he returned to me. Our less-than-traditional journey into friendship was a complicated one, but a true friendship indeed.

The rest of us made the slow trudge home.

Exhausted, filthy.

We made it deep into the woods and the rough terrain tired me out even more—weathering naturally formed mounds and hollows in the soil, the undergrowth. Ethan noticed I still hadn't returned to full-strength and offered his arm like a gentleman.

"Thank you," I said, accepting with a smile.

He returned the gesture, but said nothing as we continued on. The bond between us, the one that existed between me and each of my siblings, could be felt. In fact, it grew more powerful by the minute. I hadn't even known them for two days in this life, and already, I felt their love for me.

Mine for them.

"You're all right?" he asked as the others began to converse among themselves, rough-housing a bit like they seemed to do often. It was good to hear the day's events hadn't made them too weary—physically, emotionally. Then again, what was a flood in their eyes compared to war, bloodshed.

I gave a nod to Ethan's question, thinking over how things turned out. With my parents safe and on their way to get the help they needed, I had no complaints.

"I am," I answered honestly. "Things could have gone much worse. Thank God they didn't."

He chuffed a short laugh, agreeing.

"So, how are you ... adjusting?" was my question, followed by a laugh of my own. "Not that life has slowed down enough for you all to get settled or anything."

There was a smile on his face when he replied. "I'm alive, I have my family; what is there for a man to complain about?"

That was a beautiful way to look at it.

We walked a few more feet before I spoke again, glancing up ahead where moonlight filtered through the tall trees that created a canopy above.

"I can imagine this world is a bit overwhelming for all of you. Cars, television ... everything," I concluded.

Ethan nodded, chuckling. "At first, yes," he admitted. "However, in the supernatural realm, we see *many* odd things that aren't easily explained. So, television and tiny boxes that prepare food in a matter of seconds aren't among the strangest."

I laughed at his description of a microwave. I'd blown their minds when I made pizza rolls to snack on before we left for training.

"Well, good. I'm glad you're adjusting," I said, adding more. "And ... I'm glad you guys are here."

I turned his way when he laughed again. "You say that as if you weren't always sure you'd feel this way."

I'd accidentally told on myself, revealed I was once apprehensive.

"Mmm ... there may have been some anxiety about your return," I admitted, "but it was mostly because I was insecure."

"Insecure?"

I inhaled, deciding how to explain. "I was afraid that me being different would ... I don't know, freak you guys out?" Realizing that probably wasn't a term he was familiar with, I clarified. "I thought maybe you all would think there was something odd about me."

He let out a hearty laugh, one that lifted my spirits just at the sound of it.

"As your brother, someone who knew you for hundreds of years before this, I can assure you, there was *always* something odd about you, Evangeline."

I smiled big, feeling more comfortable around him than I ever imagined I would. "Good to hear I haven't changed too much."

"You're more like your *old* self than you realize."

Hearing that comforted me in ways he couldn't have understood.

Home wasn't too far away now. The closer we got, the more

foreign the woods became. Tonight, they were full of displaced lycans and dragons—those native to Seaton Falls, those who'd only come in weeks ago to help. They had all been pushed out of their dwellings by the flood, and now here they were.

Lost.

Confused.

Broken.

We paused a moment when Josiah, literally, gave someone the shirt off his back—a woman huddled near a small fire, trying to keep herself and her toddler warm. Overwhelmed by the gesture, water glistened in her eyes as she used the mostly dry shirt as a makeshift blanket to shield her child from the chilled breeze.

There was no telling how many had been lost tonight. Yes, our chances of surviving such a disaster were greater than had we been only human, but there was no supernatural cure for drowning.

I'd nearly proven that *myself* a short time ago.

As we passed through, angry conversations turned into fiery monologues declaring a newly deepened hatred for Sebastian. While some gathered round in solidarity, others simply cried—deep, desperate sobs for what had taken place.

But even through fatigue and the chatter, even with half a mile still separating us from home... I heard something.

Heard *him*.

... Liam.

I lifted my head the instant his raw, unbridled fury broke through the woods, assaulting my ears. Rage spewed from his very soul and I felt it from here. My entire body stiffened with tension.

I took off in that direction, suddenly forgetting the recently healed injury and extreme exhaustion that plagued me just a moment ago. My brothers flanked me at either side, matching my speed. Each time Liam yelled out, I moved faster, and so did they.

It'd been hours since anyone at home had heard from us. I was sure Elise, Dallas, and Hilda were beside themselves with worry, too, but ... none as distraught as Liam.

I needed to get to him, to let him see my face, that I was alive.

What he must have assumed when I didn't come back ...

"We have to hurry," I urged, weaving between trees and the displaced.

I tried to prepare myself for what I'd find when I made it to the house, tried to come up with something to say to justify my actions to Liam. Something to explain why I asked Dallas to do anything in his power to keep him from coming after me ...

My heart and mind both raced, wondering what it must have taken to get him—the fiercest warrior who ever lived—to meet their demands and stay put while I was out here amidst the chaos without him.

The screams billowing through the woods like a battle cry weren't screams of sadness ... they were steeped in anger. Anger like I'd never heard before. Each one sent daggers straight through my heart. I never meant to hurt him, only to protect him from what went on out here. Tonight, difficult decisions were made, but *all* were made with the ones I love in mind.

I did what needed to be done.

The seven of us burst through the door and it didn't surprise me to find Elise pacing the foyer—her face bright red with distress, her eyes tinted the same shade from what I guessed to be hours of crying. She rushed my brothers and I immediately, squeezing as many as she could in her arms.

Dallas stood nearby as well, looking just as relieved as Elise, but nowhere near as emotional. She'd practically just watched her seven children return from the dead ... again.

I knew she was owed an explanation, a breakdown of the reasons I'd behaved so recklessly, but that explanation would have to wait.

"Where's Liam?" I blurted the instant she released me from an embrace. As if in answer to my question, a loud, roar of a scream filtered up through the floorboards, from the basement, sending a chill racing down my spine.

I turned to rush that way, but a hand caught my wrist. I met Elise's gaze, confused at first, but then understanding when a key was dropped into my hand.

"You'll need this," she sighed, leveling a grave stare on me. "If Hilda had been here, her magic could have held him, but she's been out trying to aid the people since the first explosion."

I didn't wait for anyone to tell me how or why Liam ended up down there, I just went.

Taking the stairs by two, I slowed when I reached the bottom, trudging across the wide-open space toward a door at the end of a corridor, one usually concealed behind a false wall. With the façade removed, and a sliver of light filtering beneath that door I focused on, I moved ahead slowly. And there, where I stood in the shadows, my vision was met by a sight I hadn't expected.

Drenched in sweat, bleeding at the wrists where shackles had been secured around them, Liam was beside himself with rage, grief. My guess was that this setup was all they could do to keep him inside, safe, when Dallas told him what I'd done, the decision I made to head deeper into town to save my parents.

I was staring at a broken man, one who when *treated* like an animal, had begun to behave like one.

The strands of his hair were weighted with moisture, sticking to his face, neck and where they rested on his shoulders. The braces where these chains had been linked to the wall were bent and twisted in sharp angles, fresh fragments of cement on the floor beneath them. I knew they couldn't have been in this condition when he was first brought down here. These were signs of what lengths he was willing to go to in order to save me.

He'd fought hard.

Even for a human, he was unbelievably strong.

I lifted the toe of one shoe to step forward, to step out of the shadow from where I watched, but couldn't move.

I was afraid. Afraid to look him in his eyes, to tell him that holding him here had all been my idea, to tell him I defied his wishes yet again. My only hope was that he'd understand, that he'd see I had no choice but to go after my parents *and* keep him safe. I shuddered to think what would have happened if I hadn't, if the others hadn't followed to come to our aid.

His broad, glistening chest heaved as he panted like a caged beast, resting on his knees in the center of this makeshift cell I assumed had once been used to hold Maisy. With clenched fists, he punched wildly at the air again, grunting through his teeth, determined to loosen the chains from the walls to break free.

To come for me.

I had to say something—explain, apologize ... something. I couldn't just watch him in agony like this.

Even if I was scared out of my mind what his reaction might be when he laid eyes on me.

" ... Liam. I—" My voice was weak as his gaze rose to meet mine.

That was as much as I could get out, wanting to go to him, to hold him, but I wasn't sure he'd let me. Not with the promise I knew I'd broken tonight—the one where I vowed to put my safety first for *his* sake. But, in my eyes, this was different. The two I went after today weren't just random people I put my life on the line for.

Few things hurt me more than causing Liam pain, and I'd done that tonight. I'd sentenced him to hours of worrying, thinking the worst. Things that, when it concerned me, were torture for him.

Wetness touched my cheek and I swiped it away when I stepped further into the light, focusing on the blood he shed trying to break free, trying to do what he'd *always* done.

Protect me.

More steps to close the distance and those steps were met with mounting fear.

If I'd been brave enough, I could've reached out and touched him by now, but I just stood there, squeezing my hands in tight fists at my sides.

What was I supposed to say?

Before I could overthink it, a clumsy, "I'm sorry," tumbled from my lips.

The silence was so loud my ears began to ring. Nervous breaths shuddered in my chest, puffing over my lips as I waited. For words, for an outburst, but neither came.

Only a look.

One that met my gaze without Liam lifting his head, only his eyes as a wild stare landed on me. It told of the night he had, the wicked thoughts that must have passed through his mind on repeat. With his heavy brow shrouding his gaze, I nearly backed away. If it had been anyone else in these chains, someone who didn't have my complete trust like he did, I probably would have.

I wanted to fix this, wanted to help him understand why everything that happened tonight was necessary. I somehow found the courage to kneel before him at eye-level, but when I placed a hand on his rigid shoulder, the word, "Don't," spoken hard and unfeeling made me recoil instantly.

He didn't want to be touched.

My chest moved with each rapid breath. I wasn't sure what to think or say next, or even if I *should* say anything.

"Liam, I—"

"Are you hurt," his sharp tone cut in, the abrasiveness of it making my skin crawl as he surveyed me—the torn sleeve of my shirt, the remnants of blood on it and my skin.

I shook my head and answered, "No," but wanted to say so much more.

However, when he shut me down the next instant, there was no chance of that.

"Then leave," he seethed, those shoulders heaving again as the rims of his nostrils flared with wrath.

I stared, unable to blink, but only for a moment before gathering myself. If he wanted me gone, I'd go. He was angry and I understood that, but if we could have just talked about it, maybe he would have sympathized. Even if only a little.

With my back to him, I didn't feel the need to put on a brave face, so I didn't. Tonight had been filled with so many emotions, so many close calls, and so many hearts on the line.

Including Liam's.

Before I left him like he requested, I stooped to place the key to the shackles on the ground where he could reach it.

Maybe when he was ready, I'd have a chance to fix this.

CHAPTER 21

Evie

It took an hour for him to leave that cell.
Even after being given the key.

From my bedroom, I could have traced his steps—from the moment he stormed up the stairs, to his door slamming so hard against the frame it seemed the whole house shook.

Elise had come in to visit after checking on the guys downstairs. She placed her hand on mine when my expression must have told of how distraught I was, how misunderstood I felt.

"He'll come around," she assured me, offering a kind smile right after.

I believed her, but hated the idea of waiting to work things out until then. I had to get my mind off the altercation with Liam somehow, so I changed the subject.

"What's the word from the Council?" I asked.

Elise sighed before responding. "The area has been thoroughly searched for the fools who did this. They believe this to be the work of a small team that got in and out of town quickly to avoid detection. There's been no report of mutts or other activity," she went on. "Just ... devastation."

I recalled the grim scene we walked through on our way home and *devastation* was a fitting word.

"I did my best to convince the Council to allow us to open our home to a few, but it was out of the question." Another soft smile touched her eyes. "They wouldn't dare endanger the life of their queen," she said with an air of jesting in her tone that made me smile, too.

"Of course not," I yawned.

For a moment, we submitted to the silence that crept in. This was all still so hard to believe.

"Ethan says tonight's ... *mission*," she stated with a smile, "was a success."

I considered that word, success, eventually giving a nod. "Aside from nearly drowning, I'd say it was."

My thoughts went back to the look of acceptance behind my mother's gaze when we parted ways before that ambulance drove off. It was almost like ... she knew.

Knew our connection extended beyond today.

Knew we meant something to one another.

"While I don't appreciate having to hold my breath while awaiting news of whether my children are dead or alive," Elise sighed, "I do admire your courage."

My gaze met hers as she shared more of her feelings.

"I like to think I've had my moments of bravery, but they were few and far between. But you ... I think you'd risk your life every day if it were necessary to protect those you love."

I breathed deep, feeling the emotion behind her thoughts.

"Says the woman who laid it all on the line for a race of super-naturals that aren't even her own people," I smiled.

She returned the gesture before clarifying. "I did it for *both* races. We've always needed each other whether we realized it or not."

I imagined that was true.

My hand cooled when she moved hers, standing from the edge of my bed where she'd been sitting.

"I'd better get a move on," she yawned. "Hilda's been out there all night, and now that you seven are home safe, I'm going out to help as well. The people need supplies, food, blankets, clothes. The Council may have the power to stop us from opening our home, but not our hearts."

It was hard to fathom someone as naturally compassionate as her being in admiration of *me*. There was once a time not so long ago when I hated her, thought of her as the most selfish person walking this planet.

And then the smoke cleared and I discovered I was wrong about her.

So wrong.

She was a beautiful person, inside and out.

There was a look of surprise in her eyes when I took her hand before she could walk away. That look turned into confusion when I stood and embraced her. I knew she had places to be, people to tend to, but I needed this first.

I needed to hug my mother.

Something changed for me this evening. Getting to see my adoptive mom, looking into her eyes and realizing her memory was all the witches stole, and not her love for me, it gave me peace. No, she may not have remembered who I was, but she definitely *felt* who I was.

"Thank you," I breathed, squeezing Elise tight around her

neck, feeling her arms encircle my waist. "You've done so much and I appreciate it. *All* of it," I clarified.

"Anything for you," was her reply and I never doubted that for even a second.

I'd been so distant with her in the past, but that was behind us now. I wanted her to know I understood the sacrifices she made for me, understood the hard choices and decisions she made on my behalf. It was all for my own good.

"I love you," I added to everything else I admitted tonight.

There was a long period of silence while Elise must have had to let that sink in, had to convince herself I'd fully come around, but I did. I felt so much peace finally letting the last of my guard down with her, there was no doubt in my mind I was doing the right thing.

"I never stopped," she replied, and there was no missing the emotion in her voice, choking her up a bit.

I released her and saw the tears I fully expected, but I also saw a smile and it did my heart good.

She left to meet Hilda. It was incredibly late, and despite being dog-tired, I knew I wouldn't get to bed anytime soon. The air was too charged tonight. There were people out there trying to piece their lives back together, people the night's events had broken. There was no way I could just pretend things were as peaceful outside this house as they were *inside*.

Peaceful ... maybe that was the wrong word.

At the thought, I glanced up, focusing on my bedroom door. I imagined the one across from it where Liam likely sat brooding about the choices I made. I stood and turned out the light, but didn't bother getting into bed. Instead, I moved toward the balcony, stepping out for fresh air.

It was cool, but I didn't need to cover my legs or arms. The tank and shorts I put on after my shower were fine. Hugging myself as I surveyed our property, I breathed deep, doing all I could to release the tension pent up inside, but it was no use.

It killed me knowing how pissed Liam was. If he'd given me a chance to explain, I might not be spending the night alone in my bed, a bed I hadn't slept in in so long I couldn't remember the last time.

The cool metal of the wrought-iron railing touched my forearms when I leaned against it, trying not to feel sorry for myself. Not when there were so many out there much worse off than I was.

The door to my room creaked and I turned, half expecting it to have been Elise to say one last thing before the supply run, or even one of my brothers coming in to say goodnight. But what I did *not* expect ... was Liam.

My nerves got the best of me at the sight of him, causing my stomach to sink. I stood straight, my back to the rail now as I watched him cross the room, moving through the darkness like a man on a mission. It wasn't until he made it to me that I realized that's *exactly* what he was.

Stepping out onto my balcony, moonlight outlined the breadth of his shoulders. Strong hands cinched my waist the next second, and then the shock of warm lips against mine that had cooled in the night air. It was natural for my fingers to gravitate toward his hair, still damp from a shower. They tangled in the strands as I gripped them, keeping him close, letting the emotions, the *tension,* he held in spill over now. I felt it all.

The hurt.

The relief.

The need.

The struggle within him.

All at once, he wanted to give in and come to me, but also wished he'd been strong enough to stay away. I knew as much from the feel of greedy hands roaming all over me just before he'd pull back, attempting to bridle the beast.

When it came to us, there was no possibility of holding back. With the energy that vibrated between us always, no amount of anger or frustration could keep us apart. I knew this to be a fact even after he sent me away. While I didn't expect this visit to be so soon, it was a welcomed surprise.

My mouth trailed his jaw to his neck, feeling his veins pulse where my tongue met skin. I only backed off him long enough for my shirt to be snatched from my torso, my shorts to be tossed carelessly to the floor. While my back cooled in the air, my bare chest was warm against his. Leaving me only long enough to kick a pair of sweats aside, Liam returned, taking our wordless reunion where it'd been headed all along.

He was usually so gentle, so patient. But as my thighs were brought to his waist in one rough motion, I knew I'd accuse him of being neither of those things tonight. Rough, animalistic ... those words were more accurate as I stared into a set of feral eyes that only wanted one thing.

He'd always trusted me enough to share his heart, to admit his inability to live without me, and I hurt him anyway, put him through unthinkable hell, although my intentions were honorable.

As his gaze stayed trained on mine, as we connected and our souls aligned, I vowed to myself that I would never defy him like I had tonight. His life's mission had been to protect me and I both loved and respected that about him.

There were no words, and we exchanged no verbal commitment, but I meant it from the bottom of my heart when I made a promise to myself.

To him.

It would never happen again.

CHAPTER 22

Liam

The moon was still high in the sky, meaning we hadn't staggered our way into her bed that long ago. Exhausted from our tryst on the balcony, sleep came swiftly, but even *that* hadn't been enough to keep my mind off what transpired tonight.

I tossed and turned my way through a nightmare before giving up on sleep altogether. In the dream, Evangeline's undertaking had a very different outcome. One where she wasn't so lucky.

One where she *didn't* return home.

Unnerved and anxious, I laid awake, staring at the ceiling while gentle breaths puffed from her lips across my chest where her head rested. Her soft curls were scattered everywhere like a wild mane—across my arm, beneath my chin. Glancing down at her, I pushed a few locks aside to get a better glimpse of her face.

She was beyond beautiful, she was the embodiment of love.

My love.

Which was why the direction my thoughts were headed in terrified me. It was this love for her that made us both ticking time-bombs. Each constantly on the verge of detonating for the other's sake. Only, she'd become even more unstable in recent weeks.

And there was no denying the change was because of me.

I placed a soft kiss on her forehead, being careful not to wake her. She had no idea the lengths I was willing to go for her. For us.

My heart raced and I was grateful she slept. Had she been awake, there would have been no hiding it. She'd sense I was on the cusp of doing something she'd never allow, something I could no longer see any way around.

The deep, burning gashes left behind on my wrists from struggling against the shackles were not what made tonight's events so hard to move past. Being held captive by chains I could've practically bitten through before my dragon was destroyed ... it put things into perspective. It showed me, once and for all, that this was the life we would live if I didn't make a change.

Only, this particular change would first require unmatched sacrifice.

Namely ... my life—even if only temporarily.

Or, so I hoped.

It wasn't lost on me that Elise had already refused to help, pointing out that she couldn't guarantee my plan would even work, but I was beyond seeking her permission. The only way to force her hand was to take matters into my own. If I failed, it was no one's fault but my own and she'd have no blood on her hands. As cruel as this choice seemed at the moment, as candidly as it told of my desperation, it was the only hope I had left.

I was suddenly numb, emotionless for the sake of not allowing myself to feel the full weight of this decision. What was once a flimsy idea, was suddenly a plan.

I slipped from beneath Evangeline's arm, being careful not to disturb her as I then left the bed. Staring down on her, my mate, it was impossible not to sympathize with the predicament she'd been in so many times—fighting to make me understand why she willingly laid on the tracks, ignoring the train that plowed full-steam ahead in her direction.

I got it now.

And tonight, I'd be brave like her, following in her footsteps. I'd make the ultimate sacrifice, too, but this time to set things right once and for all.

It was time and no one could walk this path but me.

Evie

At first, when I turned and sunlight penetrated my closed lids, I thought the day before had been a dream. Including the part where Liam came to me, choosing to *show* me I had his forgiveness, foregoing the difficult task of finding the right words.

The pillow was cool against my cheek and I stretched, brushing wild curls away from my face as I squinted through the light, feeling the other side of my bed for a warm body.

I was alone.

Which meant, at some point after I dozed, he left.

It was a sobering realization that honestly brought with it an air of insecurity. It crossed my mind that I may have jumped the gun thinking I'd been forgiven. Maybe he opted to return to his *own* room instead of spending the night in mine.

I sat up and breathed deep, unable to find the strength to leave the bed. Yawning, my eyes wandered toward the door, and that's when I saw it, a sheet of paper that had been pushed beneath it.

I rolled from beneath the covers and ambled across the room, pulling down my t-shirt—the only thing I bothered putting on before a heavy sleep fell on me the night before. I bent to grab the paper, noting that the handwriting was familiar. I'd seen it for years, even before meeting Liam face-to-face. It was one of the few things that gave a hint toward his real age. It bore a classic aestheticism that always reminded me of letters I'd seen in movies, written by men in fancy, ruffled clothes, dipping feathered pens in ink.

My name was printed neatly at the top and I breathed deep before beginning.

'Evangeline,

Every move I've ever made has been carried out with you in mind. Before I begin, I urge you not to forget this small fact that changes everything. You may never understand the motives behind what I've done, but I couldn't go forward without at least trying to explain.

Because my love for you never has, and never will die.

To begin, an apology is owed ... for my shortcomings, my failures. I've been charged with many missions in life. Many that put me on the front line of heated battles, few in favor of impassioned causes I felt proud to defend.

But even with all the praise and titles they earned me, none were as important to me as the mission given to me by your father—to protect his only daughter, the future queen of her people.

My anger last night was never in response to your actions. I couldn't have expected anything less from a woman with a heart as pure as yours. Your parents needed you and I feel nothing but pride for what you did. What you saw when you came down to that chamber was me breaking, only feeling anger with myself for those shackles being enough to keep me from coming to your aid.

Metal and cement.

That was it.

This is not me, Evangeline. I'm half the man I was born to be, half the man you deserve. Without my dragon, I've been forced to abandon my post, forced to watch my mate put her life in danger to protect mine.

I promise to accept whatever consequences lie ahead, and I'll do so with grace, dignity. But above all, I trust your love will move you to forgive sooner rather than later.

This is all for you.

My mate. My love.

My queen.

My heart raced with each word, right to the very end. I skimmed again, thinking I missed something, but only felt more confused the second time.

What was he saying?

The message was so cryptic, so dark. I didn't understand, but knew it was bad.

Really, really bad.

Voices carried in from the hallway and the undertone of panic made my thoughts respond in kind. Whatever was off, they felt it, too.

Nearly snatching the door from its hinges, I exited to see what all the commotion was. Elise wrestled her arm into the sleeve of her long coat, still clothed in her nightgown as she rambled numbers to herself on repeat. Her face had gone pale and expressionless as she barreled toward the stairs on autopilot. Hilda followed close behind and I caught random bits and pieces of quickly spoken phrases, saying things that didn't make sense.

One of which being *resurrection.*

"What happened?" I asked, doubling back for a pair of jeans from my drawer before chasing Elise down the stairs, meeting she and Hilda in the foyer as I struggled with the zipper.

"Can one of you please tell me what's going on?" This time, I was pleading, my stare volleying back and forth between Elise and Hilda.

They barely seemed to notice my presence, my desperate questions. Being ignored, my wolf responded to the frustration, pushing forward so forcefully I had to suppress the urge to issue a warning growl. However, if they continued to over talk me, I had no problem letting it out.

Rubbing his chest with a groggy, one-eyed greeting, Ethan joined us where we stood in limbo near the door, wondering the same thing I was.

"What is it?" he asked.

Elise rushed off with nothing more than a tearful, sympathetic glance that made my heart sink before the door slammed behind her.

My gaze was locked on Hilda, as was Ethan's.

Her brow creased with worry and I had to bridle my wolf again, feeling her strength rising within.

"There's a bit of a situation," she began.

"Where's Liam?" I didn't have the patience to wait for her to find the right way to tell me whatever she needed to tell me. When she leveled that same sympathetic stare on me Elise had, I knew I was right.

Something was wrong and they weren't telling me what they knew.

"Where did Elise go in such a hurry?" Ethan countered when Hilda didn't readily answer *my* question.

"She received a text. Coordinates," she clarified.

Frustration brimmed over with being given the runaround.

"Hilda, please!" My voice quivered, feeling my body shake with anticipation for what her real answer would be to my question. *Where was Liam?*

A firm line creased her forehead when she frowned. "I'm not at liberty to say anything more than I already have," she answered.

This was unbelievable. She had to have known this was killing me.

"I'm not holding his secret by choice," she said cryptically. "Magic forbids me."

My brow quirked, unsure what that meant.

"The furniture in my study is charmed. No one who sits on or touches any piece can lie to me," she willingly shared. "Liam was aware of the way it worked before he chose to disclose his truths, the ones that lie deep within."

There was no missing the grave look she now wore.

"In turn, I'm bound by magic not to disclose anything that's been shared by anyone under the spell's influence," she clarified.

So ... she knew exactly where Liam was, what he'd done, but wasn't at liberty to say.

Magic was so tricky. There were so many rules and boundaries.

"Is he in danger?" I asked next.

When Hilda nodded, my heart and stomach sank.

Ethan stepped forward, his expression marking a sudden spike in concern. "Shouldn't you have gone with Elise then? Isn't there something you could have done if he's in trouble?"

More of that solemn look being passed our way when Hilda shook her head.

"No," she sighed. "If Elise can't fix this ... neither can I."

First, I needed to sit, so I backed toward the steps. Then, I needed to run, so I pressed toward the door, deciding I'd just ... go. I'd comb these woods until I found them.

"Evangeline, don't." The stern warning came from Hilda and I wanted to push past her, but didn't. Instead I listened.

"He sent your mother coordinates," she hinted, still magically bound from saying too much. "He needs *her,* specifically, to find him."

I searched my thoughts, hunting for morsels of information to piece together. Hints he may have left in his letter.

He spoke of wanting me to understand his reasons for whatever action this was he'd taken. He also stated that he was doing this for me, to remedy the fact that he could no longer protect me. Because he's no longer a ... dragon.

Dread and fear swam circles in my stomach like two sharks honing in on a kill.

It hit me. The truth. He was on a mission to resurrect his dragon, and there were only a few ways to do such a thing that I knew of. One was by magic, which wasn't an option for him. Because he'd been turned human by a witch, another couldn't undo that spell.

Leaving him with only one method to consider.

The *original* method.

One I wasn't even sure still worked—to die by fire and be resurrected by the original dragon, Elise.

He was planning to take the most extreme measures to restore his dragon. If he hadn't done it already ...

I felt sick, weak, deciding to take that seat on the step after all when my knees nearly gave out. I stared at everything, but focused on nothing. For a moment, the room grew dim like I'd pass out.

"Evangeline ... you must know he's been considering this for a while," Hilda shared. "Elise and I both thought we talked him out of it, which is why it didn't seem necessary to warn you before it came to this."

She didn't need to explain. I didn't blame her or Elise, I believed they truly *did* try to convince Liam this wasn't a good idea.

But I knew him.

Knew exactly what pushed him toward the decision.

Me.

My actions. Last night must have just been the last straw, the last evidence he needed to see that I wouldn't sit back on some throne while those I love were put in danger. It wasn't even a choice. Going to them, putting my neck on the line was just ... a reaction.

One that ultimately may cost me everything.

"How long do I have?" I asked solemnly, feeling my resolve

becoming firmer by the minute. I had to try to find him, had to stop him.

"You may already be too late," was Hilda's grim reply. "And besides, I can't give an exact location because all he sent were coordinates, no address."

I racked my brain, asking myself where he'd go to do this. To ... let the fire consume him in belief that Elise could fix everything. My stomach turned and I ignored it, needing to focus.

"His house," I said after a burst of air filled my lungs when I got to my feet.

"You should rethink this," Hilda urged again. "If he's already succeeded, Evangeline, there might not be much left but ... remains."

My stomach swirled again, but there was no stopping me. I grabbed a pair of shoes from the closet and slipped my feet into them. Dallas traipsed down the stairs in jeans and a tee, popping a baseball cap over his messy hair. I guessed he'd been listening, because he was clearly intent on coming, too.

By this point, Ethan had time to let the others know what had taken place, and all seemed determined to follow, to help me find the brother given to them by fate instead of blood.

My eyes welled with tears at the sight of them all, their loyalty ever present. Even toward me, the shell of what remained of the sister they once knew.

"Let's go," I said as we exited, hoping Hilda understood that I *had* to do this. If there was any chance I could stop Liam, could talk him out of this. There was still a chance we could find Sebastian's witch and do this another way.

But there was something else I knew about Liam. He wasn't the most patient man in the world. In short, I needed to prepare my heart before we got there, accepting that, like usual, the odds of him waiting weren't likely in our favor.

CHAPTER 23

Evie

W e trekked the woods, passing through makeshift camps composed of those the flood displaced. There were many still walking about, doing their part to distribute food and supplies. It was hard to get my bearings straight with all the added commotion, the chatter.

Breathing deep, I channeled my wolf, letting her keen sense of direction lead me.

"This way," I called out, prompting the others to take off running right behind me.

Hurdling large boulders and hollowed out logs of fallen trees, we drew closer. I knew we were. Sniffing the air, I picked up on the occasional hit of smoke, but knew it could have been that of the many bonfires that had been built overnight and this morning for warmth.

Still, the thought lingered that that smoke might not have been for warmth, or cooking. It may have been the result of Liam's ill-planned idea to reconnect with his dragon.

I was beside myself with worry, trying to hold it together as I ran. So hard my chest ached, drawing in surges of air as my fists pumped back and forth to move me faster.

The surroundings became familiar and I recalled the first time I willingly reached out to Liam through our tether when I sought him in the woods. It was the day Nick admitted to his real feelings for me, and also the day I fought mine for Liam the hardest.

My dragon had sent out a distress call to him when I panicked, thinking I was lost, and he answered, leading me to him, soothing me with his confidence and certainty I *still* envied. Now, this time as I ran, it was only me inside my head, praying those days I didn't realize were so good would return.

I'd been so happy to have him back, but missed our connection more than I would ever admit.

While most of me was pissed to high-heaven he'd done this, a smaller part of me understood. And maybe even prayed it worked. Yes, if he told me ahead of time, I would've done all I could to talk him out of it, for fear of the risk being too great. But now that the deed was likely already done ... my heart ... it did hope.

We were close and the once dense crowd had thinned considerably. The thought crossed my mind that, although most had no idea who I was, didn't even recognize my face or the role I could assume in the future, they flocked nearby on purpose. Whether that reason was because they had a general idea of where I resided, or if the pull had been something supernatural. Kind of like how a hive behaves instinctively to protect the queen.

Eventually, we hadn't seen anyone for miles, and there, off in the distance, I recognized the familiar outline of a single-pitched roof—one that had been my refuge on more than one occasion.

Our pace slowed and I knew this was exactly where we were supposed to be. Scanning the perimeter, we inched closer. Within a few feet, I stopped again when my ears perked at the sound of embers bursting as not-so-distant flames crackled in the wind.

A strangely brilliant, crimson light burst from the opposite side of what was once Liam's home, illuminating the bark of nearby trees. My stomach swam with a fresh wave of dread, thinking we'd arrived right in the middle of the tragic act.

I couldn't move forward. Not with the terrible images that flooded my thoughts.

Thoughts of Liam's body burning, the last traces of life leaving him.

A firm hand braced my shoulder and I looked up to meet Declan's gaze, finding nothing but compassion there.

"I'll go," he offered. "And if the deed hasn't been finished ..." His voice trailed off, but I understood, nodding.

Tobias and Josiah followed, leaving Caleb, Ethan, Ivan, Dallas and I to standby, waiting for instructions.

I paced, wearing a path in the tall grass, trampling it down into the damp soil. So many thoughts flew through my head, I couldn't possibly nail down one.

I wrestled with being angry Liam had kept this from me, to anxiously hoping Declan returned soon to tell me what I wanted to hear—that everything was okay, that things hadn't all gone to hell this morning.

I paced while Ivan and Caleb watched me closely.

When five minutes came and went, I decided enough was enough.

"Hold on, kid," Dallas called out, stepping in my path to stop me. "I don't think you understand what you could be walking into," he warned.

I stepped around him and his pace matched mine as I trudged toward the house, the strange red light, the crackling that, perhaps, unnerved me most.

"I don't care," I stated firmly. "I need to see him."

"Just wait for Declan to give the all clear," he suggested.

I shook my head, stepping over a small fence no taller than my knees. The flames blazed louder and I heard voices now. Elise's, Declan's I believed. And another noise that was hard to place—something reminiscent of the same warning growl I nearly released on Hilda not too long ago.

The sound of it made me pause my steps again, which Dallas seemed grateful for, maybe thinking I hesitated because he said something that brought me to my senses. Little did he know, I barely heard him now, honing in on that strange breathing.

Liam ...

It had to be him, and it sounded like he was in pain.

I have no idea where the strength or the will came from, but I trudged forward again, fully aware of what I might see when I got to him. There was simply no slowing down.

If he was in pain, if he needed me, I—

My feet stopped dead in their tracks, halting at the corner that had once hidden this scene from view. One where Elise, Declan, Josiah, and Tobias kept at a safe distance as the sight before them seemed to leave them all in limbo—torn between trusting that the man they'd known for centuries was still present, but also considering they ought to trust their instincts to run.

Amidst my thoughts as I stared at a very-much-alive Liam, was confusion. It was him, but ... not.

The vibrant red I'd seen from far away wasn't what I expected. They were *his* flames—their deep crimson replacing the pale orange I'd grown accustomed to seeing. And large wings stretched from his back, wings nearly twice the breadth of the ones that carried us above the trees on my first flight not too long ago. The tips of his lengthy hair moved in the draft of his dragon's fire—a fire like none I'd ever seen before.

"Evangeline, stand back," Elise warned, calling out when I

took a step forward. She came to me right away, glancing back toward Liam as if to keep a cautious eye on him.

"He's not stable," she explained in a rush of panicked breath. The look on her face left me with the impression she didn't trust him. Almost like … she was *afraid*.

I glanced up when she finished speaking, surprised to find the blindingly white eyes of my warrior already fixed on me, as if he'd only now become aware of my presence.

"Get her away from here," his voice thundered with a warning. At least … it *should* have been his voice. Instead, I heard the unfamiliar baritone of something altogether different.

Elise's gaze volleyed between Liam and I when she braced my shoulders. "He's trying to protect you," she explained quickly, pushing me back until I was flush against Dallas' chest and his hands replaced hers.

"Get her home, please," Elise urged, speaking to Dallas above my head. "I'll be in contact as soon as I can," she added before turning to address my brothers right after.

"Boys, I'll need you to stay." Her eyes drifted over her shoulder again, that look of deep concern still present. "We may need your help."

Without hesitation, they nodded and stepped up, ready to do whatever she needed.

"Come on, kid," Dallas instructed, keeping a firm hold on me as I stumbled in his shadow, glancing back until Liam was out of sight.

He was alive, he recognized me, but honestly … that was *all* I knew for certain.

CHAPTER 24

Evie

I f it hadn't been for Hilda, I would've forgotten to eat, instead
pacing the entire day, and now into the night. Her quiet
knock at my door a moment ago broke the silence I'd sat in
for hours—hours I spent wondering about Liam, questioning
whether I should have let Dallas escort me away so easily.

I should have stayed, made sure he was okay.

A silver tray lined with chicken soup and fresh baked bread
was placed on my desk and whereas I hadn't been hungry since
the ordeal earlier, I was suddenly starving.

"It's not much, but I prepared it with my own two hands," she
smiled, making sure I knew this meal was a labor of love, not just
something she conjured with the twirl of a finger.

I sat and lifted my gaze to smile back. "Thank you."

I wasn't sure when she found the time to cook. Within minutes
of my return, she rushed off to her workspace and I hadn't seen her

since. She'd locked herself in after muttering something about the Oracles requesting that she commune with them concerning '*a very sensitive matter*'. I got the impression it was urgent, but at the rate of change here in Seaton Falls, it could have been about anything from the flood to my brothers' returning.

Or ... maybe it was about what Liam had done today.

It was entirely possible they'd had a vision of what I saw with my own two eyes—him with those large wings, those bright, red flames.

I *still* had no idea what it all meant and could only hope they weren't alarmed.

Because ... I kinda was.

To my surprise, Hilda didn't leave right away after delivering dinner, instead taking a seat on the edge of my bed nearby. I peered up at her a moment, observing her as she looked around my space, focusing on a picture pinned above the lamp of my parents.

Her smile grew.

"That was a brave thing you did for them," she stated, nodding toward the photo.

I brought the spoon to my mouth, deciding not to reply. The act was one I considered to be more necessary than anything else.

"And it was perhaps even *more* brave for those who accompanied you," she went on. "Considering their emotional investment was not in your parents, but in *you*."

I paused at those words, finding so much truth in them.

"It's strange how your world has evolved," she went on, her gaze landing on me as I ate. "Just months ago, we were all so sure Nicholas was the devil incarnate," she chuckled. "And now, it seems we were wrong."

And this was why I fought so hard to save him, fought so hard to keep the Council from killing him. While no, I didn't foresee any of this, his redemption, he's definitely proven himself to be worthy of the title friend.

"It would still be wise for us to keep a watchful eye on him," she went on.

I didn't disagree.

"When he followed you the night of the flood, did he mention the sound again?"

I paused mid-chew when she asked, hating that she brought it to my remembrance. I liked to think things with Nick and I were improving, but this small detail—the maddening sound he described hearing whenever we were close—was a loud, clear sign that it was all an illusion.

"I only noticed it affecting him during combat training, but I think there was too much going on when we were in town, trying to get back to safety," I answered.

Hilda was silent, pursing her lips together while she thought.

"Do you think it means something?"

At the sound of my question, her eyes came back to mine. And then a smile, one I wasn't sure how genuine it was. It could have easily been to convey a sense of calm that didn't really exist within her.

"I have a theory, but, like all things, it will surely reveal itself in time." After speaking, she scanned me curiously, but then said nothing more of it before changing the subject.

"Don't be angry with Liam." When she mentioned him again, I peered up to find her gazing thoughtfully toward the window.

"Despite what you may think, he did this stupid, *stupid* thing ... because he loves you." It was clear she hated his decision, but it was equally clear she respected it.

She didn't show it often, but she had a soft side. Especially when it came to us. Her family.

"He told me," I replied, clarifying. "In a letter."

Her head tilted with intrigue. "Oh?"

"He wanted to make sure I understood."

She nodded. "And do you?"

I gave the question some thought, taking a sip from the glass she brought with dinner.

"Not at first, but I get it now," was my answer. "I only hope he doesn't regret it." I stared at my bowl for a long time, praying that wouldn't be the case.

"Regret it?" she asked. "Because of his state when you left him today?"

I nodded once to confirm. "He wasn't himself." It wasn't just the outward, physical changes. Even the depth of his voice shook me.

"He knew there was a chance things wouldn't go according to his exact plan," she shared. "He convinced himself this process would be no different than when Elise performed the ritual centuries ago, but what we couldn't seem to get him to consider was that, back then, she awakened *human* children. Not children who already possessed traces of dragon DNA in them. Not humans who were already powerful supernatural shifters. We can't be sure those traits, although they've been dormant within him, aren't the cause of these changes."

My brow knitted together with fresh concern.

"I've never witnessed the act myself, but from my understanding, regeneration should have taken hours," she explained. "The healing process, based on Elise's recollection, was quite grueling, lasting the better part of the night for the children of *Ars-en-Ré* ... but that clearly wasn't the case for Liam. His transition was almost ... immediate."

I hadn't done a ton of worrying today because he was alive and well when I left. I'd only been anxious.

Until now.

"Do you think he'll be okay?"

"I can't answer that," Hilda replied. "But what I can say for sure is that he's better off as he is now than he was as a human."

"Because he's not vulnerable anymore?"

Hilda shook her head. "There's that," she sighed. "And there's *also* the fact that order has been restored."

I didn't understand at first.

"I can only imagine how hard it must have been for him, having roles between the two of you reversed. He took pride in his ability to protect you, his mate, only to find he wasn't capable of that anymore, and what's worse, discovering that *you* had to protect *him*."

She smiled a bit. "But, I suppose all that's changed now. Based on what you described, Liam can hold his own once again. Perhaps even more so than before."

I had so many questions. Questions Hilda, and maybe no one else, could answer.

Pressing her hands into the mattress she pushed off my bed. She was set to walk away, to leave me to eat alone, but I stopped her.

"Thank you," I stated, smiling when she did. "For dinner. For the talk."

She offered only a gracious nod before leaving me alone with my thoughts.

All one-million of them.

Pure exhaustion—emotional, physical—it was the only way I could have possibly fallen asleep, still awaiting a meaningful update from Elise.

However, at the quiet mechanical ticking of the front door-knob being turned, I sat straight up in bed, hearing the sound all the way from my bedroom. I hopped down and rushed for the stairs, counting heads as they filed through the entrance. First Elise, then each of my brothers.

My eyes peered into the darkness just beyond the threshold,

searching for one more. Only ... there wasn't one. Elise latched the door behind my brothers and my heart crushed beneath the weight of disappointment.

I didn't know what to think, what to ask. All I knew to do was sit down before my knees gave way beneath me on the stairs.

"Well?" Hilda greeted them, doing all she could to quell the anxiousness she tried hiding earlier, but it was no use. She cared about Liam as much as she cared about the rest of us.

Elise puffed a fatigued breath between her lips. "It's been a long, tiring day," she said first. "But he'll be okay."

I stood, finishing my descent down the stairs, blurting a question as soon as I reached the bottom.

"Then ... where is he?"

Elise met my frantic question with a smile, and then an embrace.

"Waiting for you outside on the porch," she answered. "He asked me to send you out, so the two of you could speak in private."

There was more. I heard the hint of a syllable on Elise's lips when they parted, but I didn't wait for what she'd say next. I had one thing on my mind—seeing Liam.

I snatched the door open and rushed out. Glancing right, then left, my gaze landed on him. It was clear he'd thought through all the details, probably had been doing so for weeks, even before knowing for sure he'd follow through with this plan. He even remembered a second change of clothes, seeing as how the others had likely been disintegrated and he currently stood before me in jeans and a tee.

My eyes filled with tears just thinking about it—the pain he endured out there. Alone in the wilderness.

I scanned him again, taking another step in his direction, noting another change I hadn't picked up on before. When my gaze slipped to his arms, there was only skin. No ink to speak of.

The tattoos I now knew every single detail of were missing, had been burned away.

He stared back with so much hidden behind those eyes, saying nothing. Although he hadn't revealed even a hint of what thoughts ran through his head, I knew; saw right through him.

There was hope, uncertainty.

He was trying to read me, but I gave no indication as to how I felt about this reckless thing he'd done.

But, with the way my heart swelled, I couldn't keep him guessing for long.

My bare feet moved swiftly across the cool brick beneath them, right until they left it the next second when I leapt on him, sure he'd catch me. From the look he wore just before he went out of focus through a blur of tears, he expected something else.

Fear, anger maybe, but not this.

I'd gone through a range of emotions during the day, but once I saw him, the only one that remained was relief.

I loved him enough that the hell I'd been through didn't even matter. I imagined he had a similar feeling when I came back yesterday from the journey to save my parents.

"Please don't hate me." It seemed like such a silly thing for him to say.

Letting my eyes drift closed as I held him. I shook my head. "Couldn't even if I tried."

My cheek was warm to his and I noticed the difference already. The strength in his arms as they gripped my waist tighter, the energy that vibrated within him. It was so familiar, but much, *much* stronger than it'd ever been before. I guessed it had to do with what Hilda explained, about his DNA basically being super-charged now. But I didn't care if he was different. No matter what changed, he was still mine.

I leaned away, parting my lips to speak, but those words never came. Instead, I conveyed the feeling with an action—a kiss so deep I could've swore I felt it down in my soul.

He didn't need to ask my forgiveness. I understood. He was never meant to be only human. He was a dragon, the fiercest the world had ever seen.

And he was mine.

"I'm so sorry." He exhaled the words and I felt them moving feverishly over my lips as my legs cinched his waist just a little tighter.

I didn't answer, only kissed him harder, deeper. It felt so good knowing we'd been given a second chance, an opportunity to give forever another try.

I hadn't voiced it to him, but I was all too aware of how limited our time could have been. But now, thanks to an act some considered stupid, and I considered brave ... we had that back.

Our kiss slowed and my fingers came to rest at the nape of his neck just beneath his hair. I would have stayed there with him forever, but I couldn't be selfish with his time tonight.

"We should get inside," I suggested. "Hilda's been worried about you, too."

He responded with a nod while his gaze stayed trained on me, but before placing me on the ground again, another kiss pressed to my lips.

This moment, having him back ... it meant everything.

With our fingers laced, we took slow steps toward the door. My eyes traced the outline of finely sculpted muscle that showed through the back of his t-shirt as he led me into the house. Everyone still congregated in the foyer, waiting for him, no doubt. Just like I suspected, Hilda made quick work of getting to Liam first. She truly *did* miss him, and if he hadn't believed it when I told him before, he should now.

She stepped forward, placing a hand on Liam's cheek, offering a warm smile before speaking. "You're stubborn as a mule, but ... I admire your courage," she admitted.

He laughed, taking no offense to my aunt's abrasive way of even saying *nice* things.

"When you get a moment," she said as the smile she wore faded just a little, "Come see me. It can wait until morning, but ... we need to talk."

Liam seemed to notice the shift in her tone, too, but didn't address it. Now more than before, I had a deeper suspicion that the conversation with the Oracles *was* about him.

My heart fluttered a little, but I tried to ignore it.

"I'll find you in the morning then," he promised, which seemed to appease Hilda for now.

Even with her clearly deciding not to ruin the night, I couldn't shake the feeling that, whatever this was she needed to discuss with Liam ... it was about to change everything.

The house was still and quiet. We laid face-to-face, the room illuminated only by the flicker of a single candle's flame. With the sheet draped over my body, tucked beneath my arms, Liam was the opposite. He was so free with me and I envied that. Envied that the years he remembered with me made him so confident, knowing there was no real need to hide. I guessed I'd get over that eventually, just not tonight.

I breathed deep, loving that twinge of smoke I caught hints of in the air, smoke that wasn't my own. It was his, a sign he was back.

Completely.

Lacing my fingers with his, my gaze roamed every inch of his smooth skin, still in awe over the absence of curved lines and vibrant color that once marked it.

I breathed deep, trying to sense my dragon, but she still hadn't returned. I half thought she'd be back and stronger than ever by now, but that wasn't the case.

When I released a heavy sigh, Liam's brow twitched. Next, a warm hand landed on my cheek.

"I didn't hurt you, did I?" The question was weighted down by real concern.

So much so, it made me laugh a bit. "No," I said at first, amending the statement right after. "Well, actually, a little, but it was worth it," I grinned, recalling how much different it was being with him *this* time, versus all the others.

His heightened strength and virility were overwhelmingly apparent, as was his attempt at bridling both. It simply wasn't possible. The end result was a series of aches and pains in unmentionable places. Minor discomforts I was sure would disappear within the hour.

"My apologies," he crooned as white teeth flashed. A wide smile stretched across his face and I shoved him.

"I nearly believed you," I lied, rolling my eyes with the words, noting the hint of ego behind his.

He took my hand, placing a kiss in the center of my palm before bringing it to his chest where a powerful heart beat within it.

"Seriously, what's bothering you?"

I felt for her again before answering. "My dragon's still not right," I sighed. "She's still not coming forward, only my wolf."

Once, I'd been so afraid to explore that side of who I am, but over the last few weeks, my wolf was all I had. I'd come to rely on her strength, her ferocity when my own courage dwindled.

Liam was thoughtful as I stared at him—every perfect detail of that beautiful face. I know that's not traditionally a word assigned to describe a man, but it was the only one fitting for him in this moment.

The hand he held warmed when his veins began to glow—

their usual orange lava now replaced with red. It was hypnotic to watch.

"I think I may know why she's still distant," he said, blinking hazel eyes at me.

"Why?"

"Our tether," he shared, wetting his lips when adding, "I think it's because our link has been severed."

I hadn't even considered it, thinking she was merely in mourning because he'd been made human, not realizing it was the connection she missed.

"How do I ... I'm not even sure I can still do it." This was something new for me, but I was comforted by the fact that I'd only tethered myself to someone once in my former life as well.

Liam squeezed my fingers between his.

"Just concentrate. Last time it was somewhat more ... ceremonious," was the word he settled on, "but that doesn't matter. Try calling her up again."

It took a lot not to release the frustrated sigh creeping up my throat. He had no idea how many times I'd tried to bring her forward over the weeks, only to have her rebel.

But then my hands warmed, and I gazed at them, the moving streaks that stretched from the tips of my fingers, up my forearm. I almost didn't believe that she'd come when I called for her, but then it hit me; it wasn't *my* request she responded to. It was Liam's. His dragon's.

I smiled and so did he.

"Good. Now, burn blue," he said next.

I concentrated again, focusing on the moving light until the orange began to fade, dimming to allow a brilliant turquoise to emerge. It was almost laughable how much more my dragon cooperated with *Liam* than she had with *me* lately.

"For this part, I can only tell you what it felt like for me, because this isn't one of my abilities. But, somehow, you made it feel like ..." He paused to locate the memory, and then described it as best as he could. "You made it feel like a piece of me went into your soul, and a piece of your soul came into mine."

I stared, imagining it, the red pulsating in his arms mingling with the turquoise in mine. There wasn't more he could add because he wouldn't have known more than that. The rest was up to me.

My lids closed on an image of him staring, waiting with confidence in his gaze that I could do this.

I hoped I wouldn't let us *both* down by failing.

I followed what little direction he could give, imagining pieces of our souls trading places, mine finding refuge in his, his finding refuge in mine.

Foreign energy pulsed from my palm where it met Liam's and I focused on it, forcing that sensation to spread from my hand, up my arm, and finally to my chest—where I always felt that invisible thread that linked us no matter the distance.

It faded and the lights beneath our skin had died when my eyes opened again. Liam blinked at me, and I didn't miss the faint smile on his lips. I felt it, knew he could, too. Somehow, without any clue what I was doing, our tether had been restored.

"I'll never take this feeling for granted again," I promised, saddened as I recalled the moment it died before, the emptiness it left behind that night.

Liam brought me closer and his mouth melded to mine, bringing to my attention that I'd never felt more connected to him than I did in this moment—mind, body, soul.

As the kiss deepened and I held him tight, listening as he wandered inside my head for the first time in *way* too many days.

"And I'm never letting you go."

CHAPTER 25

Evie

My grandfather's estate was no longer just a safe-haven for *me*, but for my friends as well. With Officer Chadwick working around the clock the past few days, helping those who could no longer help themselves, Roz hadn't left my side, but she wasn't the only one who'd been crashing here. Chris and Lucas were becoming permanent fixtures, too, with both their moms being nurses and doing their part to aid the injured.

Our town was a mess, and yet somehow, the four of us managed to find solace.

In each other.

A night of movie watching was an attempt at forgetting the chaos that surrounded us. It didn't help, but we all needed the closeness, the comfort of being around friends after living through a disaster in which we could have lost them.

In short, we all learned a lesson in taking things, and people, for granted.

I was the first to wake, blinking into the dim light that peeked in past the heavy drapery. It was super early judging by the sun's muted, orange glow. Choosing to camp out in the living room together, the floor was a jumble of colorful blankets and cushions from various couches that we borrowed from all over the house.

Beside me, a sleeping brunette who'd never believe she snored as loudly as she did, brought a smile to my face. Slipping a numb arm from beneath her head, I shook off the sensation of pins and needles dotting my skin and sat up, spotting Chris sprawled out in front of the big-screen, and Lucas somehow wrapped tight in a blanket near the fireplace. I wasn't sure what I would've done without them here, but I'd learned how to be grateful in recent days.

There was cereal in the kitchen and I didn't feel like waiting for the others to wake up and join me, so I figured I'd knock back my first bowl, and eat the next two or three with them. These days, we all ate enough where I was sure we'd each need our own box anyway.

I moved through the dining room quietly, passing through the butler's pantry to get to the kitchen. Instead of turning on lights to brighten the large, dark space, my feet moved across cool tile, headed for the window over the sink to draw the curtains.

And when I did, I stumbled back, only stopping when I slammed into the counter, silent with shock as I stared out.

Blood rushed to my head as my heart raced, rubbing my eyes hard until they burned, but ... the image never went away.

This couldn't have been real, though.

Last night, when we went to bed, everything was normal, but now ... *this*. A macabre forest composed of wooden stakes and mangled bodies for trees. They casted odd shadows onto the ground with their twisted limbs and contorted torsos in the early morning light.

So many bodies.

Everywhere, lining the yard of my grandfather's estate.

Bile rose from my stomach and was only forced back down by fear as I sank to the floor, scrambling to understand. My entire body shook as a thought ran through my head and I fought to stifle it.

Did I do this?

Had I blacked out again and ... killed all these people?

If I *wasn't* responsible ... whoever did this might have still been out there, watching me, stalking the grounds as they waited for signs of life inside.

I had to get to the others. To warn them—either to leave here to protect themselves from me, or perhaps to stay inside and protect themselves from whoever was out there. I had no idea which action was the *right* action, so ... I sat.

Afraid.

Frozen.

The sound of footsteps trailing the same path I'd just followed to the kitchen startled me, knowing right away who it was. With her bare feet and small stature, it was easy to tell Roz's gait from the guys'.

"Get down!" I shouted just above a whisper.

Her steps halted, and for a moment I thought she'd ignore the command, but then I heard a hesitant thump as she got to the floor.

"Why the heck are you hiding?" she whispered back.

I wasn't sure what to say, other than explain plainly that the yard had been decorated with impaled bodies overnight—and that I couldn't promise I wasn't the one who had done it.

When I didn't answer quickly enough, there was a scuffle on the other side of the counter, and then she stood with a heavy sigh, maybe thinking this was a joke.

However, when she stayed silent, I knew she'd seen them, too. The bodies.

She crumpled to the floor with a loud thud this time, making quick work of ducking down again.

"What's happening?" her voice trembled, making me wish I had a firm answer that might comfort her, but I had nothing.

"I came into the kitchen and they were just ... *there*," I explained.

She was sobbing now, I heard the tears and fear mingling in her throat when she spoke again. "We have to call someone," she rambled. "I have to let my dad know the Sovereign is—"

"But what if it wasn't him," I interjected, not even realizing I'd spoken the words aloud until Roz paused midsentence.

There was silence and I wished I could have seen her face. Maybe realizing this, the next thing I heard was the rhythmic thud of her knees against the tile as she crawled around the island to me. A heavy sigh puffed from her lips when her back came to rest against the cabinet beside me and then, she took my hand.

"Nick, you didn't do this," she said gently, knowing exactly what my thoughts were.

"How can you be sure," I breathed out, staring straight ahead.

"I've been up most of the night texting my dad for updates," she shared. "I hardly slept and, honestly, just dozed about an hour ago." She checked the time on her watch to confirm. "So, if you really think you could have killed, staked, and arranged all these bodies out there in an hour, then you're either crazy ... or you're a *wizard*," she added.

My eyes slammed shut with relief.

A breath shuddered in Roz's throat. "We have to get out of here, though."

I couldn't have agreed with her more.

"Stay low," I commanded, leading the way back to Chris and Lucas in the other room. They were easy to rouse awake, all traces of fatigue leaving their bodies when I told them what Roz and I discovered outside.

Both reached for their phones right away, wanting to warn their families, Beth. Roz put in a call to her dad, which required her to share that she'd spent the night with me—an admission we would likely *both* pay for later, but for now, the bigger issue was the bodies, so he didn't scold her much. However, his exact orders were that she head home immediately.

Under the circumstances, I agreed it was best that she go to him. Especially if I was a target or some sort, which the scene outside suggested.

Richie answered on the third ring when I dialed him. He'd been so busy with his colleagues, doing all they could to help those who lost their homes, loved ones, lost *everything* in the flood. Normally, I wouldn't have bothered him, but this was the mother of all emergencies.

"Yeah?" His raspy voice came through the phone and I heard the exhaustion in it. He'd most likely been up all night trying to help.

"There's a bit of a situation," I began. "I just woke up a few minutes ago and outside ... the entire estate is covered with bodies." I was panting into the receiver, having a hard time settling, catching my breath. I still hadn't ruled out the idea of whoever did this still being out there.

"Bodies? As in, more than one?"

I nodded as though he were in the room to see. "As in maybe a hundred or more."

He was quiet for a spell, and I wondered if he had the same thought I did initially. So, to save him the awkwardness of asking his own brother if he was a murderer, I spoke up.

"Roz and the guys are here. Said I didn't move all night, so ..."

An audible sigh of relief came through the earpiece of my phone, confirming what I suspected.

"Ok, is there movement outside? Anyone on the property from what you can see?"

I crept to the window for a better look.

"I *think* it's all clear."

"Good. Get out of there," he ordered, adding a firm, "Now!"

"Okay." I was sure he knew how freaked out I was, because I'd never bent to his will that easily, not even when he still held the power to outrank me.

"Ben and Kyle are already with me, helping out, so we'll leave now and meet you at Mom and Dad's," he stated, sounding like he'd already begun the dash toward his truck.

"See you in a bit." I ended the call and turned to the others. "We have to go. Richie thinks it's a bad idea to stick around."

"Then I'm with Richie," Chris replied, his wide-eyed expression telling of how on board he was with the idea of getting as far away from here as possible.

"Did you get a hold of Beth?" I said, turning to Lucas as I grabbed my hoodie from the back of the couch.

He nodded. "Yeah, she's safe at home with her parents. I told her to tell her folks they needed to stay in and to keep the doors locked."

"I just ... I don't understand." At Roz's words, I turned toward her, breathing deep. It didn't make sense to me either.

"Why here?" she asked. "Why you?"

There was a strong possibility this was personal, not just some random act of darkness. It may have very well been a message.

A warning.

I'd chosen to spare Roz most of the details from our battle with the Sovereign. She seemed content to know everyone made it back alive, not pressing for more information. So, one of the things she wasn't made aware of, was how Evie and I came face-to-face with the Sovereign, his son.

How I was likely just as much a target for foiling their plan as Evie had been.

Only, I didn't have the protection she did.

When I didn't readily offer a response, I felt Roz's eyes burning a hole through me.

"What aren't you saying, Nick?"

I could have told her what I suspected—that this was the Sovereign's way of flexing his muscles, letting me know he was in town and knew exactly where to find me—but it would've just been speculation. So, I kept it to myself.

"We don't know it's personal," was my answer, but deep down, I believed differently.

Roz said nothing. If I had to guess, that keen intuition of hers had already determined things were more dire than I mentioned, but maybe she wasn't asking for details because she didn't really *want* them.

She dropped the issue, instead asking a *different* question.

"What about Evie?"

Grateful for the conversation shift, I blinked.

I'd already shot her a text as soon as I hung up with Richie, but didn't think to call. Mostly out of respect for Roz, but also due in part to being sure Liam would be close by.

"I know they've basically got the National Guard surrounding the house," Roz added, "but still ... you should check in to at least give her a heads up," she went on to suggest.

I slipped on my shoes while I thought about it, deciding Roz was right. I moved toward the door while the phone rang against my ear.

No answer.

I tried again, and still nothing.

"They're probably asleep," Roz chimed in again. "Normally, I wouldn't think it was a good idea to show up at the door unannounced, to wake them, but ... circumstances," she concluded, staring while I thought.

"I'll head over there," was my final decision.

"We'll drive you," Chris offered.

I gave a nod and then, reluctantly, unlocked the door, preparing to make a fast break for the cars.

Rushing out into the open wasn't ideal, but neither was sitting idle in the house, making ourselves easy targets. So, after a quick look outside, the four of us took a collective deep breath, and then ran for it—Chris and Lucas to Chris' jeep where I'd join them in a second, but first, I got Roz to her car. She climbed in and leveled a look on me that said so much, and before parting ways, I kissed her.

"Please, go straight home," I urged.

She nodded, letting me know she wouldn't deviate.

With that, making sure she was on her way first, I doubled back to the jeep and hopped in the back. The engine revved and, as we took off, I only now got the full scope of the property, the dark warning someone left just for me. There were at least a hundred, which meant this was the work of a large group. Mutts. Soldiers maybe.

I scanned the faces as we pulled off, believing many of these people must have been survivors of the flood, those forced to sleep outdoors, vulnerable.

I turned away from the scene, the death and carnage that'd been staged overnight. Had to.

Richie would be waiting if I didn't tell him our plans had changed, so I dialed him. Naturally, with things heating up, he answered on the first ring.

"Almost to the house. You're in route?" he asked.

When I replied with a hesitant, "Uhh ... yes and no," he puffed a heavy sigh into the phone.

"Now's not the time for games. Go straight to the house," he commanded, adding. "No detours."

"Don't have a choice. Evie's not answering and I need to let her know what's up."

Truth was, if *I* was being targeted, she definitely would be, too. If that hadn't already happened.

Another sigh into the phone before Richie spoke, ending our call with a very irritated, "Meet you there."

Following my directions, Chris pulled up near Evie's within minutes. On cue, the infuriating buzz in my ears began—a sound close to the high-pitched frequency emitted by electronic devices. Pulses of energy I could usually only hear, but today ... I *felt* them.

Moving all over my skin.

It wasn't far from thought how much more in control I felt when Roz was with me, but I'd have to make due this time. Besides, this would just be a quick visit to pass this information along, then I'd be gone. I closed my eyes tightly, willing myself to keep it together. When I opened them, I felt more normal.

The drive up was the exact opposite of the scenery outside my *own* home this morning. Where mine had been transformed into a nightmarish graveyard, the property near Evie's was dense with makeshift camps, shifters torn between fleeing and staying around to make sure Seaton Falls was battle-ready.

Chris surveyed as we slowed our pace. A distracted, "Wow," left his mouth at the precise moment I thought it. That I knew of, no one had been ordered to set up camp in any particular location, but from the looks of it, most had chosen to flock close to her. Maybe for their own protection. Maybe to ensure hers.

When we reached the gate to find that my brothers had beaten us here. Richie was already out of his truck, in deep conversation with one of the guards.

The guys and I stepped out, and that powerful energy strengthened even more. It was ... stifling. While I knew I was the only one experiencing it, it was so overwhelming I found that hard to believe.

What had changed that made it so much more intense?

Once it started a few weeks ago, it seemed to grow stronger every time I was in Evie's presence. I had no idea whether the change was within *me,* or ... within *her.* Whatever the case, I wanted to get this over with and get as far away from here as possible.

Both, for my sanity and Evie's safety.

"I need to speak with her."

I'd already gotten the statement out, addressing nearby guards before my feet stopped just shy of the gate. Apparently, my fast approach was seen as a threat, because I'd clearly set a few of them on edge. I guessed as much when large rifles—likely loaded with magic-laced bullets—were pointed toward my head.

What they may have perceived to be aggression, was actually desperation. I had to do this quickly so I could get out of here.

Sooner rather than later.

"Easy, Nick," Richie warned, lifting both his hands into the air, encouraging me to fall back.

"We've got strict orders not to let anyone beyond this gate," one of the soldiers suggested. "So, it'd be in your best interest to turn around and ... maybe just give her a call." The statement was oozing sarcasm I didn't find amusing.

I didn't have the time or patience for jokes. And maybe Evie didn't either.

At the thought, the buzz grew louder, taking on a strange rapid vibration now. My blood warmed in my veins, heating near a boil as I stood there, staring down the barrels of several guns. Still, even with one pulled trigger standing between me and death, I only focused on the sound, shifting my eyes toward the house.

"Tried that," I seethed, feeling my mood darken. "And we've got critical information I need to get to Evie right away. And, correct me if I'm wrong, but isn't it your job to make sure she's safe? And yet, you're stopping someone trying to do just that?"

They stared, saying nothing, completely unaware of the wolf within me chomping at the bit, begging to be set free. Only, I feared what might happen if it managed to do so.

I felt ... different. Strange in ways I couldn't put into words.

It was clear, the guards were too by-the-book to be reasoned with, so holding the gaze of one, I did the only thing I could.

I yelled.

"Evie!"

My voice rang out into the early morning air, probably carrying through the woods quite a ways.

The guards weren't amused. Not in the least, but there was no rule that could stop me, as long as I didn't try to cross through the gate.

"Evie!"

I called out even louder this time, doing all I could to wake her, get her out here so I could do my part in keeping her safe.

Behind me, the doors to Richie's truck opened and shut again when Kyle and Ben stepped out. They approached slowly.

"Take it easy, Nick," Ben tried to reason, but I was determined to get this over with.

Ignoring his plea, my lips parted one last time to call out to her. Only ... her name didn't come out quite right. Intertwined with the syllables were undertones of a deafening roar that shook branches of nearby trees. My voice ricocheted through them, causing birds to abandon their perches and take flight.

When I gripped the sides of my head and stumbled back, it was Kyle who steadied me, draping an arm across my shoulders as I fought against the oncoming darkness. My head ... it rang with disgusting thoughts that couldn't have been my own. Couldn't have been, because they were images of tearing a girl limb from limb.

A girl I managed to love in two different ways in one lifetime.

A girl I considered a friend.

"Get me out of here," I pleaded, only mumbling loudly enough for Kyle to hear. "I can't ... I can't be here. Something's happening."

He didn't hesitate. At those words, he turned me from the others, ushering me toward Richie's truck before I had the chance to do something stupid, something I couldn't control or undo.

"Let's go!" he called out over his shoulder, causing our other brothers to fall in step.

We were nearly there, nearly on the path to freedom, to safety.

But then ... a door opened.

The slight creak of hinges seemed to be the only sound I heard in that instant, and the wind carried a familiar scent to my nostrils, awakening evil within me I didn't realize truly existed until now.

My hands ached to end a life, and *only* one life.

Hers.

I turned, knowing I shouldn't have. Knowing it would only fuel me more if I looked into her dark, unsuspecting eyes, but I couldn't help it. I stared at her as only she and I seemed to exist in that cone of silence, and for the first time since this all began, I didn't see Evie.

I saw ... a target.

A deep, guttural roar billowed from my gut and burst from my lungs. Those rifles that had settled when it seemed I'd decided to walk away were raised again, and despite knowing the soldiers were all too willing to pull the triggers, I couldn't stop myself. On this day, I wanted the blood to run cold in Evie's veins.

Wanted it so bad I could taste it.

My brothers, Chris, Lucas ... they all struggled to hold me, all pleading with the guards not to shoot, all knowing there was only so much time they could stall them.

My will was ironclad. Both feet planted firmly in the soil and I somehow managed to inch forward even with so many fighting to drag me in the opposite direction.

At the door, Evie stood in shock, watching the scene that unfolded before her very eyes. A vision of separating her head from her shoulders filled me with bloodlust. All I needed was one second.

One to end that incessant vibration emanating from within her.

It became clearer to me than it had ever been before. *This* was the reason I'd been born, my life's purpose.

I was meant to liberate Evie's soul from her body.

On this day, suffering a gruesome death at my hand, she would breathe her last breath.

Evie

Triggered.

That was the word that came to mind as I stared, frozen in place, watching someone I no longer recognized claw his way toward the gate.

His face was distorted in strange ways, and thick, dark veins became visible through his skin. This was not a transition into the wolf I'd seen manifest in him before. This was something different. The beast I stared at today bore little physical resemblance to the guy I once trusted with my life, and even *less* resemblance in behavior.

This monster ... it was wicked, the embodiment of evil.

When I was first awakened by the sound of my name being yelled, I had no idea this was the scene unfolding outside our front door. But now ... I knew what brought him here.

An insatiable hunger to end my life.

My instincts should have been to run, but I couldn't move. A strange mix of disbelief and sadness warred within me. I struggled to grasp the concept of how someone who'd very recently played a huge part in saving my parents' lives was now crazed, drenched in sweat and nearly tearing his clothes from his body with rage.

All the while, he kept his deadly gaze trained solely on me.

I had no idea what changed, what made him decide that right here and now was the time to end me. Seemed we'd all been dreading this moment for so long. Even Nick himself.

Commotion behind me barely registered. I sensed my brothers, Elise, Hilda, and Dallas.

But I *felt* Liam.

A large hand nearly swallowed my arm whole, moving me aside when his massive frame replaced mine in the doorway. As his shadow fell on me, it was clear he aimed to stand in as Nick's target should he manage to break free.

"Don't act rashly," Hilda warned as she pushed her way through.

An onslaught of quickly spoken phrases like, *"Excuse me"* and *"Move it,"* flew from her mouth as she elbowed her way to the front door.

Liam answered without taking his eyes off Nick, speaking through gritted teeth and a firm jaw.

"I've waited long enough to kill him," he seethed, adding, *"Too long."*

I could only imagine what must have been going through his head, recalling a moment similar to this—one he hadn't been able to prevent in the distant past.

Beyond the gate, a powerful scuffle made my skin crawl. Although Liam had blocked my line of sight, it wasn't hard to imagine Nick growing more enraged as the seconds passed.

"Permission to shoot?" I heard one of the guards say, his voice followed by the distinct chirp of a walkie talkie. My heart raced with that question, knowing it would only be a matter of seconds before a response came back, giving him the go-ahead to take Nick down.

Or ... at least to *try*. I wasn't completely convinced there *was* a way to stop him.

Not if this was his destiny, a fate forged in magic centuries ago.

"We need answers," Hilda's voice rang out again, this time louder than before as she moved me further back into the foyer, giving her access to Liam.

He was tense, full of rage as his body somehow appeared larger than usual. Beneath his skin, red trails pulsed through his fists, up his arms, the veins of his neck, dispersing at his rock-solid jaw.

It wasn't far from my mind that he was different, that we still hadn't seen all the changes his new transformation brought forth. But as he stood before me now, the difference could definitely be felt.

His new strength called to my dragon stronger than I ever experienced. She seemed to feed off his heightened energy, making me antsy as my heart raced.

"Liam," Hilda said gently as the soldier asked for permission once more, bringing the situation to an urgent crescendo. "He's been activated," she reasoned. "Shouldn't we find out why?"

Her inquiry went unanswered as Liam's stare never left Nick.

"I need a moment with him," Hilda insisted, finally managing to slip past Liam, and out onto the porch.

My lips parted to speak, to stop her, but Elise got the words out first.

"Are you insane? He'll tear you apart just to get to Evangeline," she warned.

Managing to peer past the massive arm of my warrior, I watched her—my fearless aunt who saw beyond the chaos of the moment, and saw an opportunity.

My heart raced twice as fast now, praying this didn't end badly for her.

But then, a strange wind seemed to kick up out of nowhere,

knocking bare branches against one another, creating such a ruckus it became difficult to hear. Trees shuttered and almost groaned with the force of it.

Hilda's steps down the walkway toward the wall were unhurried, unfazed by Nick's display of power. She showed no signs of concern whatsoever.

That's when I noticed the change in Nick, how tension left his limbs, his expression. In a way he was suddenly ... submissive. As if he'd been lulled into this state.

Magic. She used magic to quiet him long enough to gather whatever information she sought.

"Nicholas," she called out, raising her voice to be heard over the sudden wind. "I need you to explain what you're experiencing?"

The guards turned, passing an incredulous look Hilda's way for having asked such a simple question, but she didn't falter.

"What are you seeing?" she went on. "Or feeling. Or ... hearing?"

Some of the awareness seemed to return to Nick, but the blind rage settled just beneath the surface. He blinked, finally focusing on Hilda more than the bloodlust.

"Is it the sound?" she went on, trying to help him pinpoint what I guessed must have been a myriad of sensations attacking him all at once.

To my surprise, he nodded—the first coherent action I'd seen from him since I opened the door.

"What do you hear?" she asked next.

His eyes closed, shielding their blue centers while he worked to calm himself. It was still clear he didn't want this, didn't want to be the monster fate had damned him to become.

"It was ... like electricity at first, but now it's ... *different*." he explained, his voice still not sounding like his own. It was deep and raw, animalistic.

"Different how?" Hilda shot back.

That otherworldly wind howled now, swallowing Nick's answer before I could hear. When I touched Liam's arm, intending to move him, a stern look was cast over his shoulder, landing on me.

"You're not going out there," he asserted, making no apologies for not bending to my will.

I peered up, sympathizing with him more in this moment than he'd ever know. My hand slipped down his arm until our fingers were laced.

"Then come with me," I suggested. "I need to know." My gaze stayed locked with his when I added more. "We *both* do."

While I knew this ran much deeper for him than needing closure, *answers,* I couldn't imagine that wouldn't help, wouldn't give him peace of mind.

A reluctant look landed on me first, but then, he finally gave in.

I emerged from the house slowly, mostly hidden behind him, of course. It didn't surprise me when my brothers' footsteps followed. My intent was never to go all the way to the gate; I just wanted to be close enough to finally know. For so many reasons I wanted ... no, *needed* ... to understand.

Liam and I stood there, side-by-side, listening as the mostly one-sided conversation continued.

"I need you to tell me exactly what you hear," Hilda pressed once more. It felt like she had an angle, inside information that just needed confirmation, but that was only a guess.

"It's ... her heartbeat, but ... different," Nick struggled to answer.

"Different how?" Hilda shouted above the wind I was now certain she caused. Although, I was also certain the trick would only work for so long.

"Focus, Nicholas! Different how?" she asked again.

This time, drawing out an answer I don't think any of us expected.

"There are two," he forced out. "Two heartbeats."

Hilda fell silent, keeping her back to Liam and I as she processed the last of Nick's explanation.

"Take him away from here," she ordered, speaking directly to his brothers. "Get him to the Elder's chamber and demand that they lock him in a cell, keep him under watch with as many witches as they can spare. I'll be there as quickly as I can to explain whatever they need to know."

Richie nodded, showing no signs of protest. He and the others hauled Nick toward the truck while he was still a bit dazed by the spell.

"He was coming to warn you," Chris called out, prompting Hilda to halt and give her full attention.

"Warn us?"

Chris nodded, still seemingly in shock by the strange turn of events.

"This morning, outside his grandfather's estate, someone arranged at least a hundred dead bodies across the yard. He seemed to think it was some kind of message," he concluded.

Hilda stared a moment, and then gave a quick nod. "Thank you. We'll be on watch."

With that, Chris and Lucas climbed into a jeep, following the convoy that pulled away from our property.

Hilda approached Liam and I, and there was no missing the grave look on her face. Maybe it was the answer she pulled from Nick, or the information from Chris. Or maybe it was everything, the doom and gloom that seemed to follow us wherever we went.

"This all coincides with what the oracles shared with me yesterday when we convened, the reason I needed to speak with you," she added, addressing Liam directly. "I didn't fully understand the breadth of the situation at the time, because I was missing pieces, but ... now it's so clear."

I felt Liam's body tense beside mine.

"*What's* clear?" he grumbled, his gaze hard and unwavering when it settled on Hilda.

She wrung her hands and I'd never seen her nervous before, but guessed this was what such a thing might look like on her.

"I came up with a theory years ago, one I never shared with anyone. I found myself wondering why the Liberator didn't simply come for you when you were young, a child like he would have also been at the time. You would have been an easier mark. *Certainly* easier to kill," she explained. "So, I found myself asking a strange question: *What if it was never about you?*"

I frowned, when she finished speaking, unsure if I had a hard time following because my mind was still reeling from basically staring death in the eyes, or if I was just missing something.

"But that doesn't ... make sense," I stuttered, trying to mask the frustration.

"It does with what Nicholas just shared." Her response only made me *more* confused, even when she explained further. "The buzzing ... it was energy, new life just beginning. And now, weeks later ... he hears two heartbeats. Yours and another."

My gaze followed Hilda as she came closer, placing her palm flat on my stomach when she reached me. I continued to stare with the words she said next.

"Four weeks from conception ... that's when a heart beats on its own for the first time."

I staggered back a bit with the realization of what she suggested.

"It was never about you, Evangeline," she reiterated. "It was always about your heir."

Both knees weakened as that word rang inside my head—*heir*.

"We now know that when the original Liberator came for you

... it was because you were with child," she clarified. "Which is, consequently, the reason Nicholas has been activated today."

Four weeks ... I did quick math in my head, realizing what Hilda proposed wasn't entirely impossible, but ...

"Now that we know, there's no time to delay. If Nicholas is right about what or *who* is coming ... we need to hide you," she urged, linking her hand with mine before adding, "... *Both* of you."

To find out what happens next, get your copy of the final book,
FATE OF THE FALLEN, today!
https://www.racheljonasauthor.com

Love ARCs, random giveaways, and fun bookish conversation?
Come hang out in my Facebook group for readers,
THE SHIFTER LOUNGE!
https://www.facebook.com/groups/141633853243521
Can't wait to chat with you :)
For all feedback and inquiries, email me at author.racheljonas@
gmail.com

A NOTE FROM THE AUTHOR

Thank you so much for reading Season of the Wolf, *The Lost Royals Saga, Book 4.*

If you have enjoyed entering the world of the Lost Royals, show other readers by leaving a review!
Just visit my website for all available portals where to review the book:
https://www.racheljonasauthor.com

Join my readers' group for more news The Shifter Lounge
https://www.facebook.com/groups/141633853243521
and my Newsletter today!
https://us14.list-manage.com/subscribe?u=
73f44054c9dda516cc713aea7&id=ad3ee37cf1

THE LOST ROYALS SAGA

NEXT IN SERIES

In the end, it all comes down to love ...
The saga concludes with the final installment,
FATE OF THE FALLEN.

**They've laid it all on the line—their lives, their love—
and now they can only hope it's been enough.**

An unexpected turn of events has changed everything. Suddenly aware of a life more valuable than their own, Evie and Liam need a fail-proof plan to survive what's to come.

Only, with their enemies closing in ... they're out of time.

Their worst nightmares have arrived in full force and it will be impossible to avoid them all. So, when things fall apart, who will be the first to rise against them? Who will be the first to head into danger for the ones they love?

And worst of all ... which member of the Seaton Falls clan will lose everything?

As the story concludes, the stakes have been raised and no one is guaranteed to make it out unscathed.

Join Evie, Liam, and Nick in the fifth and final installment of THE LOST ROYALS SAGA.

Grab your copy of "Fate of the Fallen" today!
https://www.racheljonasauthor.com

THE LOST ROYALS SAGA

NEXT FROM RACHEL JONAS

There's a spinoff of the Lost Royals Saga!
Own the DRAGON FIRE ACADEMY trilogy today!

Four dragon warriors.
A beautiful shifter hybrid.
An island with a dark secret that could bring them all to their knees.

Seriously? Four dragon warriors need to stalk my every move? I get it; they think I'm dangerous, but I'm only on their island to learn. Not to destroy it.

This is another unfortunate side-effect of being the freak who descended from all three supernatural lineages. The bloodthirsty dragons, the destructive wolves, and the disloyal witches. Some believe that, when I transition in a few months, there's a slight, teeny tiny chance I could unleash hell on the supernatural world. Call me crazy, but I'd know if I harbored that kind of power inside me.

... Wouldn't I?

My entire life, all I've wanted was to be normal. Hence the reason I didn't think twice about trading in my crown for a stack of books. I've got three terms on this island to prove the naysayers wrong, including my chaperones—Kai, Ori, Paulo, and Rayen.

These four are gorgeous, but also ominous as heck. Babysitting me has clearly taken their focus off something they've deemed more important. So, now they go out of their way to make my life a living hell, with hopes that I'll give up and leave.

Thanks, guys.

You could cut the tension between us with a knife, but what's weird is I don't hate them all the time. There are even odd moments when I catch them watching me. And not in their usual "wish-you-were-dead" sort of way.

Even if I survive the academy, there's still no guarantee these four and I won't kill each other before graduation.

Grab book 1 now!
https://www.racheljonasauthor.com

LOST ROYALS SAGA

ABOUT THE AUTHOR

Rachel Jonas also writes as Nikki Thorne.

Hey, I'm Rachel! Consider this your formal invitation to hang out in my private Facebook group, THE SHIFTER LOUNGE. You'll get fun book convo, exclusive giveaways, and other random acts of nerdiness!

Don't usually talk to strangers? No worries! Allow me to introduce myself. I'm a Michigan native, wife, and mother of three who made a career of indulging the voices inside my head :) With several completed series, and stories in both the paranormal and contemporary YA/NA romance categories, there's something for everyone!

Happy reading!

Don't forget to follow me!

Twitter: @author_R_Jonas
IG: @author.racheljonas
Rachel's Facebook: https://www.facebook.com/author racheljonas/
Reader Group: https://www.facebook.com/groups/141633853243521/
Amazon: amzn.to/2BHiLlS
Goodreads: https://www.goodreads.com/author/show/16788419. Rachel_Jonas
BookBub: https://www.bookbub.com/profile/rachel-jonas
Nikki's Facebook: https://www.facebook.com/nikkithorneauthor/
TikTok: https://www.tiktok.com/@racheljonasauthor